SECRET KEEPER

LAS VEGAS VIPERS BOOK SIX

STACEY LYNN

Secret Keeper

Las Vegas Vipers Series

Book Six

Stacey Lynn

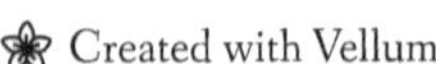 Created with Vellum

ONE
RYANN

Nerves knitted themselves together so tightly inside my stomach they were an Irish infinity symbol. Every nerve in my body was lit up, it was a wonder I wasn't shining like a glowworm. The sounds around me were harsh to my ears, overstimulating my senses, and I had considered turning around on my red high heels at least three dozen times since I stepped through the doors of the Las Vegas Vipers training facility and offices.

There was only one person standing in between me and seeing my father for the first time in a decade.

Susan Graff.

Her deep red painted lips pressed into a thin line as I tried to inhale a calming breath. She was my father's gatekeeper. His assistant. A woman who I could tell had the patience of a gnat and a complete inability to withstand bullshit.

She'd been scowling at me for the last five minutes while I waited for her to finish a phone call, eyes narrowed, probably trying to determine why I looked familiar, but also not.

"Is there anything I can help you with?" she asked and shuffled papers on her desktop without taking her eyes off me.

"I want to speak with Vik Boucher."

"Do you have an appointment?"

"No, but he'll want to see me." There was no way I was going to schedule an appointment with him. He probably would have told her to cancel it.

"Mr. Boucher is a very busy man. You can not waltz in here, demanding to see him if you can't tell me your name and what you want, at the very minimum."

It was foolish to consider I could show up and demand to speak with my father without letting anyone know that he *was* my father. Considering it'd been a decade since I saw him, more than that since my mother left him, I doubted anyone knew I existed.

If this wasn't important, I wouldn't be here, but I needed his help even if I was loath to ask him for it.

"Fine," I all but seethed and curled my hands into fists at my sides. "Tell him Ryann is here and would like to see him."

"Ryann?" Thin, perfectly tattooed eyebrows rose into harsh points above her eyes. "Ryann who?"

"That's all he'll need to know."

If I could have had my mom's second husband, Paul, adopt me to rid myself of everything my father ever gave me, including my last name, I would have. Too bad she didn't get remarried until I was eighteen.

There was no recognition in Susan's eyes, staring at a woman in her twenties with a boy's name, which told me everything I needed to know about how much—or little—my father gave a shit about us.

I'd done my research. Hell, I'd followed him for years. He'd been coaching in Vegas for so long that he was an icon in the professional hockey world. Most coaches didn't stay with one team for this many years, so I'd checked up on him in case he was hired by a different team and had to move. While he continued to lead one of the hosting winning teams in the NHL, the chance of that was slim.

Reluctantly, she lifted a black phone to her ear and pressed a button.

"I'm sorry to interrupt. However, you have a visitor—"

My father's deep voice barked something I couldn't understand, but the woman in front of me shot me a look.

"Yes, sir. I know. I tried telling her she didn't have an appointment and you're busy, but she said to tell you Ryann is here to see you."

Her eyes widened. His voice, muffled through the line, went lower.

She gave me a quick scan and slid her gaze toward his office. "Yes, Vik. I said a woman is here. Her name is Ryann—"

"Send her in."

That came through crystal clear. Barked out as a harsh command, Ms. Graff licked her lips and set down the phone without saying goodbye.

"He said you can go in."

I decided to put the woman out of her misery. I'd been a pain in the ass. I could only imagine how difficult my father was to work for. "My dad is a peach, isn't he?"

Before I turned toward his office, her jaw fell so harshly it was a wonder it didn't slam into her sleek computer screen.

MY DAD WAS OLD. At fifty-five, he wasn't *old* old, but he'd aged since I'd last seen him in person. Granted, that was before my mom moved us to Reno and I'd forced my oldest sister, Braylen, to drive me to this very office to let Dad know we were moving. I was so certain he wouldn't want us so far away that he'd fight for us. Take my mom to court for shared custody.

Instead, he'd crossed his arms over his full chest and said, *"I see."*

I see.

That was it. Like he couldn't be bothered at all to take ten minutes and talk to a daughter he'd barely seen in the two years since their divorce.

That was a decade ago, and I was no longer the same stupid young teenager who truly thought if I *tried* hard enough, wrote enough letters, sent enough pictures, that my dad would actually start giving a shit about us.

Those hopes were long gone.

I needed help, and he was the best man for that.

None of that meant seeing him again, standing near a wall of windows that overlooked an ice rink didn't make me tremble in my heels or grab hold of the first chair I could find to support my body weight.

"Ryann," he said, and it was drawn out, almost scared or on a breath.

My name from his lips made the room shake. Maybe that was my knees knocking together.

All the dreams I'd had of having a dad who would love me even if I wasn't a son who could someday become an NHL player like he had once been, crashed into me, making the room spin and my dad's, now slightly wrinkled, suntanned face blur.

My mouth, dry as Nevada's summer heat, turned to sandpaper and I forced myself to lick my lips and steady myself.

I pushed off the chair and dropped my hands to my sides.

"Vik," I said, and if that hurt him, he showed it with a blink.

No expression was on his weathered, rounder face other than that blink. I wasn't sure what hurt more.

No excitement at seeing me? Or no reaction to me calling him by his first name. Considering his parenting skills, or lack thereof, calling him Dad was out of the question. Father was pushing it.

We studied each other for a moment. His shoulders rolled back as his spine stiffened, and he returned to the far side of his desk.

"You look well," he finally said as he sat down and gestured for me to take a seat.

A seat. In his elaborate office, where he made millions and millions and had more Stanley Cups than any other coach in history. He offered his daughter a *seat*. Not a hug. Not a smile.

A goddamn fucking chair.

I sat. Crossed my leg over the other and brushed down my skirt. "You look old," I retorted, and that painful yin and yang in my chest—wanting to love the man while hating him—squeezed painfully tight.

"I see your mother raised you with manners."

"At least she raised me," I sniped right back. "And don't ever mention my mother again."

He blinked. Rolled his lips together and nodded. "Apologies. I'm sorry. You've shaken me, showing up here. It's been a long time."

Whose fault is that?

I didn't ask the question. I wouldn't like the answer I received.

"Ten years," I stated, and if he remembered the day I ran from his office, hysterically crying all the way out to where my sister had parked her car and waited for me because she'd refused to see him, he didn't show it.

Not even a blink.

"What brings you in today?"

Perhaps I could have started this meeting different. It was possible he'd read my energy, pulled tight with tension and nerves and very little excitement, and reacted accordingly. Perhaps I could have walked in, said, 'hi Dad,' and smiled, and we would have gotten off to a different start—like him asking me how I was. If I was done with college. How my *sisters* were doing. We could have shot the breeze, gotten caught up...

But this was better.

I'd handed him my heart enough times only for him to drop it like trash.

"I'm here to ask for help."

"Help?" He flinched in his chair, pushed aside a file folder, and rested his forearms on the desk. "How do you need help? Money?"

Please.

Mom made enough. Paul made more. We weren't swimming in millions like Vik, but we did fine for ourselves.

"No. Not money." I shook my head. "I need a job."

I dropped the handle of my red slouch bag off my shoulder and pulled out my resume. As well as awards for high school academic achievements, varsity letters in track and cross country, and my college transcripts.

I told myself it was so he could see I was qualified.

It also had nothing to do with qualifications, and I was self-aware to know. The little girl who still wanted to earn his love. The little girl, all grown up with daddy issues a mile long.

But that was obvious to me when I went to college and majored in sports marketing. Because I might not have been a collegiate athlete, might not have ever stepped foot onto an ice rink because I wasn't a *boy* like he'd wanted, but I'd still studied sports for years because I wanted to have something in common with him.

Good Lord, I needed a stiff drink.

He took the offered file from my trembling fingers and set it in front of him.

"You need a job."

"Yes." I sat up straighter. If he wasn't going to read the file, I could speak for myself. "I graduated this summer from the University of Nevada in Reno. I have a three-point nine-grade point average and a bachelor's degree in business marketing, sports emphasis with a minor in social media management."

"I see." He pushed his thumb to his cheek and settled a large, meaty palm on the file and yet it stayed closed. His eyes never left mine. "It's a difficult field to get into."

"I know."

"And you came to me."

Well, you are my dad... even if he couldn't help me with the hockey team, there was football. He had to know people there.

"I did," I admitted.

After several beats of his intense gaze on me, he swiveled, giving me his profile and began typing on his computer.

Hope filled me, bubbled in my stomach, loosening the knot inside, and I waited patiently, spinning my foot in a circle, my hands clenched lightly together in my lap.

Done with whatever he was looking up, he turned back to me.

"I'm sorry. It appears we don't have any open positions at this time, but I can send your file to human resources. Should something open up—which is doubtful with the season getting started—they can contact you if they feel you're qualified."

No.

He said *no.*

A burn hit the back of my eyes. I would *not* cry. Not again. Not ever again in front of this man.

This horrid, horrific, completely shitty human being in front of me.

"I know that," I said, and surprising myself, my voice didn't waver. "But you're the coach. Friends with the owners. Or maybe other teams? I was hoping you could—"

"Use my position to manipulate and scheme just so my daughter can have a job that isn't needed? I'm sorry, Ryann, but I can't do that. If there's anything else..."

"No." I stood, glaring daggers at my file he was holding hostage with his palm, and lifted my eyes to his. "No. I'm sure I know now that there's not a single damn thing I need or want from you."

My walk was steady.

My ankles stiff.

My voice didn't crack until I was safely encased inside the elevator and the tears didn't fall until I was back in my hotel room.

And then I made the second dumbest decision of the day and called my mom.

TWO

RYANN

"Come on." Hayden threw an arm around me in the booth and tugged me toward her. My insane sister then broke out into a rendition of "Let It Go" so horrible, tables near us were cringing. Not like Hayden cared what anyone thought of her.

Across the table, Braylen slid another shot glass in my direction. "Drink up, and then can we stop talking about this? It's my weekend, and I refuse to let a man who doesn't give two shits about any of us ruin it."

Braylen was our oldest sister. Hayden the middle. While Hayden had long since given up hope of any contact with our sperm donor, she also never seemed to have my baggage, nor Braylen's intense hatred of him. Braylen was only harsh when his name was mentioned and while I hadn't actually said his name since we sat down for dinner, my red, swollen eyes and fading splotchy chest told the tale enough.

"Fine." I rubbed said splotchy chest, took my shot like the good little baby sister I was, and finished my glass of water. "I'm sorry. I should have waited."

"You should have told us," Hayden said. "So we could all show up and give him a piece of our minds. Maybe that's what we need."

"We don't *need* anything, at least not from him," Braylen stressed. "We have Paul. And Mom."

A mom I'd made cry, not for her, or her poor choices in a first spouse, but because I was hurt. Pretty sure Paul wasn't home because if he had been, his ass would be on his way to Vegas to give good ol' Coach Vik a piece of his mind. Followed up with his right hook.

"And you have Blake."

"Exactly." Her shimmery pink lips curled at the corners. "There are good men out there. Amazing ones. Like Paul and Blake. I could name another handful of them. Just because the one who made us isn't one, there's enough good ones out there so spending time thinking of him is a waste of our time."

"And energy," Hayden agreed. She nudged my shoulder. "Right?"

"Right." I nodded, resolute in my determination to put this day away from me.

And my dad in my rearview—permanently.

I pulled out my phone and opened the camera app, flipping the screen so I could check my makeup and ensure there wasn't spinach or steak in my teeth. While Hayden did the same, I swiveled my phone and snapped a selfie with her shoving her fingernail between her front teeth in the background.

"You're such a brat." She stuck out her tongue, so I clicked the camera button again.

"Girls," Braylen chided, and it wasn't possible for her to sound more like our mom.

I flipped the camera and took a picture of her scolding face.

"Sorry, *mom*," Hayden and I sang.

She rolled her eyes. "Come on. It's my bachelorette party, and I'm stuck with my bratty little sisters. Take me to go lose the money Blake gave me on roulette and slot machines and then get me drunk."

"You invited us," I reminded her.

She signed away the dinner bill. She'd refused our help. Her soon-to-be husband Blake was quickly moving up in his own little corner of the finance world. I didn't understand a word of what he did when he tried to explain it to me, but I knew he made a boat-load of money, and he'd insisted on covering our weekend. Since I was still currently jobless outside of working part-time in Paul's ophthalmologist office, I wasn't complaining.

She grinned at us and stood from the table, arms held out wide. "Because I love you and you're the best."

"But I'm better," Hayden whispered in her ear.

My middle finger, fingernail long and sharp and hot pink, shoved into the soft area above her hip. "Bitch."

"Pest."

"Good fucking gracious," Braylen muttered. "Let's get outta here before I put you two in timeout."

PIAZZA ROMANO WAS *LUSH*. To die for. My eyes had been the size of saucers since we walked in and wedged ourselves to a high-top table close to the dance floor, closer to the bar, but far enough in a corner we weren't in a major walkway. Ritzy Italian dripped from the walls and the bar, making everything elegant. Old-world Italian and dark rich hues of deep reds and golds, if I believed in vampires, I'd say we walked straight into the air wicked den of iniquity.

My pulse raced with regret from the day and the fervent need to wash it away. Music slid against my skin, making goose bumps spread like wildfire. Everything about this was exactly what I needed.

"Holy crap," Hayden exhaled with a smile that almost split her cheeks. "The men here are *gorgeous*."

"Good thing we all got separate rooms, then, huh?" I teased and brought the straw of my tequila sunrise to my mouth.

"Absolutely."

"Please don't let me have to hear you two tonight," Braylen moaned and dropped her head into her hands at the table, elbows propped on it.

"I haven't found a guy I've been interested in enough to get dirty with for too long. I've forgotten how to ride a bike. I think it might actually be rusted."

Braylen snorted. Hayden ignored us, off in her own little world of internal debauchery taking place in her beautiful, blonde-haired brain.

"Look at *them*," Hayden shouted, and her arm gestured up, pointing to the second floor. A security guard was at the top and bottom of the stairs, men the size of The Rock, with arms crossed over their chests. "So damn hot."

I leaned forward. The bar was dark, and the lights flashed on the dance floor, but the cordoned-off area upstairs was dimly lit, just allowing me to make out faces.

"Which one?" I asked, shouting over the music.

Hayden grinned at me. "*All* of them."

Nut. She was an absolute nutcase of a woman, which was why she wasn't just my sister but my best friend.

"Come on." I sucked back my drink, slid my hands down my skintight, hot pink dress that matched my nails.

All of our dresses were the same, bought online in different neon colors. Easier for us to find each other in a dark club, and while we could have gone classier with blacks or silvers or whites for Braylen's upcoming nuptials, she'd insisted on more of a sister weekend than a bachelorette hullabaloo with the rest of her bridesmaids.

Our tanned skin showed above our hips, cutouts, and our boobs were barely being held in place by the tight fabric, but if there was one thing I could thank my dad for, it was good genes. We all looked almost exactly like his sister, an aunt we'd never met but my mom told us about. Unlike us, all between five-four and five-six, our mom was taller, waifish, and raven-haired to our natural golden blonde we'd all dyed over the years to varying degrees of platinum and blondes.

I gathered Hayden and Braylen's hands, and we headed toward the dance floor. It gave Hayden the perfect spot to keep an eye on the men above and as we formed a tight circle, hips popping and swaying and knees bouncing to popular dance songs, I threw my hands up, lost myself in the music and the men above.

Damn. Hayden was right. Most of them were deliciously appealing. A whole buffet of men who tossed back beers and threw back shots, sat around several pushed-together tables. A few headed down the stairs to dance and went back up a few songs later with girls wearing half the amount of clothing of ours—a feat in itself, trailing behind them.

What would that be like? To be the kind of beautiful woman men like *that* would simply pluck off the dance floor. It'd most likely end up being for one night only because there was no way those men were the settling-down type. Not at their age. Not with the looks. I didn't know if they were for a bachelor party or a guys' trip, but as I caught sight of a light-haired, blue-eyed man with a chiseled jaw so strong my knees wobbled at the sight of him, I didn't care.

I *wanted* him. And so I turned, thrust my backside out and trailed my arms around my waist, dipped fingers into the cutout above my hips and dragged them up my sides, around my chest. I glanced back to see if he'd noticed me at all, and instead of being at the railing where I'd sworn he saw me before, he was on his way down the stairs.

His gaze in our direction.

Steely, deep-set eyes I couldn't quite see the color of, but he and three guys he was with moved closer.

"They're coming this way!" Hayden shouted in my ear. "And I get the dark-haired young one!"

Thank God we wouldn't have to fight over the blond.

"Wing-womaning it up like a boss," Braylen chimed in my other ear. She shouted so loud her spit hit my cheek and I stuck out my tongue.

The men approached, dressed in confidence and slick black pants, tucked in dress shirts. They moved like they had full awareness of every muscle in their body, with gleams in their eyes that dared anyone—man or woman—to challenge them.

And they were *hot*. Scorchingly so.

The blond stepped toward me, and with heat rising at the tops of my eyes, spreading slowly through my veins, he settled a hand at my hip. His cool skin brushed my on-fire flesh and then I was turned around, my back to his front as he settled in behind me, all the cool, calm, collected confidence of a man who was absolutely, one-hundred-percent used to women doing whatever he suggested.

I was one of many, no doubt.

And I didn't give a damn.

As we started to move, one of his hands rested softly at the peek of skin above my hip, his other hand trailing slowly down my arm to my hand, where his fingers easily laced between mine.

Next to me, one of the other men, dark and dangerous and looking like a grump on a stick, stepped back from Braylen and shook his head. He said something I couldn't make out, turned away and walked off the dance floor.

My brows puckered. Braylen watched him leave with a smile on her face because she didn't care one bit about having strange men dancing with her, before she turned to the remaining man who bent down to hear her. Braylen lifted her left hand, showed her three-carat emerald-cut diamond to him. No doubt warning him he wouldn't be getting anything from her.

"Your friend is married?" A rich, raspy, and heavily accented voice was in my ear.

I turned to him. He was taller than me, but not too tall with the four-inch spikes for heels I had on, and I should have braced myself. Up close, the man wasn't sinfully sexy, he was drop to my knees and rip his dick out of his pants mouth-wateringly delicious. His eyes were pale blue, so close to clear, and the deep set of his eyes gave him a fierce expression.

"Sister. Engaged!" I shouted back. "If your friend is looking to score, he won't."

The man nodded and turned back to Braylen and his friend, but if there were doubts about what I'd said, they vanished when I saw the man take Braylen's hand and spin her in a circle. His other rested at her lower back, ignoring all exposed skin and he kept a polite distance while he *danced*. And he was not grinding nor faking moves. This was a man who had been trained to dance.

"Unbelievable," the man said in my ear again, and there was a quiet laugh I felt in the shaking of his chest vibrating against my back. "The fucker is good."

"You didn't know?"

The man smirked at me, spun me around so my chest was to his, and tilted my chin up with the knuckle of his fist. "He is new."

New?

Such an odd way to word a friend. I shrugged it off because facing this way, I could feel him. I could explore him everywhere. I could sense the power in his thighs on his leaner frame, and I could inhale the scent of freshly adorned cologne or shaving gel.

And so I quit caring. Braylen could take care of herself. Hayden too. But this man?

I wasn't going to miss a moment of enjoying every second I could spend with him.

THREE
ALIX

I had never felt so drawn to a woman before, especially not some beautiful creature who was probably only in Vegas to celebrate a major life event, who would be gone tomorrow. Puck bunnies were a dime a dozen in my life. Women who followed teams and players simply for the fact of thinking they'd bag a professional athlete, either permanently or for the honor of being able to say, *"Remember that time I fucked..."*

Hotels were insane when we traveled. Word getting out what hotel we were staying in, and by the time we'd arrive back after a game, the lobby would be filled with women, tugging up their skirts and tops barely covering their nipples, all for the sake of one of them catching our attention.

It might have made me a first-class prick, but it was *awesome*. I hadn't had to work for a woman's attention since I was drafted to the NHL in America from where I used to play in Switzerland.

But this? Me seeking out a woman who was with two others who looked so similar to her, it was obvious they were sisters, if not triplets? This was different. I wanted to *earn* the honor of her time. Take it slow. I wanted to haul her off into a storage room and slip my fingers deep beneath her extremely short hemline, and I wanted to get her phone number and old-fashionably court her for weeks before a first kiss.

And yet, as soon as she mentioned her sister was engaged, I surmised my first assumption.

She was here for fun. She'd most likely be gone in a day or two. That slow courting I desperately wanted to give her wouldn't happen. And she was too good for a storage room.

We danced until sweat dripped down my spine and her hairline gleamed with it. One of the women had returned to a table, then went to the bar and returned with drinks she handed to her sister. The one with Ryder Bromann, our new teammate who shocked the hell out of me by being able to fucking *move* like he was in a dance competition, took one of the drinks and then handed one to my woman—whose name I didn't know but would quickly fix.

"Need a break?" I asked her as she brought a slim straw to her mouth. Lips full, pouty pillows of smeared lip gloss that instantly made my dick take notice.

She smiled and almost knocked me on my ass with the beauty of it. Grabbing my hand, she tugged us to where their table had remained cleared, an incredible feat. I opened my mouth to invite her upstairs but stalled.

My team was there, and while they'd respect any woman we brought around, I didn't want to share her. Didn't want to know if she knew who we were, didn't want to see her fall over herself if she was a fan. No, tonight, I didn't want to be Alix Halvrick, center for the Las Vegas Vipers and hopefully this season's Stanley Cup Champions.

I wanted to be Alix.

A man who could win her by being *me*.

"I'm Alix," I told her, and could not stop myself from touching her. My fingers pushed blonde curls off her shoulder where her dress strap was so thin it was holding up the fabric by a wing and a prayer.

"Ryann. You're a good dancer."

"Ryan?"

"Two n's." She held up two fingers. "And before you ask, yes, it's a boy's name. I know."

She said it playfully, but there was something tightened at the corner of her eyes. "And a story attached to it, I take it."

She shrugged and whatever sadness had tightened her eyes deepened before she washed it away with a sip of her drink and a smile that I felt like a punch to the gut.

She was *stunningly* beautiful.

"My dad wanted boys."

"Dads can be assholes." Because shit, I knew that. My own wasn't much to write home about. Never really had been but grew worse after my mom died.

She pointed a hot pink fingernail that matched her dress toward the other girls. "My sisters, Braylen and Hayden."

They were all equally gorgeous. It was clear there was an age difference between Braylen, the one engaged, and her, but there was something that made Ryann better.

More intense. A visceral reaction had tightened my shoulders and made me want to stand up straight and punch any man who checked her out, even though I was guilty of doing the same thing.

"I have a sister. Arya."

"You also have an accent," she teased with a gleam in her eyes and that straw resting against her bottom lush lip.

"I do," I said and was prevented from saying more when a server appeared, a fresh round of drinks I'd been having upstairs, and a couple of shot glasses. The waitress was the private cocktail waitress we'd had all night. "Thank you, Seila."

"Your friends thought you could use them. And a fresh round for you, miss?"

"Tequila sunrise, please. And two more for my sisters? But they can go on our tab."

She didn't even glance at me to question it. Didn't hesitate.

She didn't *know*. She had absolutely no clue who I was and wasn't that just fantastic?

This night kept getting better and better.

TWO MORE SHOTS and a couple beers later for me, and I had a pleasant buzz and a beautiful woman wrapped around my arm, leading me down the hallway of her hotel, six floors below Piazza Romano toward her room.

We danced for hours, until her sisters came up and said they wanted to head to a different club. Ryann had nibbled on her bottom lip, arched a blonde brow and there'd been a question in her eyes.

Did I want to leave?

"We have a long day tomorrow, but we can go somewhere else and talk if you'd like?"

"My room? Downstairs?"

Absolutely yes. I waited while she hugged her sisters, promised them I'd take good care of their sister.

"You better." It was Hayden, the non-engaged one. Her wink said she knew exactly how I was going to take care of her sister.

And yeah... I wanted that, too, but I also didn't want to stop talking with her and I wanted to spend as much possible time with her as I could. Ryann glanced at me, giggling as she pulled her keycard out of her dress top.

"Anything else hiding in there?"

She laughed, shaking her head like I was adorable. But truly... what else was beneath that skintight dress? I hoped she'd let me see.

The door clicked open like a shot. Lights left on either by forgetfulness or safety reasons, blared bright and I followed Ryann into the room, already reaching for the hot flesh above her hips, over a scrumptious backside I'd spent hours trying not to shove my hard dick against on the dance floor.

"Ryann," I rasped as my hands made contact and tugged her back to me. Her hands went to mine at her hips, and she spun, smiling up at me, a smile so wide and free I almost didn't want to kiss her.

Almost.

"I've had fun with you tonight."

I leaned in. "Me too."

We hadn't just danced and gotten drunk and fondled each other on the dance floor. At one point we moved to a quieter corner and *talked.* Talking was not my strong suit. Between my accent and the noise, it wasn't the easiest thing for me. But neither had I ever *wanted* to talk so much.

Amazing, truly, this woman out of nowhere managed to pop the lock on my voice, and more than what I meant to say, tumbled out. After she mentioned her dad, I told her some about my own. How he expects me to move home, how he's forcing my sister to get engaged to a prick so similar to him, she continues to threaten to move here to escape.

She told me she moved to Reno when she was a teenager. She worked in her stepfather's eye doctor practice until she could find full-time employment. I told her I travel a lot for work.

Nothing we said were lies, but they were not full truths either.

I normally barely spoke to the women I took to bed, but her not knowing who I was both thrilled me and bothered me. Hiding who I was from her. What I did. And yet it seemed wise.

For reasons I could not put my finger on.

"Do you want a drink?" she asked. "I have a full bar."

I wanted to drink her, all night. All morning. I wanted to drink in her very essence so I would never forget a moment with this beauty.

"Sure. I will take one more."

Perhaps she was nervous. She hadn't appeared so. She was all confidence and smiles and gave everything sexy on the dance floor. More than one man had tried to interrupt us, only backing off when they saw the feral gleam coming from me. Like hell anyone was touching her and forcing me to watch it happen.

Her lips brushed against mine softly, her lip gloss long gone and the scent of her perfume mixed with her sweat, somehow a heady combination. "One more. Get comfortable. I'll be right back."

She slid my hands from her hips, stepping back, not letting go of my fingers until the last moment and then turned. As she moved backward from me, a sly little smile on my vixen's face, she slipped out of her heels, instantly making her so much shorter—so much more perfect for me—

Pretty sure I growled when she bit her bottom lip. "I just need a minute."

She turned and then scampered down a small hallway. I stepped farther into the room. This wasn't a typical, tiny hotel room with nothing more than a bathroom and king-size bed we usually traveled in. This was a suite with a small living room, a hall that led to what I assumed was the bedroom and her bathroom. But the view was insane, Caesar's palace nearby. The Eiffel Tower even closer. The room overlooked the lights of the Strip that were still bright and lively at two o'clock in the morning.

Considering how late it was, and how much alcohol I had to drink, I would most likely be throwing up in the trash can at practice tomorrow afternoon, but as I unbuttoned my dress shirt and stripped out of it down to my black tank beneath, I couldn't find it in me to care.

I was in her small kitchenette, digging into the fridge until I found a beer and grabbed a few options for Ryann, when soft, padded footsteps headed my way.

I stood, turned, and almost swallowed my tongue, almost had to catch my eyes as they jumped out of my sockets.

"Sorry," she said, cheeks blooming a beautiful shade of pale pink. She gathered her hair off her neck and wrapped it up into a thick plastic clip. "I had to get out of my dress."

She had her hands lifted above her head, causing her new dress —a baggy T-shirt that shouldn't have made my mouth dry—rise to the tops of her thighs, *barely* hiding the secret of whether she'd left underwear on or not. Or if she'd been wearing any at all.

"You are stunning," I said, managing to find my balls and remember English.

The dress hid everything I'd explored with my hands. It was a pale, worn gray with a slight rip at the neckline and a few small holes at her shoulder. It was either worn from years of wear or purchased like that, but my dick liked the idea of it being old, worn, something she threw on to be comfortable and felt she could do that around me.

She blushed again, shaking her head, but took the second beer on the counter. "Thank you. I could say the same about you."

Her gaze, blue-eyed, a little glassy but not droopy, telling me she wasn't too drunk, trailed over my shoulders, the veins I knew ran a map down from my arms, and across my chest. "I could say the same about you. You look chiseled from marble."

Statues in Rome, men with dicks smaller than mine, popped into my mind. I took the compliment as intended.

"Come on." I held out my hand and waited until she slipped her palm into mine. "Come talk to me."

"Talk?" she asked, nibbling on the corner of her bottom lip, blush darkening.

"For now." I leaned in, brushed my fingers along her jaw, back to her ear. She shivered beneath my touch, lips parting, and I slid my fingers back to her chin, gripping it gently before tipping her head back. "For a bit."

FOUR

RYANN

Let's go to Vegas, my sister said.

Have a one-night stand, my other sister said.

Mind your own business, I'd said to both of them.

Now, with Alix guiding me to the couch in my small sitting area, in a room Blake paid for, three suites for all of us, I wasn't sure one night with Alix would be enough.

Sex and seduction dripped from him with a playful dance to his moves that told me he didn't take himself too seriously. He liked to lead, based on his moves on the dance floor, but wouldn't be overly bossy. I'd expected him to take me as soon as we crossed the threshold, but he must have noticed the sudden rush of nerves because he didn't.

He waited.

Removed his dress shirt while I'd had to stretch and groan and wrestle myself out of that skintight, sweat-dripping dress. And his arms. Sweet mother-of-pearl, the man had muscles and veins for days that had forced me to swallow instead of lean in and trace the lines from his shoulders straight to the backs of his hands. With my tongue.

He sat down and kicked his feet up on the chaise portion of the couch, guiding me to him so I was close, facing him, my feet draped over his lap.

And I *let him move me like that*. Just sat there, allowed this man I barely knew to put me wherever he wanted, and why was it so *hot?*

His thumb brushed over my ankle in a slow, sweeping motion. He placed his beer on the side table next to the couch and shifted so he was sitting with his back to the corner, more facing me.

"Now that I can talk without noise making it difficult. Tell me where you are from."

Oh, dear heavens. He actually wanted to talk.

The man kept surprising me. For a moment, I faltered. We'd glossed over my crappy father earlier, and I couldn't talk about where I was from without thinking of him and my incredibly shitting morning with him.

Alix's thumb put more pressure on my ankle, bringing me back to him, the stretch of my tanned legs over his muscular ones, and the pressure of his thumb on my skin was arousing. It'd either been too long since I had sex, or I left my common sense on the dance floor.

"Here." I cleared my throat as his brows rose.

"Really?"

"We were raised here, mostly. Then my mom moved us to Reno when I was a teenager."

"And your sisters? What are they like?"

"They're my best friends." I shrugged.

It said it all, really. Braylen kept us grounded. Hayden was the troublemaker and the most social of all of us. I was the people pleaser. We butted heads as easily as we worked together, and an argument barely lasted more than an hour until we either burst into fits of giggles or tears. Wine usually settled the tears, though. And hugs. We were big huggers. Which was probably why I didn't leave it at that.

"Braylen's the oldest. Her fiancé works in finance, so I don't expect them to stay in Reno forever. Blake has lofty goals for himself, what he wants for his family. Hayden is our wild child. She's a travel blogger, so she's constantly on the move, sending us videos of her travels that usually include activities like cliff-jumping or something that terrifies the hell out of the rest of us. We're close. Probably more than most sisters."

We'd had to be. And as soon as I turned eighteen, my mother's role shifted to us being more friends than mother-daughter, so she was one of us, just with the dark hair we didn't inherit.

His thumb kept brushing, rising higher, dropping to above the arch on my foot. Up my shin, down to the top of my foot before he'd grip my ankle, run a hand along my other leg.

Every time he headed up my legs, my core tightened. I was already wet, probably flushed because my blood was heating as he kept his gaze on me, glancing at my lips occasionally while I spoke.

"Do you still have family here?"

"Not really." I took a swig of my beer.

"There is, but you are not close to them. Got it."

Another brush of his hand grazed the back of my leg. One finger trailed toward the back of my knee and goose bumps erupted on my legs. Alix grinned seductively, never once glancing down.

He simply watched my expressions and had to know he was turning me on.

"How...?"

"You have the most expressive eyes. I drown in them."

It could have been the accent making his words sexier than they should have been. It could have been the way his riveting blue eyes met mine and held... a beat, two... then more before either of us could look away. It could have simply been this man, with one hand draped over my shin, his thumb slowly brushing along my skin, that made my body pulse with the need to *move*. To grind.

Yet he seemed in no hurry, so my torture would continue. It was heaven. Hell. A mixture of enjoying this game, the slow seduction of it, and the desire to *know* him.

"And you? European, based on your accent. French, or am I wrong, and it's Canadian?"

"I am from Switzerland."

"The French side," I surmised. "Near Geneva?"

Light hit his eyes.

"*Correctment*," he purred.

Yes, purred and tilted his head.

"You've spent time there to know the difference, *oui*?"

Oh, oui, oui, baby. With a voice like that, I'd say oui, oui to anything.

"We've spent time traveling Europe, Southern France. A few trips to Switzerland and down to Italy. You come from a gorgeous homeland."

"It holds nothing on you, and that is not a line."

Like I cared if it was. He could read me his grocery list, and I'd be equally enthralled with him.

"Thank you."

"I mean it." He leaned forward, lifted his hand that was on my leg, and cupped my cheek. His thumb made a soft, teasing motion along my jaw, and his blue eyes turned scandalous as he caught me shiver. "I have enjoyed my night with you."

"Me too."

"But I think I will enjoy this more." He licked his full lips, leaned in, and I gasped in a breath right before those lips pressed to mine.

There was the faintest taste of beer beneath the stronger scent of *sexy masculine man*, and he kissed me senseless, until I was breathless, until I was shifting my legs and gathering them beneath me so I could rise on my knees, leaning into him.

Alix's mouth opened, lips parting, and his tongue slid into my mouth like he already knew every exact way to kiss me to turn me into a tightly wound, needy mess.

I whimpered at that first taste of him, his other hand sliding to my lower back, and I was moved, held until my legs were straddling him. As he lowered me, my core rocked against a hard, thick length that couldn't possibly be real.

"You are delicious. So special," he muttered, rasping the words against my lips as his hands dove into my hair. He dislodged the clip from my hair and tugged me closer to him until my breasts scraped against the thin cotton of my shirt and pressed to his chest where his heartbeat was thumping a rapid pace, reminding me of horse hooves on dirt at my one and only horse race.

"Shit," I rasped, rolling my hips against him.

He groaned into my mouth, hands sliding down my back until he cupped my backside. He stopped then, fingertips at the hem of my yoga shorts hidden beneath my oversized shirt, and dropped his head to my couch. "Is this okay? Too fast? I can slow—"

"Down?" I laughed, husky and throaty, and shook my head. "I'll kill you if you do."

Lips quirked at the corners and thank God I was sitting because my knees turned to jelly at the rapturous look on his face. "I do not wish to die."

"Then take me to my room?"

"Where I can devour every inch of you like I've been dreaming of for hours? Yes. I think we have talked enough."

I laughed, and he kissed it away, but we were both still smiling as he stood, pulling me with him, and as our tongues touched again, the smiles vanished, and there was only need and want and a desperate desire to rid both of us of our clothes and feel the weight of his body on top of mine.

This woman. My mind was spinning. I was what the Americans on my team called a player, which I would argue with because I didn't play with women. I respected them too much to play with their hearts, but I did take the opportunity to enjoy a wide variety of women. Ever since I moved to the States for hockey, it was easy to find a woman for a night, or a few weeks, but I had no intention of settling down until I could provide a woman with a stable, secure future that wouldn't involve being shipped off to a new team and a different city whenever my management team felt like they'd had enough of me. I had no wish to find a woman, start a family, and then continue forcing them to change schools and make new friends.

Yes, I wanted all of that someday, and there were days—especially most recently when I was missing my sister and my mum—when I reconsidered.

Perhaps that's what this connection to Ryann was. Me, lonely, wanting to find a woman but not wanting to drag her across the country with me, that had knocked me on my ass the first time I heard her throaty chuckle in my ear while we danced so close together. I already knew the shape of her body even hidden beneath this oversized shirt.

Which I was currently desperate to tear off her so I could trace my tongue along the length of her body, pull her nipples into my mouth and test their sensitivity.

I also wanted her clothed so we could keep talking. That would have to wait though. My dick, currently pressed and scrunched in the confines of tight boxer briefs and pants and wedged against her hot core, was dying for priority.

Tomorrow.

I would come back tomorrow after practice. Take her on a date if I could remember how those went, and then test myself on the memory of her body.

Her room was dark, which wouldn't do, so I carried her to the side of her bed and flicked on the lamp. A low glow illuminated the room, and I pulled back long enough to see her shadowed profile.

"Beautiful," I whispered and set Ryann on her feet, my hands going to her shirt. "Can I?"

"You have my full consent to do whatever you'd like," she teased, her hands already tugging at the waistband of my pants to remove my black tank. "As long as I have the same."

"Anything." My voice was already hoarse, in part from screaming at the club. Mostly from lust, watching her confidence as she removed my shirt.

Also, the thoughts *anything* brought to my mind was vast. Creative. And more than a little bit filthy.

This would not be a typical, hurried and frenzied meaningless meeting.

She might have been a stranger to me, although after some of our talk tonight, it felt as if I had known her for years. She was not there with me in that moment, in her hotel room because she knew my career—she just wanted me, and for the first time in a long time, I had no desire to use it as a tool to get a woman into bed with me.

Stripped of her oversized shirt, I lost my breath at the sight of her. Her breasts were not only full, plump, and perky, they were bare of any covering.

"Shit. I need you." I drew her closer to me as I moved us toward the bed. "The things I want to do to you are endless."

At the first surprised hitch of her breath, I made my move. Cupping her cheek with one hand, I trailed my other up her arm until my thumbs were at her throat, my lips skimming her jaw.

"Alix," she whispered, a breathless plea to end the torture I was currently providing and yet I could not. Would not until I drove her mad with desire and then gave her endless, unspeakable pleasure.

"You are a treasure," I told her, and then I kissed her. My lips met hers, and I traced the seam of hers with my tongue, silently seeking entrance that was given. Our tongues met and a beautiful, needy sound escaped her lips. This kiss was already different than the previous ones.

Unhurried and warm, filled with lust as electricity zipped down my spine at the quiet, pliable touch of hers.

"I have need of you," I murmured and pressed my hands down to her backside until I lifted her up and moved forward, setting Ryann down on the bed until she was splayed before me, an offering... a gift, clothed in tiny, skintight shorts that barely covered the parts of her I wanted to discover the most.

I brushed my hands up her legs, reveled as she shivered at my soft touch, and her legs opened, spread, feet planted to the bed until my fingers met the waistband of her shorts. "May I?"

"Only if you take off your clothes and join me."

I stripped out of my pants faster than I slapped a puck into a goal, and soon, Ryann's hips were lifting as I pulled down her shorts until all of her was exposed.

Her sex glistened, and beckoned me to taste her, so I climbed on the bed, my hands at her inner thighs, spreading her open, and I trailed my tongue up her inner thighs, avoiding what I wanted most. Her hips rolled, searching for that first touch of me, and I avoided it, despite the need burning in my chest and my hard dick demanding I take her.

I kissed her hip bone, the soft skin at her stomach, and then up to her breasts, where I lapped at her nipples, her dark pink, hardened buds.

"Oh." She gasped as I sucked one into my mouth, flicked her other one with my fingers and alternated, tasting every inch of her I could while her hips continued to roll, and her hands ran up and down my back. My arms. Hot pink fingernails scraped my scalp and tugged on my hair until I brought my mouth to hers.

I speared her mouth with my tongue, devoured hers in a kiss, and pushed my hand down her body until my fingers were at her slick, wet folds.

Her pussy *dripping* for me.

"You like this," I confirmed and brought the evidence of her pleasure to my mouth, sucking it off my fingers.

"I need more. Please."

I kissed her again, and this time, I did not tease. I pressed a finger inside of her, quickly added another, and as I fucked her with my fingers, her nails dug into my hips, my back. Our kiss was frantic and sloppy, the sounds of sex and moans—both hers and mine—whispering off the walls, growing in intensity, and as she braced her feet in the bed and clung to me, I tore my mouth off hers to slide down her body until my mouth was *there*.

My tongue slipped inside of her, and I groaned against her sex at that first hot and wet taste of her. "So fucking sweet. So wet." I shoved my two fingers back inside of her. Twisted. Moved them slowly as I slapped her clit and held her hips down with my forearm braced across her hips.

"Alix!" She called my name like a need, and I gave it to her until she was a trembling, soaking wet mess, and as she came, I sucked on her clit and added a third finger. I drove her to the cliff with her bringing pain to my scalp from her fingers.

She cried out, her body trembled, and it was only once she was coming down that I bathed her hips and her legs with my tongue and mouth until I was standing at the end of the bed, grabbing a condom from my pants I'd dropped earlier and shoving out of my boxers.

"Shit," Ryann rasped, one arm draped over her eyes. "I might be done. That was... that was good." She peeled her arm off her face and dropped it to the bed.

"Yeah?" I asked, because if she was done, I would deal, but I surely hoped like hell she was joking.

I stroked myself, and let her eyes roam my body until a sensual little smirk curled her lips and she shook her head.

"No." Her arms rose in the air and her hands wiggled. "Come here. Now, I have need of you."

I chuckled as she repeated my words from earlier, complete with a faux accent. "Your accent needs work."

"I'll practice," she promised, and as I lined myself up at her center, she kissed me, smiling a smile I wanted to see more of that quickly morphed into something much different when I pushed inside of her.

I sheathed myself in her hot little body in one slow thrust and then braced my hands on the bed, took in every one of her features and expressions, committing them to memory all while trying to hold back on coming too soon.

And then I moved. Ryann took every punishing, forceful thrust with pleasured moans and cries for me. Her trim legs wrapped around my waist and pulled me closer. I took her hands, shoved them into the bed next to her head, and I worked her until she pressed her lips to my throat, bit down while she came again and from the pain of that bite I hoped like hell she'd leave her mark all over me.

"Shit. I'm going to come," I rasped against her shoulder.

"Yes," she hissed while her walls clamped around me, pulled me deeper, and sucked me in, and it wasn't just the hot fucking or the sex or her sexy, lithe little body, it was this connection I felt around her.

She didn't pull me into her body. She was a vortex, twisting me up in a way I feared a night with her would not be enough. Reno was less than eight hours away. We could make something work.

I came, groaning Ryann's name against her throat, both of us wrapped up in a pleasurable embrace before I smothered our cries by kissing her again until we were both breathless.

Rolling off her, I curled her back to my chest, my hand on her stomach. I drew lazy circles onto her flesh with my thumb and kissed her shoulder.

"I did not think when I went out tonight, I would meet someone like you."

Her breath hitched, and her hand covered mine. "Me either, Alix. Me either."

We lay in silence for several minutes until I slid off the bed. "I need to go get us cleaned up. Be right back."

She hummed, a sound that was near sleep and when she whispered my name and asked me to stay, I wasn't sure if she was awake at all. After I used the restroom and returned to the room, a soft glow coming from the lamp to see her exactly where I left her, her blonde hair splayed out all over the pillows and draped over her shoulders, her quick fall to sleep was confirmed. I didn't hesitate before rejoining her in bed.

There was no way I was leaving until morning, not without getting her full name. Her phone number. And most likely, another delicious round before I had to get to the arena.

Warm, calloused palms scraped along my inner thighs, pulling me from sleep with a gentle start.

"Oh," I rasped as my eyes opened. Alix was there, leaning over me, his hands spreading my legs and kissing the crease of my thighs.

"Good morning."

"Morning—" I barely finished the word before his tongue took one long, leisurely swipe against my sex and my head fell back to the pillow. Good morning *indeed*.

"I woke up hard this morning, your hands all over me, and I couldn't resist." A gentle flick at my clit pulled a groan from deep in my throat.

"Please." I flipped a hand in the air and laughed. "Continue with your day."

"With pleasure." They were the last words spoken, intelligible ones, anyway, before he dove back to my sex, and teased me with hard and gentle licks, long swipes, and circles at my clit. He added fingers and pressure and his grip tightened on my thighs. Despite the fact I'd already had more orgasms in a night with him than I'd had in some entire relationships, he took me to the peak quickly, threw me over it, and brought me back down before I could even try to withhold the temptation to climax so quickly.

"You are good at that." I laughed, breathless, brushed hair off my face, and forced my other hand to loosen my grip on the sheets. Alix hovered over me, his blond hair so thick and somehow perfectly in place, I was almost jealous, but there was no time for it to take root before he was bending down, brushing his lips along the column of my throat. Back to my ear.

Good *grief*. How could I still want more?

The man was incredible. In bed. Out of it.

An alert dinged on a phone. His. Mine. I had no clue until Alix paused his teasing exploration of my jawline and turned, frowning as he saw the time on the clock.

"Shit," he rasped. "It's ten o'clock."

And? I wasn't an early morning person by any means, but apparently, he was.

"Got somewhere to be?"

He chewed the bottom corner of his lip before his rich blue eyes met mine. "Practice later. It's fine."

Jumping into an ice bath couldn't have chilled me quicker. My hands went to his chest, pushing, putting space between us. "Practice? For what?"

Puzzle pieces clicked together so quickly that the full picture became clear in a blink. The accent. The body. His flexibility.

I'd just spent the night with a—

"Hockey."

Fuuuccckkk.

He stood, crossed his arms over his chest, and I forced myself not to drool over those abs. The thick bulge beneath his boxer briefs. "I play for the Las Vegas Vipers."

No. He couldn't. Of all the damn shitty luck I had so far on this trip to Las Vegas, and this had to land straight into my lap as well.

I jumped from the bed, noting the shock in his eyes when I

moved so quickly. He frowned as I whipped the bed sheet around my body faster than he'd made me want to drop my panties.

"You should go."

"What?" A side of his lips twitched, and he settled his hands on his hips.

I was already moving, tucking the sheet tightly around my body. Shit. This was bad. So very, very bad.

If my dad ever found out about this, he'd never speak to me again—which... whatever.

I nodded my head toward the hotel door. "You need to leave."

"You are messing with me, yes?"

Oh, I'd made a mess, all right. Shaking my head, I bit my tongue. "No, Alix. Last night was great. Incredible."

"Unforgettable, no?"

Oh dear. That accent. My knees wobbled as his blue eyes skimmed the length of my body like he was imagining every single freckle he'd kissed and already memorized. The sheet burned against my flesh.

Unforgettable was right. In all the good ways and bad.

"And this morning." I flipped out a hand toward the bed. "Well, that was... wonderful, too. But it was just a night, and you have plans. I do too, so thank you."

For making me forget no matter how hard I tried, my father would never like me or my sisters. Hell, I wasn't even all that certain he liked *women* in general anymore.

"You are not joking." He shook his head, dazed. Probably getting pissed he was still rock hard, and he'd figured he'd get to fuck me again after working his magic with his tongue and fingers.

"No. Please leave." My chin trembled.

God, this epic, gorgeous man. Kicking him out was the last thing I wanted to do. Had he kept his mouth shut, I'd be enjoying the weight of his body, the powerful thrust of his hips against me. The thickness of him sliding inside of me. I'd concocted plans last night to not leave an inch of his body undiscovered before I had to go back to Reno tomorrow.

And one stupid word ruined it.

Just like it'd ruined everything else in my life.

Freaking hockey.

He scowled, somehow managing to look sexy doing it even though it was directed at me, and tugged on his black dress pants from the night before. Then his tank top.

"I do not understand what just happened," he said, shaking his head. Frustration clear—in more places than just his face. "But I will be back later, to talk. Last night..."

He sighed, scrubbed his hands through his blond hair. "That might have been the best night of my life," he admitted, the frustration ebbing out of his tone, softening his voice and somehow thickening that gorgeous French accent.

My heart thudded against my chest. It'd definitely been the best night of mine.

If only it could have stayed the night forever.

"I'm sorry." For so many things, but also for the trouble this could bring him.

He pressed his full, pouty lips together and nodded. "Me too. You sure?"

"Yes." Unequivocally. Even if it hurt to be so certain.

Alix shoved his wallet into his back pocket, snagged his keys where he'd tossed them on the dresser and left, not looking back.

Somehow managing to break my heart as the door slammed shut.

As soon as he was gone, I dove across the bed and grabbed my phone.

"What?" my sister, Braylen, answered, voice thick from sleep, tequila, and too much screaming. "This better be important if you're calling me this damn early."

"I just had the best night of sex and maybe everything else in my entire life."

"The sexy blond guy?"

"Yeah."

"So why are you calling me and not enjoying him?"

"Because he's a Viper."

There was only a beat of silence before the sleep cleared from her throat, and I knew she was now sitting, fully awake. "Get your ass to my room for mimosas or Bloody Marys. Now. I'll call Hayden."

SEVEN
RYANN

I was shit at keeping my word.

After September's messy visit to Las Vegas with Braylen and Hayden, I'd sworn to myself I'd never return to this town. Moreover, I promised I would never seek out my father, walk through the halls where he worked and coached.

And yet, stupidly, there I was, three months later, waving a hand to my dad's assistant, Susan Graff, as I entered, and she told me to head on in.

He called me two days ago, right before Christmas, and left a message about a job opening the team currently had. But no, my dad didn't stop there. He'd already purchased me a ticket if I still needed help finding a job.

Yes, I was definitely still looking for a job. So far the only option I'd found was working with the women's swim team at UN-Reno and it paid less than part-time, which meant I was still shelving files in Paul's office, working fifty hours a week and barely managing to scrape by while living in the garage apartment of my childhood home. But hey, I'd moved out of my childhood bedroom – look at me going places.

My desperate desire to move out and be independent was most

likely what had me considering this foolishness and forcing myself to not entertain a single thing regarding the last night I spent here, with a man who'd required multiple battery changes to my favorite personal toy since.

I knocked on Vik's open door, and he turned from the wall of windows. The same exact place he'd stood the last time I came to see him.

Déjà vu hit hard and fast, and it wasn't the first time I wondered if that was his thinking spot.

"You came." His voice was lighter than last time. Skin the same rich tan, bald head just as bald. But there was something different about him, too. A softer edge making his hard jawline and stance seem gentler.

"I did. You wanted to talk about a job."

"I did. I do," he corrected and wiped a hand over his mouth. "Can we sit?" He swung his arm out toward a sitting area. Small table, six chairs circled it. I would have preferred the buffer of his desk this time for a job interview, but slunk over to the table, dropped my purse on top and slid into a chair.

My father took the seat two away from me, angled toward me. "How have you been?"

"Um. Fine. I thought you called about a job." Lord knew the man certainly had no interest in a reunion. Not with the way he'd left things last time.

"I did. And we'll get to that, but I wanted to explain. The last time I saw you... that didn't go well."

It hadn't. I'd relived it too many times. It hurt every time. Despite my anger with him, I was still the stupid little girl who wanted her dad to love her, even if I knew it'd never happen.

"I was in the hospital a few weeks back."

Surprise had my back straightening. "What?"

"We'd gotten back from a five-day away trip. I didn't feel right. Chalked it up to stress and whatnot, but by night, I couldn't... well, it scared me enough to call an ambulance."

"Are you okay?" And why did I suddenly care so much? This was the man who never showed a single ounce of caring about his daughters once we left. Hell, before then.

Still, my heart was speeding, and my face cooled as blood drained from it.

"I am. Now. I told the team I had the flu. They don't know. I thought I was having a heart attack. Turns out it was a pulmonary embolism." I must have given him a confused look because he explained. "A blood clot in the lungs. The symptoms can be similar to a heart attack, but regardless, I was in the hospital for a few days."

I was still trying to process this, still imagining the worst-case scenario—glad that he was okay, pissed he didn't let us know.

"You learn a few things when you're alone in a hospital room, the fear of the end of your life right in front of you."

My lips were practically fused together. He hadn't called. And he *could* have.

Reading my thoughts, he nodded. "I could have called. Wanted to, but with the way I treated you last time, I wasn't so sure you'd take my call."

He had a point there. A valid one. In fact, I hadn't answered his most recent call either, but waited to see if he left a message.

"I'm glad you're okay and you got help when you needed it," I told him. That was true. Getting a call saying my father was dead, even if we hated him, would have been worse.

"Thank you. That means something to me, to hear you say that. I'm assuming your sisters might not share your thought."

"I'm not really sure I want to talk about them with you."

"That's fair." Although he certainly didn't seem pleased about it. He clasped his hands together on the table. "That event was a wake-up call for me. I have done a lot of things wrong in my life and lying alone in a hospital room forced me to evaluate myself." He shoved a hand over his mouth, curling it as he exhaled a harsh breath. When he spoke again, his tone was lower. "As hard as it was and as difficult as it is to admit, I didn't quite like realizing the guy I've become, the man I failed to be. I'd like to explain some, if you could—"

"I'm not really sure I need to hear your excuses." My chest squeezed as I said it. Did I want to know more about my dad? Yes. But excuses were pointless, and there was too much between us. "Is this why you called me about the job? To get me here to listen to your apologies?"

"That's my first step." He stood from his chair, grabbed a file on his desk and pen, and brought it back. Sliding the file toward me, he twirled the pen in a circle.

The only sign he might have been nervous.

I'd always had a soft spot for my dad. Even when Mom left, I understood why. He hadn't been a good husband. Or a decent father. He was absent at best, emotionally distant when he was there. The mood in our home would deflate like a popped balloon as soon as he'd walk in the door.

In truth, my mom was probably a single mom as soon as Braylen was born. At the time, he'd just started coaching as an assistant with the Vipers. Mom told us when we were older, she always thought things would get better. Once he proved himself. Once he adjusted to having a family and a career. That day never came.

That didn't mean once we left and I wasn't with him, I hadn't cried at night. Missed him. Wanted him to come fight for his family —or at least his daughters.

But a lot had changed since then. September's run-in topping the list.

"What's the job?" I finally asked.

Even with my job at the university, I'd still tried to apply for jobs. But most would take me too far away from Mom, and I wanted to be close. Vegas alone was a trek. At least seven hours away. But Hayden was always on the road. Braylen was now married, and while we were all still close, I was who Mom had left.

Paul, obviously. She was happy. Wanted us all to spread our wings and follow our dreams. When push came to shove though, and it came to entry-level jobs I'd received interest in, they were all on the East Coast and I couldn't bring myself to pull that trigger.

Perhaps, I needed them more than I cared to admit.

"It's a legit position, just so you know," he said and gestured with a dip of his chin toward the file folder. "The team needs an assistant for the travel coordinator, and our staff that handles all of our gear can always use a set of extra hands. It's simply too much work for one person, and our former assistant recently decided to stay home after she had her baby in the off-season. Callie, our coordinator, has been struggling, and I'm concerned if we don't get her help, and quickly, she won't last the season."

It wasn't marketing. But it was something with a professional team. I flipped open the file and scanned the requirements and duties. All seemed pretty self-explanatory until I realized—

It involved traveling with the team. Right there. Black and white. Travel assistant is required to attend all road games with the travel coordinator to facilitate ease of transitions between locations, whether that is transportation to and from the hotel or games, managing hotel check-ins, and returning to Las Vegas.

Oh shit.

That meant a lot of time being with Vik. It wasn't him that had my stomach rolling and a pulse beating at the tops of my thighs.

Being on an airplane with Alix. Staying in the same hotel with him. Bus rides.

Team dinners if staff was included.

I'd be around him all of the freaking time, at least when we traveled, and it was hockey. They traveled a shit ton.

My eyes grew as I took in the salary. "This is real?"

My dad smiled. It was possibly the first smile he'd ever shot my way, and I hated it as much as I wanted to pull out my phone and snap a picture to remember it. He smiled like Braylen, and it was unnerving. If I ever told her that, she'd probably never smile again.

"Starting salary. It's the league standard, you can check with other teams if you'd like."

I'd definitely look into it. I'd come to him for help with a job, not a salary that blew my mind. I wouldn't have to live in a studio apartment. Hell, I might be able to get a two-bedroom with that amount, and I'd save on groceries since I'd be traveling so much. Plus, my car was nearing a decade old. Didn't have a lot of miles, but something sportier would be fun…

My mind ran away from me. The possibilities I'd been dreaming of since college graduation were now clearing into my reality.

"All this because you had a health scare? This is your way to make amends? Because I very clearly remember you telling me you wouldn't help me before."

He inhaled a deep breath and glanced out the windows down to the ice rink below, where there were a handful of skaters. None of them were wearing Alix's number though.

Because of course I'd gone home and turned into a stalker, and I'd now watched more hockey games in the last three months than in my entire life.

I couldn't stay away from him, even seven hours away.

"I did say that, you're right. I also said we didn't have jobs available, and if one did open up, I'd let HR know. I've also talked to them. And I looked at the resume and file you showed me last time. You're qualified for this, maybe more than. But yes, I was also hoping, maybe in a small way, this could be an opening for us—for me—to start to amend things with you."

"Is that a requirement for the job? Being forced to spend time with you?"

"No." He said it so quickly, I jolted. "I am not trying to coerce you into that. There are no strings attached to this. If you want the job, it's yours, but that's the last favor I pull. You keep the job or lose it based on your performance, and that performance will be tied to your reviews with Callie and human resources." He leaned in and softened his voice to a tone I could never remember him using. "Like I said, I regret many things now. Perhaps it is too late, but I was born a competitor, and I still am, so I like to believe it's never too late. Outside of traveling with the team together, I won't force you to spend time with me. Anything personal is entirely up to you, but I am hoping, eventually, you might open that door."

Tears burned the back of my throat, and I pressed my tongue to stop them before they could spread.

I was a twenty-three-year-old woman, and I never thought I'd see the day when my father actually wanted to talk to me.

"I don't know," I admitted. "But I'm not saying no to you or the job."

"That's fair."

"If I do accept it, when would I start?"

I'd have to move. Find an apartment. Rent a moving truck. Go home and face my mom and sisters and Paul and Blake and tell them all what I was doing. Deal with the fallout.

It'd take time.

"We really do need someone soon, as soon as you can, actually, and I do know that's asking a lot. The team has a few hotel rooms we use for players after they're traded or called up to give them time to get settled. I do know one is available if you'd need that."

Now *that* was a favor. Guaranteed. A smile teased my lips, and I pressed them together.

"I only ask one thing."

Of course, he was going to. "You just said no strings."

"This isn't strings, it's a request."

It sounded absolutely like it was *not* a request, but I'd bite. "What is it?"

"Do not date one of my boys."

Heat flared at my chest. Outward. And none of the reasons I expected. Because the very idea of him mentioning his players should have first, brought back memories of Alix. But no... his *boys*?

"Right." My jaw tightened and my limbs began to shake. "Your boys. Curious. Do you have that *request* with every staff member here? Or just the evil *girl* you had a part in bringing into this world but ditched because she'd never be one of your *boys*?"

He blinked, and it was amazing he could be so absolutely ill-prepared for me to think anything different than what he'd just said. "That's not what I meant, Ryann."

"You didn't answer my questions." Red speckled at the corners of my vision, making him blur, and if one Vik was bad enough, this was way worse. "Do you have this talk with all the staff?"

For a second, just a brief pulse, he actually looked embarrassed. "It's not technically against policy."

"So, it's just your wicked little female you brought into this world that you don't want poisoning your precious little boys."

"That's not what I meant, but I know them."

Ha. If only I could let him know how well I knew one of them, too.

"And?" I was not letting him out of this easily.

A muscle twitched in his cheek, and I was pretty sure, unfortunately, our expressions matched. Equal frustration, part rage.

"Forget it. Just forget I said anything."

Oh, how quickly he could backpedal. If I wasn't already near the verge of tears, I'd push him, but he only made my head spin. Was it for my protection? Did he think they were all cheating assholes? Or was he keeping them from *me.* And for what purpose.

I should have known I'd never get a clear answer out of him, he'd already shown his card. His *boys* would always be more important than his own flesh and blood.

"Out of curiosity," he started, and I swore his voice thickened. "Your sisters... do you think there's a chance—"

"No." I shook my head. And if there was a chance in hell before, it'd be negative five hundred after I told them what he just said to me—*if* I told them. "That's never going to happen. Especially with Braylen, and besides that, you'd have to get through Blake first, and I can guarantee he wants to kick your ass."

"Blake?"

Oh shit. He didn't know. Of course he didn't, but the fact he hadn't known still made a lump lodge in my throat. Braylen insisted on not even bothering to send our father an invitation to her wedding. Even Mom tried to convince her but she wouldn't be moved. She'd practically forced me to take a blood oath when I came to see him in September, so I wouldn't mention it to him.

I licked my tongue over the front of my teeth and met my father's eyes—blue eyes that matched mine from the slight downward tip at the outer corners and thick black lashes. "Braylen's married. She and Blake were married in September, the week after I came to see you. We were here for her bachelorette party weekend."

"You were all here..." He trailed off and turned back to the ice rink. Definitely his thinking spot. Every time he was uncertain, his gaze went to the window where he'd stood earlier. "You were all here, and I wasn't nice to you." He glanced back at me. "Married. Wow... that's... she's happy? He's a good man?"

Thick brows arched into perfect half moons.

The retort, *a better man than you*, hung heavy on my tongue and I swallowed it down. "They're happy. And he's great."

"She hates me."

"You abandoned us." It came out cold, but it was the bitter truth, and I'd been too young when we left to know the full scope.

Now I was a grown woman with male trust issues a mile long due mostly if not wholly, to the man sitting across from me.

"It's not like any of you called."

Anger rose, hard and fast, forcing me to my feet and shoving my hands to the top of the table. How many chances was I going keep giving him only for him to continue proving how big of a *dick* he was?

"We were *children*. Your children. It wasn't our *job* to keep in touch with you, it was yours, to love us and protect us and *want* us... regardless of what chromosomes we were born with."

His mouth dropped, and I must have imagined the regret in his eyes before he nodded. "You're right. I'm sorry. I've made many mistakes."

Love for a man I always wanted to love me swirled, mixed with anger, until my fingertips buzzed and my head swam. I grabbed my purse and shoved the file inside. "I need some time to think. I can't —I can't do this with you, not now. And I don't know if I can work with you. There's too much."

Shit. He was handing me the job, the help I'd asked for, and he'd been sick. But having to see him every day? Listen to those jabs that showed no responsibility or remorse? That could be asking too much.

"Maybe this was a mistake," I muttered, and as he opened his mouth, I didn't give him a chance.

I fled.

Out of his office, bypassing the elevator as he shouted my name, and straight to the stairs. I charged down five flights of stairs, tears blurring my view, and I sniffed them back, and pushed through a door. It wasn't the main floor. But my thighs were burning, and if I kept crying, I'd risk breaking an ankle in a quiet stairwell.

Not how I'd want to see my dad again.

I was wiping my eyes, spinning around, trying to find an elevator, and as I reached a corner, a shadow crossed into my path. I didn't have time to spot before that shadow turned into a fully formed body and I slammed right into it.

"Oh!"

Two hands reached out, grabbed my wrists, and tugged me back to my feet, my ass inches from the carpet.

"Thank you. I am so sorry." My hair was askew, my mascara probably streamed down my cheeks, and as I blinked away tears, I cursed.

"Ryann?"

I closed my eyes as his voice, my name, thickened with his accent and surprise, and so beautiful, rolled through me.

And just like that... I did the one thing my sister warned me not to.

I ran straight into Alix freaking Halvrick.

"Hi, Alix."

EIGHT

ALIX

This was not possible. This could not be happening.

How in the hell did the woman I hadn't been able to stop thinking or talking or dreaming about since September fall into my lap? Literally.

And at the Vipers' training facility of all places.

Hell, yesterday I was sitting on the couch next to Emmersyn, Kane's wife slash fiancée, while we gave him shit as he decorated their Christmas tree, still talking about Ryann.

The girl who kicked me out after the best night of my life.

The woman I hadn't been able to move on from.

The woman I'd had no desire to move on from because my dick apparently stopped working the moment the door to her hotel room clicked shut behind me.

Three long, torturous months without sex. Without women.

Without Ryann.

"What are you doing here?" I asked.

She stepped back, forcing me to release my hold on her, but I wanted to dive back and grab her. The first touch of her, even if I didn't know it was the moment I caught her, sent a whip of electricity through me.

"I... uh..." She glanced back in the hall where she'd come from and swiped beneath her eyes.

Mascara was running.

Her eyes were red.

"Were you crying? What's wrong?"

"Um. Nothing. I have to go."

"You cannot."

She stepped away, and I reached for her. She moved before I could get a hand on her, skirted right out from beneath me, and hugged her stomach with her arms.

Her blue eyes, wide and glassy, glanced behind me. "What?"

"What?" Was she kidding? "I have not been able to stop thinking about you, that night. And now you are here, *here* of all places, where I play, and we cannot talk?"

Wait...

"What *are* you doing here?"

There had to be a reason. My mind came up blank. "You do not work here."

She huffed, pressed fingertips to her forehead, and shook her head. "No."

"Did you come to see me?" It was a long shot. But if she wanted to find me, I'd told her I was a Viper. She was smart enough to figure it out. "Because if you did, Ryann, I must say, I am damn glad to see you."

I was turning into a fool. Every word I spoke, she took a step backward, slowly, like I'd frightened her. A reason for her being here made sudden sense. "Are you pregnant?"

"What? God no." Her jaw fell. "Oh my God. No. I'm not pregnant, Alix. No, but listen, I really need to go. So can you just... like forget you saw me?"

"Forget?" She had to be kidding. "I have waited for this moment."

"Ryann?"

Coach Vik yelled from a distance. His heavy footsteps echoed on the floor, and I turned to Ryann as she cursed.

Oh no. No way. This was not happening.

"Coach?" I asked as he closed in on the corner, appearing right from where Ryann had come from.

"Alix." He said my name with surprise, and then both of them swiveled and faced a now ghostly white Ryann. "Hey. Have you seen my daughter?"

"Daughter?" I choked out.

We all knew they existed. He had three of them....

Oh shit. Blood rushed from my face so fast it was a wonder it didn't spill to the floor beneath my feet.

Three sisters... September... a shitty dad...

"Fuck," she cursed again in a harsh whisper. Blue eyes glared daggers at me as my world was officially rocked.

There was no way to avoid this. No way to play dumb, even if the word daughter sounded like a foreign language I didn't know coming from him.

"I, uh, think she's right here." I pointed my arm around the corner. Based on the look on her face, she wanted to bite my hand off. Kick me in the balls.

At least my sudden, forced departure now made sense.

Ryann Boucher.

I'd fucked our coach's daughter.

"Hey, Vik." From what she'd said in September, it didn't surprise me she called him by his name.

"Hey." He shoved his hands into his typical team day practice forest green athletic pants and rocked on his heels. "You ran out so fast I needed to make sure you were okay. I'm sorry again for..."

"No need." She held up a hand, stopping him. "I'm fine."

Coach glanced at me, jaw grinding.

Pretty sure this was a family moment I wasn't supposed to be witnessing.

Also, definitely positive Coach was nervous. Hell, I'd seen him less nervous when we were playing for the Stanley Cup.

"I know this is difficult," he said. "But will you think about it? My offer?"

He glanced at me again.

It was definitely my cue to leave, but I couldn't. My feet were frozen to the floor even as the carpet was being yanked straight from beneath them.

She hitched her purse on her shoulder, glancing at me before quickly ignoring me. "I will. I'll let you know after Christmas."

"Okay. And the other thing..."

"I can't give you an answer to that."

What? What are you talking about? Why are you crying? How did he hurt you? All the questions I wanted to blurt out roared through me like a rare thunderstorm.

"I'll call you," she finally said. "Either way, but I need to get going now."

"All right. Thank you for your time."

He rocked back on his heels.

I was an obvious fly on the wall who should have left as soon as he showed up. He made that obvious by turning to me. "Don't you have practice to get ready for?"

"Yes, sir," I muttered, glancing at Ryann.

She studiously ignored me.

"I need to go," she said again. "Bye, Vik." She turned, and walked away.

There was a punch to the goodbye, and it hit my chest. Most likely, that was for me *and* her father.

I had to let her go.

Because somehow I knew, if Coach ever found out what happened between the two of us—good relationship or not with her—he'd either kill me or trade me before I could blink.

"See you on the ice," I told him, and left in the opposite direction.

How in the hell had I pined for so long for the woman I could most likely, never ever have?

Just my luck.

———

INTRUDER ALERT! *Intruder Alert!*

"Honey, I'm home!" I called out through Kane's townhome as his special alert for me blared. Being next-door neighbors, we saw each other every day, even when we weren't at practice or on the road. Okay, maybe it was because I always stopped by, but it was Kane's fault.

He was a hell of a cook, and after a day like today, there was no way I wanted to eat alone.

I'd gotten my ass handed to me at practice, earning more than one curious look from Coach but hard as I tried to focus, I failed. I never failed at hockey.

"Oh my God, do you ever eat at your own home?" Emmersyn groaned from the kitchen but when I saw her, she was smiling.

"It is not my fault your husband and fiancé is an excellent cook."

Emmersyn snorted. Her dark brown hair was back in a pony-tail, and she was chopping an onion at the counter. "Stop. Husband is fine. He's being silly about this second wedding thing."

"I'm rarely silly," Kane said, jumping off the stairs, forgoing the bottom two steps. "What's up your ass today? You looked like shit at practice."

I grabbed a beer from his fridge, even if the whiskey on his kitchen counter seemed more necessary.

"Thank you, friend. Thank you very much for that."

"It's true."

"Everything okay?" Emmersyn asked, knife in the air, onion forgotten.

If she was cooking, I'd need to head home. In the months since she'd moved in here, that same night in September that should now never be mentioned again happened, Emmersyn had cooked very few meals that hadn't set the oven on fire.

I really didn't want to go back home.

"I have good news and bad news," I said and plopped my ass onto a stool across from her at the counter.

"Good first," Emmersyn said. She set down the knife, and Kane kissed her temple.

"Thanks for the help. Get some wine and have a seat while I finish up."

"Oh thank God you are cooking," I moaned, now starving for whatever he was going to make.

"Shut up." Emmersyn punched me in the shoulder. She had the strength of a mosquito, but I said nothing. "Good news. Tell me, tell me."

"The good news is I found her. The blonde?"

"Yes, yes. The woman who got away. Love of your life," Kane groaned. So I had talked about her. A lot. "And that's great. How?"

I ignored him and Emmersyn's happy squeal. "And I know her last name now. Want to know what it is?"

"What?" Emmersyn asked.

I waited until Kane looked up from pulling more vegetables out of the fridge. It was possible I was dramatic.

"What is it?"

"Boucher." I grinned a grin that put off Joker vibes and waited for them to understand in one... two...

"No fucking way," Kane gasped.

Emmersyn followed. "Isn't that Coach Vik's—"

"Last name?" I nodded. "Yup. I fucked and fell in love with one of Coach's long lost, never talked about, never seen daughters. The youngest one, because that night when I met them in September, it was her sister's bachelorette party, remember?"

"Oh shit." Kane choked on a laugh. "You met all of his daughters that night. We all did."

"And Ryann was at the offices today. Crying. Running from him. I ran right into her."

"Why was she crying?"

"No clue. She wouldn't tell me a thing and couldn't wait to get the hell away from him. And me." I was pretty certain on the last part.

"What are you going to do?" Emmersyn asked. "I might be wrong, but I'm thinking a relationship with the coach's daughter might not be a great idea, especially if they're not close."

"I can't have a relationship with her." I couldn't. "Not only for that reason but because she wants nothing to do with me. At all. And now I get it."

At least I had one answer to a host of unasked questions.

Why had she kicked me out and gotten almost pissed, definitely regretful, as soon as I'd mentioned practice?

"Shit, Alix. That really sucks."

"Tell me about it."

Emmersyn dropped her arm over my shoulders and rested her head against mine. "I'm sorry, Alix."

"Yeah. Me too."

She squeezed. "We'll find you someone. Someone who deserves you. You're a good guy."

"I am very awesome." I nudged my shoulder into hers. "Instead of marrying this grumpy asshole again, you should run away with me. We could go get hitched at a chapel. Tonight. You game?"

Emmersyn laughed so hard she snorted. "Sorry, Alix. I think I'm stuck with the grumpy asshole."

"Hey. What'd I do to you?"

"Oh please," I said and waggled my brows. "Tell me what he did to you. Tell me, tell me."

She slapped a hand over my mouth. "Shut up, Alix."

"I liked her," I mumbled. Peeling Emmersyn's hand off my mouth, I repeated it. "A lot. And the way she looked at me, today? There is no chance, even if she was not the coach's daughter."

"Well, maybe the good thing is if they don't have a good rela-tionship, you won't have to see her again and can really move on."

That did not sound like a good thing at all. Neither part of her idea.

I shrugged. Drank my beer.

I ate Kane's delicious steak and grilled vegetable dinner and let Emmersyn mother me by watching a movie and insisting I stay there for a while so I wasn't alone.

Not a bad night.

But their company did not help.

I hadn't spent more than two minutes with Ryann today, and none of it was good, but I already missed her.

NINE

RYANN

Happy New Year to me.

A new job. A new start in Vegas four days into the new year.

The decision hadn't been easy. Braylen had gotten so pissed off I was considering this and hearing about Dad's health problems that Blake almost gave her a Valium to calm her down. Hayden was traveling in Kenya on some safari for a national travel magazine, so we weren't able to talk long, but her parting words to me were, "your funeral."

Helpful, my big sisters were.

Mom was the one who pushed me to do it. "This opens the door to the rest of your life. Take the opportunity and keep your eyes and ears open for new ones. Traveling with the team will get you in contact with other teams. You never know what can happen, but you'll always wonder *'what if'* if you don't."

My mom was the wise one. It still amazed me after how miserable she'd been when she left our father that she could let us talk about him with none of the residual anger we still had. But then, she'd long since said she'd healed and moved on from my father. Plus, she had Paul.

So, there I was, stepping foot inside the Las Vegas Vipers'

training facility as an employee. While Vik wasn't my boss, I had no doubt we'd have our fair share of run-ins, and every time I considered the possibilities of how they'd occur, a razor-sharp pain speared my chest.

I'd spoken with Callie over the phone. She called me shortly after I texted my dad the day after Christmas and told him I'd take the job, but I needed a week. After our short introductions and her welcoming me to the team, Callie got straight to business. She gave me the hotel and room number where I'd be staying. All I had to do was give my name at the front desk when I arrived and they'd hand over my keys. When I checked in yesterday, she'd also left a bag of clothing. Vipers gear. From flared yoga leggings to T-shirts and sweatshirts and polo shirts, I was now the proud owner of an entire dresser drawer full of branded athletic and casual work gear for the team I'd despised for half of my life.

I was all set.

Or, at least I would be, as soon as I could find a way to contact Alix to let him know what happened between us was a one-time thing. It could never happen again. Not while I was employed there, especially. But I couldn't have another surprise run-in with him again, either.

No, this time I'd be prepared to see him. I'd be mentally prepared to not drool at the sight of him, in his tight Vipers T-shirt like he'd been wearing last time with a casual pair of joggers and running shoes.

His hair as perfect as it'd been that last morning.

His eyes so deep-set and sexy I'd almost fallen into his hold when he said my name instead of pulling myself out of it.

Yeah.

I'd get through my orientation and first day. Figure out a way to contact him. Then we'd meet somewhere public. I'd say what I had to say.

And then we'd be done.

Officially employed under the same company, for all intents and purposes.

"Ryann?"

I swung my head toward the elevators, where a stunning redhead was headed my way. Hand outstretched, she was dressed in casual clothes like most of the other employees who had crossed the entryway so far. Flared leggings on the bottom, a forest green polo with the Vipers gold logo at her chest. I'd gone with bootcut jeans and simple tan ankle boots and had on the exact same shirt as she did.

"Callie. Nice to finally meet you. And congratulations on the new job. I hope we can make it work."

"Thank you. And I'll certainly try my best."

She had a kind smile, a sweet voice I'd immediately liked on the phone, but she also had keen, assessing eyes. Everyone would obviously know at some point that I was Vik's daughter, and I could already imagine their questions. Whether it was about how I got the job, or what my father was like as a dad, or whatever... they were coming. It wasn't a matter of if, but when.

Callie, however, didn't ask anything. After we shook hands, she turned back to the elevators and started talking.

Straight to business.

"This is the main level lobby, obviously. This entrance is for employees only. There is an underground parking garage you'll have access to by the end of the day. Players have their own entrance, which takes them directly to their locker rooms and weight rooms. Our entrance here is also shared with the public through those doors." She pointed to the far side of the lobby. "Youth hockey leagues are held here, practices, open skate, birthday parties, etc. So we try to keep the players and staff as separated as possible while still being accessible."

The elevator doors opened, and she kept talking. "I figured, even though we'll primarily be working on the fourth floor with most of the day-to-day staff like marketing and social media management, I'll give you a grand tour today, so you have a general idea of how everything works. The guys have early morning work-outs now and then hit the ice, so while they're out there, we'll head down to see their stuff so we're not in their way. As a general rule, we don't have much interaction with the team when we're not trav-eling, but you'll get to know them really well."

Pretty sure I didn't need to know the players any better than I already did. I definitely knew enough about Alix. I knew him enough to know that if he wasn't who he was, if I wasn't who I was, I'd be absolutely jumping at the chance to spend every waking minute with him.

I shook my head. Focus. I was here to work. To prove to Vik I could do this and to take a step toward the future I truly wanted, one that would be far away from Las Vegas with any stroke of good luck and hard work.

"In addition to the traveling and coordinating their stops and any plans they have with spouses or children joining them, we also work with other family who might fly in to see a game. The tickets and hotel rooms are paid for by players or the individual, but they normally want to stay in the same hotel, so we coordinate that. We also work with the team chef for meals on their flights."

"Their meals?"

They had meals prepared by chefs?

"Yes." We stopped on the second floor. "The team's head chef and cooking staff plans and prepares meals and food orders on this floor, along with the equipment cleaners and the equipment ordering staff. But while the chef's team will prepare meals at the arena, they get taken to the airport, where we help ensure everyone gets their correct meal. Sometimes, we board the bus here to get everyone to the airport terminal together, and we hand those meals out on the bus. All depends on the times of take-offs and such."

She paused and took a breath while my head continued to spin.

"Be prepared. There will be nights we'll fly out straight after a home game and on those nights, we don't typically fly out until eleven at night. This job will mess with your schedule, but I promise it's rewarding and fun."

"Okay." I wasn't a huge fan of flying, I did enjoy traveling, and was a night owl in general. None of that sounded bad and it wasn't like I had a partner waiting for me at home or anything.

No, for the first time in my life, I was truly on my own. The realization didn't bring a smile to my face like I expected it to.

As I followed Callie, I learned way more about what went on behind the scenes with a professional team than I could have ever imagined. Skates cleaned and sharpened after every game. The laundry. How it was all packed and loaded onto planes and buses and shipped. Managing their dozens of sticks and the rest of their extra gear, purchasing their preferred brand of hockey tape. We'd work closely with the equipment team that traveled with the team to ensure everything we could possibly need got to the next destination, down to every single accounted for water bottle they'd use on the bench and puck brought in for warm-up practice time.

It was fascinating. And as I followed her, floor by floor, through the facility, I pushed aside all my daddy drama, my boy drama. I took a minute to be thankful.

I might not be doing sports marketing *right now*. But I had reached my dream of working for a professional team, even if I got a little help along the way.

I HELD MY BREATH, anticipation killing me, as Callie pulled open the doors to the locker room.

"The locker rooms at the arena where games are held are nicer, obviously, but the layout is similar, so the guys don't have to search for anything. Athletes tend to be superstitious so if they throw their gear by someone else's locker during pre-season practices, that's how it is on game days for them. If they move during the season for whatever reason, they get moved at the arena, too."

The room wasn't anything extravagant but plenty spacious with a semicircle of forest green wood benches. Lockers above for their gear. The floor was a dark wood, scuffed but still shining. It was also currently a mess, with gear tossed on the floor, on the top shelves, skates hanging from hooks.

A light from the ceiling snagged my attention, and I looked up.

"Oh shit," I gasped and pressed a hand to my chest while Callie chuckled.

An illuminated snake's head, complete with fangs, was coiled, face pointed down directly over me, mouth open, prepared to strike.

Still trying to gather my breathing, I laughed. "I was not expecting that."

Their logo was two entwined vipers, but I hadn't expected to feel like one was slithering along the ceiling, ready to eat me.

"You get used to it. The one in the arena where they play is even larger."

Great.

"Guess I'll need to get over my fear of snakes." They were everywhere. On the staff members' shirts. Running up the legs of some chino pants or athletic joggers I'd seen employees wearing. Painted on the walls. The floors.

"The physical therapy room is through there." She pointed to a far corner. "Showers and everything on the right door just past there. At the arena, at the far back right corner, there are double doors that lead to their lounge area which gives them space to relax after games or focus before them. That lounge area is connected to a family lounge where family members with passes can hang out, or drop off their kids for babysitting if they would like. I'll show you the arena the next time we're there, but unless we're attending the game or flying out right after a home game, we don't actually spend much time there." She paused, clicked her fingernail against her chin, and shrugged. "I guess that's it. At least this gives you an idea of where the team spends most of their time. We don't intrude, but we do sometimes have to hunt them down, so you do need to be comfortable with the possibility of seeing anything in the locker room."

And just like that... thoughts I'd been trying to avoid returned.

Because I could walk in on Alix *naked*.

Not what I needed. "Thanks for the tip."

"I usually shout out 'woman in the room' and give them a few moments to cover up. They're respectful. We've never had a problem."

That helped.

Also, made me a little sad?

I shook my head and scanned the room. I'd studied the roster names and photos on Google over the last week, at least trying to put names with faces to make the adjustment easier. Had I spent more time on Alix's pictures? Maybe doing a deep dive on Google to see him in a variety of forms, clothing—or missing clothing?

I'd never tell. At least, not Callie. It was no surprise then when I found his locker. Cleaner than some of the others. Organized. He was next to Kane Anders and Ryder Bromann, both men who'd been at the club on the dance floor that night. Kane had been the one to pull away almost immediately, based on the online photos I found.

"This helps," I told Callie.

I *had* to stop thinking of that night if I wanted to have any chance of keeping this job. It happened. It shouldn't have. It was time to move on.

"Thanks for the tour." The whole thing had lasted a couple hours. "What next?"

She grinned. "Now we go upstairs and get to work. The tech department should have your laptop and iPad ready to go, so we'll spend some time going over that and you can spend the rest of the afternoon filling out paperwork. There are a few new hire modules you'll have to take on the computer. Sexual harassment, that kind of thing."

We started walking out of the locker room, right as the man I was trying to forget about shoved open the door so loud it banged against the wall.

Both Callie and I jumped.

For entirely different reasons, because I recognized that thick, short mop of blond hair. Had dug nails into that scalp. He had his helmet in one hand and was looking down and looked even broader and somehow *better* in pads and a jersey.

At our sounds of surprise, Alix glanced up. His deep-set, rich blue eyes snagged on me and quickly looked to Callie.

He froze. Eyes widened on me in complete and utter shock before he wiped it away. His mouth opened. Closed.

Then a scowl twisted his thick lips. Lips I'd imagined running over my breasts so many times they tightened painfully beneath my bra as he blinked and glanced my way again.

Not good. Not good at all.

"Hi, Callie," he muttered.

"You okay, Alix?" she asked.

"Twisted ankle. I'll be fine."

With another piercing look aimed at me, like *I* was responsible for his twisted ankle, he hobbled off, equally as graceful and athletic in his skates and gear as he'd been on the dance floor.

"He's a really nice guy," Callie said quietly. "He must be in pain. Usually, he stops and chats regardless of what's going on."

As if I needed the reminder of how nice he could be.

"I'm sure our next meeting will be better," I assured her as we headed down the hall back to the offices.

If only it were the truth.

Based on the fierce look I could still feel as we left Alix behind, there was no doubt our next meeting would be any better.

TEN

ALIX

"You're going to have to shake this off." Kane plopped down on the bench next to me.

After I'd twisted my ankle doing mundane drills Dominick's youth team could handle, the last thing I expected to see was Ryann. The woman I'd been thinking of while skating and took a skate edge too hard. Fell right on my ass as I lost my footing. I hadn't stopped thinking of her since I saw her last week.

The last place I expected to almost run right into her again was in the same building.

Standing in my locker room.

It took a second to register she was with Callie, our travel coordinator. A thousand questions pummeled my brain when I took her in, saw her dressed professionally, like she was working, and that she was with Callie. Who had spent more than a little time complaining during our last away series about not having an assistant and desperate for one, because Debbie, her old assistant, decided to stay home after she had a baby. Said Coach had talked to someone right before Christmas about the job and was waiting to hear back.

And I'd run into Ryann, fleeing her dad's office right before

Christmas.

Fuck me to the Alps and back.

"She's here. And I think she's working with Callie."

"No shit? Did you talk to her?"

"What was I supposed to say?"

Kane grunted as he tore off one of his skates. "Can you go find her? You know where Callie's office is."

"I will not."

There was no way Ryann would want to see me. Not in the office at least.

"I get you've been hung up on her for a good long while, Alix, but maybe you need to work on letting this go. You haven't been right since you saw her."

"I know." She was in my head, an itch I couldn't scratch and couldn't get rid of. "Fuck me."

My head hit the locker and I closed my eyes. At least my ankle wasn't sprained. I'd been back on the ice after icing it for twenty minutes and taking a couple of ibuprofen.

"A nice soak in your hot tub tonight would make me feel better," I told Kane.

He laughed, shaking his head. "It's all yours. Emmersyn and I are going out for dinner anyway. Just be gone before we get back. And no, before you ask, you can't come with us."

"I will go to Malley's. They'll feed me."

Kane stood and rolled his eyes as he tossed a towel at me. "Or you could finally learn to cook."

"Why would I do that when I have you?"

"To grow up?" he suggested.

"That does not sound like any fun at all."

Kane laughed. We stripped out of our gear and showered. By the time I was done, Arlo and Ryder both said they'd meet me at Malley's later. Couldn't be a late night. We had a game tomorrow, but it wasn't until seven, and we wouldn't need to be at the arena until one. We could have one drink. Play some pool and relax.

Ryder was still new to the team, and when he was traded after Max left, we'd all felt that hole in our team. But Ryder was a great guy. An even better player. He was no Max, but he'd slotted into our team line-up with ease. And so far, was helping us stay at the top of our divisional standings.

I was sliding into my Lamborghini when my phone beeped, lighting up the screen on my dash.

A text from a number I did not recognize.

I pressed the button to read it, and the mechanical, female French voice I used for my Siri echoed in my car. "Hey, Alix. This is Ryann. I found your number in the team files. I probably surprised you today, but I'm working for the Vipers now. Can we meet and talk? Or you can call. But I think we might need to meet. You know, to talk."

It was the first time I despised my French-accented Siri. Too bad it couldn't have been Ryann's voice.

There went my plans for a hot tub and Malley's.

Because hell yes, we were going to have a talk.

A long one. And I hoped I could keep my hands to myself this time.

***

TURNED out Ryann was staying at the Sunset Resort and Spa and Casino. It was the same hotel where the team kept rooms for long-term use for players either traded to the team or called up from our minor affiliate until they could get settled in a more permanent location. Given that she was apparently moving here from Reno, I shouldn't have been surprised.

It was close to the practice arena and only fifteen minutes from where I lived, so I agreed to meet her at the attached steakhouse for dinner.

I was there early, unable to help myself, and found myself obsessively checking my phone at the table to see if she'd cancel.

This was good, though. We did need to talk. Although what we wanted to talk about were probably two different things.

Hers, probably pretending that night did not happen.

Me, planning on when it could happen again.

"Hey. You're here." Ryann stood across from me at the table, running her fingers down a chunk of her hair, twisting it at the end while she glanced around the restaurant.

I stood immediately, gesturing for her to take the seat across from me. "I am. Sit. It is... good to see you."

My chest was tight and so was the crotch of my jeans. She was gorgeous, dressed in a simple black skirt and a light pink top. It was sleeveless, wrapped around her chest and had a bow at her hip. The shirt drew my eyes to her cleavage, the perfect amount I could still remember sliding my tongue through and the shiver that rolled through her when I did.

Oh yes. We would be doing that again.

Definitely.

"You are stunning," I told her.

"Thanks, but um..."

She still had not sat down. Looked like she would call this a bad idea and flee to the safety of her room.

"I will behave," I promised her and waited for a quick grin to burst free from her nerves.

She slipped into the seat across from me and draped her napkin over her lap. So graceful. Perfection.

"I'm surprised you know how." A teasing smile was on her face that vanished as soon as our eyes met. She gestured to a fresh glass of water that had already been delivered.

"It is yours, yes. And also, you probably already know I rarely behave."

A blush crept along her chest as she drank her water, fiddled with the menu, and both of us seemed at a loss to say anything. But she'd called this meeting, so I would let her run the show.

For a while.

Our server appeared, took our drink orders. We both stuck to water, and I placed an order for the spinach and artichoke dip with pita bread before telling him we'd need a few more minutes.

"The dip is delicious here," I said once he left. "You may try it if you like."

"Thank you. And thank you for meeting with me. I didn't know how to contact you before today, and I'm sure you were surprised when you saw me."

"All three times for different reasons, yes," I admitted, and that blush spread to her collarbone.

She squirmed, pressed her hand to her chest as if her fingers would cool the heat she had to be feeling. A sick thrill shot through me that I could affect her so easily. So deeply.

Which put us on even footing since she did the same to me even if I was better at hiding it.

"I'm going to take a guess here."

She patted the napkin in her lap. "Okay...."

"You met with your dad. Maybe back in September. Definitely last week, and he offered you the job as Callie's assistant. You took it, and now you're here. Living in Vegas, working with a man I believe you do not respect much or think much of."

"Good guess," she whispered, and there was pain in her eyes.

"I'm a smart man. Debbie left to stay home with her child and Callie spent our last away trip calling us all children and assholes and how she could not wrangle us alone."

"What a wonderful thing to hear on my first day of work."

I laughed along with her smile. "We're not assholes. We are... focused on the game... and not usually much else."

"Noted." Her lips twitched. Fought that smile that had so easily broken free on our night together.

She ran her finger up the goblet of her water glass, gathering condensation before rubbing her fingertips together. They were no longer the hot pink that matched her dress from September, but a deep, rich red. Professional.

She meant business.

"This job... is it what you wanted? And with your dad?"

"He's my father or sperm donor. Not my dad." She snapped it so quickly, frustration blooming, before she blew out a breath. "Sorry. I went to school for sports marketing, so yes, this opportunity helps. Back in September, when we were here for Braylen's party, I'd gone to see him. It was the first time I saw him since I was thirteen."

I'd known he had little contact with his ex-wife and daughters, but thirteen? "That is a long time."

"Almost a decade. I asked him for help, and he said no. So, no, I'm not really looking forward to being around him. But I need the job, and it's not an easy field to get into."

"And it is better than filing eye charts?"

Her long lashes blinked several times. "You remember."

Her part-time job working for her stepfather who sounded like more of a dad to her than Vik ever was. Yes.

"I remember everything," I told her, lowering my voice in a way that told her exactly what I remembered.

Everything about that night.

A new blush stained her cheeks, and she flinched. She might as well have poured her ice water on me. "What happened that night cannot happen again."

"I assumed you would say that."

Our server returned with our appetizer and refilled our waters. We took a couple minutes to quickly glance through the menu and both ended up with the filet, salad, rice pilaf, and broccoli.

Once he left again, I dipped a piece of pita into the dip and scooped some up.

"So we're in agreement then." Ryann eyed the dip like she wanted to give in but kept her hands pressed to her lap. "We'll forget it happened and have a strictly professional relationship from here on out."

"Oh no. I did not agree to that."

ELEVEN
RYANN

Alix was everything I remembered and more. He was confident. So damn sexy, my body was burning from the nearness of him. It was taking everything I had to remain in my chair and not reach for him. To remain focused on why I called him, why we needed to talk.

It shouldn't have shocked me at all that he didn't agree with me, but what did surprise me was his bluntness.

"Excuse me?" I asked as he chewed a mouthful of dip and bread that had my stomach growling. I had been so nervous all day I'd barely managed to enjoy a cup of soup from Panera when Callie DoorDashed us lunch.

"Eat." He pointed to the appetizer and brushed off his hands before taking his napkin in his lap like mine. "It is good."

"I think maybe we should talk about this."

"About the dip? Nothing to talk about. It's delicious. You should have some."

I fought an eye roll. I hadn't expected him to be so difficult or look so darn attractive while doing it.

"No. That's not what I meant, and you know it."

"Talk all you want." He scooped another bite of dip and

brought it to his mouth. "I will have you underneath me again. Bent over in front of me and on top of me. I believe it is only a matter of time."

It shouldn't have had me squirming in my chair so badly, the tops of my thighs pressed so hard together I could feel the moisture from my underwear. Good grief. I was wet for this man who essentially just ignored my wishes.

"Alix—"

"Have you thought about that night? Me? Since then?"

His words were so nonchalantly spoken. His blue eyes were anything but as his gaze dropped to my chest and the burn against my flesh he ignited there with a look.

"I have thought of you. Went back to your hotel later that day and looked for you. Even after I knew you checked out, I went back the day after to try to find you. I have not stopped thinking of you since then. Ask Kane sometime. Or his wife, Emmersyn. They know."

The heat he created was doused in a moment. "They know? About us? Me?"

He leaned his elbows on the table, grew closer to me and dropped his voice to a rumble that did insanely hot things to my nipples.

How would I survive the rest of the season having to interact with him so frequently if I couldn't handle a meal?

"Kane is my best friend. My neighbor. He knew how much I thought of you after that night, yes. And yes, I told both of them when I saw you last week. They will not say a word to anyone, but you do know that Ryder Bromann, the man who danced like a professional that night, will recognize you too, right? And he knows we went home together? Some of my other teammates will as well."

"They can't say anything. If Vik finds out—"

I hadn't even brought up how he'd asked me not to date any of his players. Or how we hadn't mentioned that since. When it came to Vik, the less interaction we had, the better.

"He won't. I will ensure they stay quiet."

If Vik found out, I had no idea what he'd do. "I could lose this job, Alix, and I need it. Desperately. I need—"

I needed a dad who wasn't a total tool and I needed to not be sitting across from the one man who had the potential to make my life difficult in more ways than one.

"You have my word. I will talk with them. But they are my brothers. A family. We will stick together on this."

As difficult as it was for me to trust any man, I had no choice but to give it to Alix. It wasn't like I wanted to hunt down Ryder or any of his teammates and have that conversation with them.

"Okay," I finally said.

"Now eat." He pushed the plate in my direction, and this time I didn't ignore it.

A hum escaped my lips as the first taste of the warm dip hit my tongue. Immediately, Alix's eyes narrowed, and his gaze stayed on my mouth, my lips, as I chewed.

"Stop looking at me like that," I mumbled.

"Like what? Like I want you?"

He was going to be the death of me. "Yeah."

"Impossible. I have wanted you for almost four months. I do not see that stopping any time soon."

"Alix—"

His name was a warning, one he caught because he grabbed a triangular pita bread piece and pointed it at me. "But I can promise you that while you are working, I will be professional. Treat you exactly like I did Debbie or how we treat Callie."

"Thank you." His eyes glimmered with enjoyment that made me not so thankful. "Wait... how do you treat Debbie and Callie?"

He winked. The hot, sexy jerk winked at me and sat back in his chair, fully pleased with himself. "I guess you will see when we hit the road next week, won't you?"

A flutter of excitement shouldn't have bubbled in my stomach at the thought. My nipples hardened into painfully tight points, and I once again fought the urge to squirm beneath his pleased and enticing gaze.

"You promised professional."

"While you are working, yes. You have my word."

Our food arrived, and he changed the subject to if I was looking at apartments nearby or wanted suggestions on areas and neighborhoods.

The rest of the dinner went by slowly and too quickly, because ending it meant I needed to say goodbye.

This was for the best. And yeah, it'd be great if we could get along. Maybe become friends.

After I was back in my room, safe behind the door and able to relieve the ache sitting so close to him caused, his last words about my job came back to me.

While you are working, he'd said.

So what would he do when I wasn't....?

TURNS OUT, since the team spent the afternoon of games at the arena instead of the practice facility and we weren't needed at the arena until the days we left for games, we really didn't see much of the guys at all. Unless special arrangements needed to be made for someone, like their wives joining them on a trip, which rarely happened, or needing a room for family to stay in, Callie said they hardly came to the floor we worked on.

Callie had told me my first day she'd give me an official introduction to the team before we left on our first road trip and now that the time was ticking down, anxiousness was fluttering in my stomach.

Tomorrow would be my first real test when we met the guys at the airport before we flew to Calgary. From there, we'd hit Edmonton and Vancouver, come back to the States for a game in Washington before returning to Las Vegas. I'd only been working there for a week, and had been promised multiple times that while the work we did while at home was routine, and easy to manage unless there was a disaster like a hotel fire causing us to make last-minute changes—which had only happened once in the last five years—Callie assured me, the job was easy to understand, simple to get a hold of.

The true challenge, she promised me, was once we were on the road. Just thinking of the plane rides, four cities in six days, was enough to have me trusting her. The travel alone would take some adjusting and then throw in the men....

"Herding twenty-five males who live with noise-canceling headphones on is worse than wrangling muddy pigs."

She frequently compared the team to children, pigs, cats, and the occasional headless chicken, but she said it with a smile and laugh.

"They're fun, too," she reminded me as she prepped me for the first away trip. "We'll eat some meals with them. We grow close, even if we're staff and they're not, but most of the coaches and the players are genuinely good guys. Don't hesitate to grab a drink with them if you see them in a bar, or join them for one of Braxton's famous smoothie runs. He's a protein smoothie junkie and keeps a spreadsheet for the best shops closest to our hotels."

"He does?"

"Cross my heart and hope to die." She made the sign of the cross and winked. Callie was young, turning thirty on this upcoming road trip, and she'd already forced me to agree we'd go out for a birthday shot with her in Vancouver. She was fun. Professional. Took her job seriously but didn't take herself anywhere close to serious. Her long-term boyfriend, Weston, was a poker dealer at one of the casinos and she was hoping they'd get engaged soon.

"He better, or I'm kicking him to the curb. It's been four years now. What's he waiting for? Retirement?" she'd mumbled one day when she asked if I was single and about my family.

As far as Vik went, I saw him more often. His office might have been on the upper levels, but more than once, we'd gotten in the elevator at the same time. Or the rare day he'd been in the staff lunchroom, he'd ask to sit with me.

Based on the surprised looks of other's faces, I highly doubt he spent a lot of time there but had been there in hopes of running into me.

So far, he'd kept his infrequent questions settled on my job and introduced me to other coaches he was with.

Every time he did, eyebrows rose in surprise, and I figured it had nothing to do with him doing his daughter a favor, but that the daughters so many had heard about weren't involved in his life actually existed.

This morning, though, I couldn't stop myself. I'd finally managed to gather my nerves and ask Callie about it. "About a year after your mom left him, I heard he took down any reminder of you guys in his office. Since then, most of the staff are new, some coaches too, so all we heard about was that he had daughters but didn't have much to do with them."

It shouldn't have hurt as much as it did.

Didn't mean I didn't call Hayden and Braylen to let them know.

Hayden sighed, asked me if I was surprised.

Braylen cursed him out in language more colorful than a sailor's and then asked if I was sure I wanted to keep being around him.

I assured her I was fine. We hung up, I opened a bottle of wine, and after glass three, stared at my phone and the text I'd received from Alix while on the phone with Braylen.

I'd left him on unread, but three glasses of wine in, texting him back seemed like a great idea. If anything, it'd get my mind off my dad.

Alix: Ready for your first big trip tomorrow?

He'd texted a handful of times in the last week. All as

mundane as this one. *Hope you're enjoying your new job. Found any good apartments?* Or my favorite... *You should try Hacienda Del Ray by the hotel. Great food, excellent margaritas.*

I thanked him for the food recommendation because who wouldn't but hadn't responded to the others.

He texted enough to let me know he was thinking of me, infrequently enough to not be pushy. But there was no way I was forgetting what he'd said about being professional while I was working.

What would happen when nightfall came, and I was technically off duty?

Fingers shaking, I typed him back. **Nervous. Also, don't really like flying**.

Probably should have thought of that before taking the job, but all things considered, my options were limited.

Less than two minutes later, my phone dinged with his reply.

Bet I could help you with some of those nerves.

Ha. As if. Being around Alix made me one giant ball of nerves these days. The few times I'd seen him at the practice facility, he'd done nothing more than shoot me a wink or dip his chin in a greeting. Ryder, the fantastic dancing guy from that night I couldn't forget, had ridden an elevator with me once. Shook my hand, told me it was nice to officially meet me and asked how my sister's wedding went. That was it.

So far so good.

What are you doing now?

The text followed his first.

Since daydreaming of him and the night that couldn't be forgotten or named wasn't what I could say, I snapped a picture of my glass of wine sitting on a laptop desk on my hotel bed with a rerun of *Grey's Anatomy* on in the background and sent it to him.

My screen darkened with an incoming FaceTime call and my grip tightened on my phone.

I should have known if I opened the door an inch, he'd throw it wide open.

I looked like crap, makeup long since washed off after getting home, my hair in a loose, messy braid draped over my shoulder. It was possible I had salad in my teeth from dinner, and despite the still hot temperatures outside, I was in an oversized hoodie sweatshirt.

Still, because I was a masochist, I tapped the video button.

Alix's face blurred before clearing, and yeah... this was a mistake.

He was shirtless at minimum. Lights flickering behind him and the setting sun shadowed half of his face. Bubbles appeared, and there was the soft roar of a motor in the background.

"You're in a hot tub," I said, surprised at the sight of him and the view and, well... everything on my screen.

"I use Kane's a lot. He and I are neighbors."

"And he and his wife just let you use the hot tub whenever you want?"

"They're out."

"Out? The night before a game?"

We had to be at the airport at five in the morning.

"Just dinner. They'll be back soon and I'll give them privacy, but since I'm alone, with no one who wants to hang out with me—" He pouted, pushing full lips out and winked.

"Poor Alix with no friends." I played along. Harmless banter wouldn't hurt anything.

Right?

"That is right. And it makes me very sad. I think you should come give me a hug." He flashed me a cheeky grin that made me roll my eyes.

"Do you always pout until you get your way?" I tsked twice. "Not very manly, really. And a major turn-off."

He sat up straight in the hot tub. Bubbles swirled around him, only giving me peeks of his chest. Bummer.

The man had a fantastic chest.

"I believe you remember how manly I am, and I bet if I were there, even with my pout, you would be turned on."

He was right. I wouldn't lie and deny it, but this wasn't helping our current predicament.

"What do you want, Alix?" I sipped my wine and settled back into the bed. "Really?"

"You."

It was one word, said with such sincerity, such honesty and intensity, it shot a spark straight to my core I'd be relieving myself of as soon as we got off the phone.

"But," he continued. "If I cannot have that, then I will settle for friends."

"You lie." I laughed. "I know this game. Let's be friends while I try to get in your pants. Oldest trick in the book."

"The only game I play is hockey. And I would never play with a woman's heart." He shoved his hand through his hair. Sighed. "I missed you," he admitted with such quiet sincerity my heart leaped to my throat. "If I cannot have all of you, I want to be able to have you in that way at least."

My head tilted to the side. "And do you always turn on your friends?"

"So you admit you are turned on by me."

I laughed. Walked right into that one. Before I could do more damage, I shook my head. "Good night, friend. I will see you tomorrow."

"Bright and early, sunshine."

His face froze on the screen before it went dark.

And it was the look of disappointment on his that lingered in my mind after I tossed my phone to the bed and slipped my hand beneath the sheets.

I might have finally found a man who truly wanted me, who I was equally attracted to, and he was the one man I could not have.

Disappointing was right.

TWELVE
RYANN

Callie had not been kidding about the stress of the job once we traveled with them. I arrived at the airport at four thirty in the morning, a half hour earlier than the team had to be there. My eyes were so swollen and tired I could barely see, and the second cup of coffee I was currently drinking had done nothing to wake me up but was doing a great job of perking up my anxiety.

By the time I made it to the hangar where the team's private plane was settled with the loading stairs ready to go, I was thankful for the chill in the air keeping me cool.

"Okay, so once they get here, I need you to check them in and hand them their breakfasts. They'll be able to eat them before takeoff."

"Got it." Check them in and feed them. Easy-peasy even if my nerves were spiking.

"I'll be taking their luggage, tagging it, and making sure it all gets loaded on the cart. Once the coaches and the team are on the plane, you can board."

"Sounds easy enough."

"And then once we get to the airport, we do it all over again as they're unloading."

There was a lot of hand-holding and checking in I was learning, but it made sense. Wouldn't do to take off before a player showed up, although she told me that only happened in emergencies.

We'd arrive in Calgary at eleven, be at the hotel at noon, where we'd have to check them in again and get them their room keys. They'd have time to eat lunch and take a nap before heading to Calgary's arena for a short afternoon skate, dinner, relax and watch films, and warm-ups. Then the game, then back to the hotel where at every stop we'd check them in, load them off, and make sure they all got back to the hotel.

We'd start the entire process over tomorrow, except we'd only be taking a three-hour bus trip to Edmonton.

I could have slumped over with exhaustion from thinking about what the next six days would look like. At least tomorrow, we'd have the day off to explore Edmonton since they didn't have a game until the following day.

All I had to do was get through this first plane ride and day, and I'd be fine.

"This is Garrett Dubiak coming," Callie whispered in my ear, and my nerves lit up my system with adrenaline.

This was it. The moment my job really began. I wanted to dance a jig as much as I wanted to puke.

She continued talking softly as he headed toward us, pulling a small carry-on, another bag flung across his body. "He's almost always the first to arrive, always ten to fifteen minutes early and has the cutest twin boys. His wife Lizzie brings them to the games all the time." She smiled at him as he reached us. "Hey, Garrett."

"Morning, Callie. Who's this?"

"This is my new assistant, Ryann. She's going to be taking care of you guys with me, so be nice to her."

"Always." He held out his hand. "Nice to meet you, Ryann."

"You too, Garrett. Thank you."

We shook hands, I checked him in. He grabbed his breakfast in the prepared meal containers, all labeled with their names, and headed up the stairs to the plane.

"Not so difficult, is it?" Callie asked.

"I think I can handle it," I assured her.

In truth. The time flew by. As the guys made their appearance, usually by themselves or in pairs, Callie gave me a quick intro, giving me a brief personal history of them when she could. Halfway through, my nerves had settled, and it was easier to smile when I greeted the men, when my first obstacle stepped directly in front of me.

"Ryann. How's everything going so far?"

My dad, flanked by both the goaltending coach, Dan Campbell, and one of the defense coaches, Jay LaMonde. Dan was the youngest coach on the staff, retiring from the game three years ago from Tampa Bay. Jay was older than my dad by several years and had some slight graying at his temples but was a man who had definitely aged well.

"It's going well." I glanced at the iPad and scanned the list of men. The team would travel with twenty players, plus staff and coaches. "Only ten more to check in."

"Good. Good. And you? You're settling in?"

Vik rarely asked me about my actual life. "As well as can be expected. I have tours at apartments set up when we return next week."

"Take all the time you need. The room isn't going anywhere."

Masculine voices, rich and full of laughter despite the ungodly hour, echoed down the hallway where the guys were entering from.

Vik turned back to me. "I'll let you get back to work, but if you have time tomorrow, I'd like to see you. Maybe lunch today?"

"Um. Sure."

It was hard to spend time with him, harder to say no to the man. And he appeared to be *trying*. How much I was willing to give him remained to be seen.

"Good. And thank you, Ryann. I appreciate the chance."

He said it so quietly I almost thought I imagined it as he walked by me. I didn't have time to shake off my nerves from being around Vik before I turned and was face to face with the man I'd been dreading seeing and most excited to see.

"Good morning, Alix." I checked him off as I hid a smile.

"Good morning, sunshine."

Oh... he *did not*... I glared at him and looked at the man next to him.

"Kane Andrews." He held out his hand.

"Hi. Ryann. I remember you."

"The asshole who ditched us on the dance floor." Alix rocked back on his heels, seemingly pleased with himself. "But that ended up good for me, yes?"

Kane shoved his elbow into Alix's gut and rolled his eyes in my direction. "Ignore this asshole, we do."

"That is not true. You all love me!"

"Keep dreaming," Kane muttered, but he was smiling. As Alix spurted noises of his displeasure at not being loved, Kane leaned in toward me. "It's nice to finally meet you. I've heard a lot about you, but anyone who was there that night won't say a thing. You have my word."

Heat rose from the tips of my toes and shot up my body. "Thank you."

"You're welcome. And we're glad to have you on the team." He stepped back and patted my shoulder as he continued on, grabbing one of the few remaining meals.

"Here." Alix held out his fist. "This is for you."

"What is it?" I lifted my hand, and he dropped a small, pink bag cinched at the top. Kate Spade was imprinted on it and my eyes grew four times their normal size. "Alix..."

"It is a pressure point bracelet. Supposed to help with motion sickness, and there is lavender oil in the bag as well. You said you didn't like flying." He shrugged and shoved his hands into his suit pants pockets. "I thought it could help."

He winked as more men came down the hall and left without a word.

The next few men didn't go as smoothly. Mostly because Alix's surprise was hard to get over.

As was the way he left.

If he thought his gift was supposed to help settle my nerves, he was dead wrong.

I didn't open the bag until I was in my seat on the airplane.

He hadn't just gone out last night, bought me a present *after* we'd gotten off the phone—he'd engraved the bracelet.

To my friend. From yours. ~A

It was the simplest, most meaningful and special gift I'd ever been given.

I turned, found Alix several rows behind me on the airplane and on the opposite side of the aisle.

His light blue, intense gaze met mine, like he'd been waiting for this moment.

Thank you, I mouthed to him.

He nodded once, lips kicking up at the corner into a grin—right before he blew me a kiss.

Friends, my ass.

Kane dropped down in the seat next to me. We spent so much time together, living next door to each other, riding to practices and the airport together we usually sat with other teammates on flights and bus rides. It kept us from being too isolated and stuck in our own heads.

I was not surprised he did not follow our normal scheduled pattern.

Not after meeting Ryann.

"If you keep staring at the back of her chair like you want to take a bite out of her, you're not going to last one away trip without getting caught."

I gripped the oversized earpieces of my noise-canceling head-phones that were draped around my neck. "She likes my present."

"And once she realizes how much work you had to go through last night to get it for her, she'll think you're more psychotic than cute."

"Any attention is good attention, no?"

"No, jackass." Kane laughed though and dug through his bag for his own headphones along with his iPad so he could watch game film.

The man studied the game more than anyone else I knew. Not me. My job was to be fast, be open, and make good passes. I trusted my wingers, both Joey and Arlo and Braxton to be ready when I needed them.

We'd played together long enough now that we could win games while sleeping.

"She is pretty," Kane muttered, leaning toward me. "Don't you dare tell Emmersyn I said that either, but I can see why you like her."

"She is more than pretty." I sighed, and I was sounding like a lovesick fool. "She is perfect. Months I thought about her, and now she is right there, and I cannot have her. It is driving me crazy."

When Ryann texted me last night with the picture of her glass of wine and television show, all I saw was the bed. The rumpled white sheets. My dick went hard, jealous over hotel sheets that got to rub against her skin when I was not allowed.

Had I been in my own hot tub, and not my best friend's, I would have relieved myself as soon as we got off the phone. Or hell, while we were on it, so she could wonder what I was doing with my arm beneath the water, guess at why my lips would part and my jaw would grind together.

Kane might call me a jackass, but I was not asshole enough to do that in my friend's hot tub.

I had done it in my shower, as soon as we hung up, before I rushed to stores trying to find something that could make flying easier.

I had, after all, told her I could help her with her nerves. And this way, whenever she looked at the bracelet, she would think of me.

Once Callie boarded, the sign everything was locked and loaded and ready to roll, Coach Vik stood from his seat in the front row next to Jay LaMonde and slapped his hands to the backs of the chairs.

"All right, men. Time to forget about all the bullshit you left behind today. It's our first road trip of the new year and we all know Edmonton on Friday wants nothing more than to knock us out of our first place standings."

There were whoops and hollers, and jeers at the team that was closest to us in standings and had the ability to do what Coach threatened. He lifted his hand, silenced us as the doors to the airplane were locked and the metal stairway pulled away. "We all know they don't have a chance in hell at beating us, but let's not lose focus on Calgary first. All right?"

"Yes sir!" And "Yes Coach" and a variety of phrases were shouted in agreement.

Vik glanced toward Ryann, a question in his eyes, and she must have nodded, understood the silent question because he turned back to the team.

"Now, I know there have been rumors this week. Personal ones, about me. My family." A pin could have hit the deck and echoed like an avalanche for how quickly the team quieted down. Coach cleared his throat, glanced again at Ryann and back to us, meeting each and every one of his players in the eye. "I know Callie introduced you to Debbie's replacement this morning. Her name is Ryann, and some of you may not know, but she is my youngest daughter."

"The fuck?" was whispered from somewhere behind me, but there was white noise in my brain, because all I could do was stare at the back of Ryann's chair.

Was she really okay with this? Of course it'd be known, but I imagined her there, lips pressed together, small hands fisted in anger for her father and now being thrown into the spotlight.

"She has earned this job of her own merit, and I expect every single one of you, like I always expect, to treat her with the same respect you give the entire coaching staff and the rest of the Vipers team. Understand?"

Another round of "yes sirs" and "yes Coaches" were mumbled, these quieter. He had just knocked half the team off their asses and left Ryann flung out to sea, without any escape to get away from the man who had now caused over two dozen men to stare at the back of her head.

The asshole.

It was not a bad thing to introduce her and explain who she was, but he could have done it when she could escape if needed after.

"All right. Game faces on. We'll be landing in a few hours. I'll need you all focused as soon as we hit the hotel."

I stared so hard at the back of Ryann's chair, willing her to turn to me, to make sure she was okay.

But that would not happen. She would not turn to me, not for any reason, especially with her dad so close.

"You'll figure it out." Kane nudged my shoulder.

"Figure what out?"

"How to help her. How to win her over."

"You believe that?" For the first time, I was having doubts.

"Fuck yeah." He punched my shoulder and slipped his head-phones over the top of his head and his ears. "You don't lose at anything. Ever."

"Correct. I am pretty awesome."

"Don't worry about her, focus on the game. The rest will come at the perfect moment, just think of me and Emmersyn."

His wife, who showed up on his doorstep, literally. Who he then fake married and fell in love with.

"You're right. I will not worry."

"Of course I'm right. I always am." He smirked, kicked his legs out into the aisle as far as he could, and closed his eyes.

I did the same.

I might not study game film like Kane did, but I knew how to make a game plan.

I just had to create the perfect one where Ryann would lose her ability to resist me. No problem at all.

I ENSURED I was the last person off the bus when we pulled into our hotel parking lot hours later. A quick nap on the plane left me still tired, even as anticipation for the first away game of the new year made my blood sing. We might have had a few days at home to enjoy the holidays, but this was the mid-stretch of the season, where rankings were set in stone, where the mettle met the road.

Injuries would occur, exhaustion would set in. By March, games would be coming down to who wanted the Cup more, and I was damn focused to ensure it was the Vipers who would want it the most.

All of that was in my mind, currently streaming in the background while I set my sights on the woman in front of me, my current battle with the potential for my greatest victory.

Or loss.

But I did not like to lose, so I would not think about that potential ending.

"Here are your room keys." She held out the last remaining cardboard envelope.

I took it from her, making sure my fingers brushed over hers as I did and since I'd kept my gaze on her, I caught the flutter of her eyelashes as our skin made contact. Too long. Too many months I'd gone without holding her. Talking with her. Laughing with her like I'd done that night.

Sliding one of my keys out of the packet, I handed it to her. "Have a drink with a friend later?"

"Alix..." she sighed my name and I refused to let disappointment set in.

"For the record, Ryann, I will make this offer in every hotel we are in until you give in."

"Stubborn jerk."

"Not a jerk. Optimistic. Focused. Confident. And I think you like all of those things about me."

"Ryann!" Callie called her name, and she swiped the card from my hand.

"Yes?"

"Everyone checked in?" She came toward us with purpose on heels that clicked on the tiled floor. Callie always dressed to impress on away games like us guys had to do, but it wasn't required for staff. I preferred Ryann's sleepy look, wearing a Vipers polo shirt, dark green with the gold logo resting above her left breast and the skintight, flared leggings she wore.

She looked comfortable. Casual.

No less beautiful than she'd been in a hot pink skintight dress that exposed the softest parts of her.

"They are," Ryann said, and tucked the card into a folder she was holding. "Alix was the last one off the bus."

"Good. See you for lunch then?"

The team and traveling staff would have a catered meal in one of the hotel's conference rooms. Coach always insisted on it for lunches before we headed back to our rooms to relax.

"Oh. Um." She shook her head, looking unsure for a moment. "I'm sorry. Vik asked me to have lunch with him. I think in his suite."

"Oh. Okay, then. I'll see you when we need to board the bus."

Relief loosened her shoulders. If she thought it strange Vik wanted a private lunch with Ryann, she didn't act like it.

Callie tossed her a smile, a nod to me, and spun, headed toward the conference rooms, past the registration desk and to the right.

"I should go," she mumbled. "And see if she needs help."

"You're okay with that? Eating with your dad?" Her dislike of him ran far and deep. But she'd taken the job, and I'd caught them talking occasionally in the halls. Maybe a couple weeks of working with him had changed her already.

She shrugged, hugging her iPad and folder tight to her chest. "It depends on what he wants to talk about. I should go."

Yet her feet didn't move and even as she said it, she sounded unsure.

As if the mention of her father stole all her joy and happiness.

"I'll see you on the bus then. But if you need anything, you know how to reach me." I nodded toward the folder where she'd shoved the card and rocked on my heels.

"Just because I took the card doesn't mean I'll use it."

"Okay."

Ryann huffed before a timid smile broke out. "You are infuriating."

"I know."

Shaking her head, she stepped around me. "Good luck tonight, Alix."

I wouldn't mind getting lucky with her, but I doubted that was what she meant.

"No luck needed," I assured her, calling out to her back.

On the ice... or with her.

Both took skill and determination.

Lucky for me, I had those in spades.

Vik texted as soon as I got settled in my room, asking me to choose something from room service. Once he placed our orders, I received another text telling me our food would be ready in forty-five minutes.

Which gave me forty-five minutes to pace the small hotel room, smaller than the one I was currently living in back in Vegas, and worry not only about what Vik wanted to talk about over lunch but have Alix's hotel keycard burn a hole in my pocket.

At least, it did, until I flung it to the desk and reminded myself how dumb it would be if I used it. The team all stayed on one floor. Staff and coaches on the floor above them. Sneaking to Alix's room for a drink—or any reason, because I highly doubted a miniature vodka from the minibar was what Alix really had in mind—would be tempting career suicide.

All it would take was one man to leave his room, see me entering or leaving Alix's room, and I could lose my job weeks after I started it.

The more I considered the possibilities, the risk Alix was asking, expecting me to take, especially on my very first road trip, the more furious I got.

I sat down on the bed and grabbed my phone and texted him.

I will not be using this card. And it's not okay you offered it to me.

Tossing the phone to the bed, I went to the bathroom. It was twenty minutes before I had to be at Vik's, and I still smelled like stale air and airplane. I flipped on the water and grabbed a T-shirt from my suitcase. A six-day road trip where I was only allowed a small suitcase, and a carry-on, packing had been a challenge. Callie assured me I'd get used to it, and gave me tips on packing cubes, and what I truly needed.

It wasn't like we were hitting clubs and being tourists, we were working, which meant most of my shirts held the Vipers logo or were casual, something I could wear on an afternoon off or to work out in the hotel's gyms.

I wasn't a huge gym rat, but I figured after all the time we'd spend sitting on planes and on buses, I'd needed the occasional job or workout to stretch my muscles.

The shower loosened muscles tightened from the early day and traveling, and by the time it was over, I felt slightly human again. I'd left my hair up, twisted into a clip to keep it dry and after a fresh reapply of moisturizer and some concealer, blush, and mascara, the purple circles beneath my eyes were gone.

My phone sat on the bathroom counter, the screen lit with notifications.

It is just a drink.

In your room. Where anyone could see me. You might have all the money in the world, but I need this job.

Then the hotel bar. Tonight. Team will be there and others always join us.

He was frustrating. Was headstrong and cocky and all the things I typically despised in men.

No.

It was the only answer I could give him. Sure, maybe I could have a drink with the rest of the team. Get to know them a little bit. Hang out with the rest of the staff who traveled as well.

Someday, I would.

But not my very first night. I wasn't just a new employee, I was the coach's daughter and even if everyone knew we didn't have a relationship that didn't mean eyes wouldn't be on me. That I might be judged more harshly than others for the decisions I made.

Lord knew Vik would probably throw a fit if he found me drunk—and it wouldn't be because he cared about me, but because of what it could say about him.

No. Drinking with Alix and his friends, many of whom knew I already spent a night with him was not a smart choice.

Understood. Maybe some other night. Hope your lunch goes well, but if not, I am here if you need to talk.

And just like that, I questioned myself.

Because Alix knew. He understood. We'd spent a lot of time that first night together talking about our fathers and our families and our sisters. Of anyone, if I needed to vent or rage, he would get it.

Thank you, I texted back.

His response came immediately. Complete with a handful of smiling emojis. ***That is what friends are for, no?***

I heard his accent through his text and a shiver sparked that familiar excitement I still wasn't used to getting when I was around him.

He was frustrating, yes. But did he also have to be so tempting?

"COME IN, COME IN." Vik waved out his arm, stepping back and holding the door open so I could enter.

"Thank you." Like me, he'd stripped out of his travel clothes and was in a fresh pair of black dress pants and a short sleeve polo shirt. I had no doubts he'd be redressed in a suit before the game. But for now, that we were both casually dressed helped settle my nerves.

"Lunch should be here any minute," he said, and turned toward the small fridge. He had a junior suite, something I knew he generally chose even though he could have a larger one. But these kept him closer to his teams, which was something Callie told me he preferred. Not to father them or babysit them, but because when they were on the road, the closeness brought the team together. "Would you like a drink? Or water?"

"Water would be good."

He grabbed two from the fridge and set them at the table. I took a seat across from him, and wished he would have had music on, or the television. Some background noise to cut through the thick, awkward silence that always fell in our first few moments alone together.

If the hotel had crickets, we'd be able to hear every song they sang. For now, it was broken by the cracking open of water bottles.

"I found Hayden's Instagram," he said. If I wasn't watching him so closely, I would have missed the way the water bottle trembled in his hand. Nerves. It shouldn't have made me happy.

Mostly because, really?

He'd never bothered to look before?

"She's talented. And she's where now? Norway?" It wasn't exactly a guess. She always tagged the locations.

Last week she'd been in the Sahara although I knew she had to go to Europe after that so I wasn't really sure. "She mentioned doing some camping in arctic domes for travel magazines."

He shook his head. "I wouldn't have expected something like that from Hayden. She must spend a lot of time alone."

I bit back the comment asking why he thought he'd know

anything about her. Starting a fight before my filet came—and yes, petty me ordered the most expensive dish on the menu—would make me ruin a delicious meal.

"What makes you say that?" I asked instead, because hell, she was fifteen when we moved away. Maybe he remembered something I didn't. Knew something I didn't, although it was doubtful.

"She always wanted to be surrounded by people. When she was little, it was never just enough for her to have Braylen or you around. She was always begging your mom for playdates. To surround herself with her friends. A day didn't go by when she wasn't wanting to be with your mom, out and about, going to the stores. She just... she had so much energy. It's difficult to picture her alone, sleeping in the wilderness."

That she had a team with her for safety's sake and they'd become her friends probably hadn't occurred to him. Mostly because he was right, Hayden was always surrounded by people. Fed off their energy and then dished it back out tenfold.

But that was always why she loved traveling and photography. She wasn't restricted to one place for too long and it fed her adventurous spirit.

The fact he couldn't realize how perfect it was for her because of that grated on me.

"And you?" I asked. That bubble of frustration started to simmer. "How often did she beg to spend time with you? And how often did you say no, if you were around at all?"

He flinched, took a sip of his water, and was saved having to answer by a knock at the door and the call for room service.

"I'll get that," he muttered and once he'd turned his back to me, I cursed myself.

I'd been the one to come to him. Wanted to work with him. I'd agreed to spend time with him.

What did I think would happen? That he'd completely ignore the past? It was all he had of us.

The creak of the cart pushed the thought to the background and he slid our plates in front of us. That awkward tension back in full force and with it, my simmering anger.

"I loved your mom," Vik said as he removed the dome from his plate. "And before you snap back at me that I did a shitty job of showing it or reminding me how much I fucked up, please hear me out."

His jaw shoved forward, indication of his irritation with me, but screw that. He deserved every uncomfortable second of it.

I nodded, clenching the fork like a knife in my fists like a savage but stayed quiet.

"I loved your mother, I did. Jennifer was this light, this quiet peace, and she provided that so easily. And yet, when she chose to step out of the quietness she preferred, she was a ball of fire. The life of the party. She was your quiet bookworm self when you were little and Hayden's need for constant excitement all wrapped up in sensibility, I imagine would still be Braylen today."

I stabbed a piece of steak with my fork and shrugged. "You're not all that wrong."

He sighed, heavy with regret or maybe acceptance. "She gave me everything I ever needed, without ever demanding anything in return, and I needed that. When I took the Vipers coaching job as their expansion team, your mom stepped right to my side from the moment we met and stayed right there. Loyal. Helpful. She was the calm to the storm I needed while I was surrounded by pressure some days so heavy I thought I'd break from it."

"Mom's the most amazing woman on the planet."

"And I fucked her over. Treated her like shit and let her down at every corner, I know, Ryann. I *do* know that."

"And us," I told him, and it was a damn shame the steak was so delicious because my stomach was quickly curling into a tight ball, stealing my appetite.

"And you," he conceded, and not even a bit reluctant to admit it. "I know that. And I know there aren't enough sorries and apologies and excuses and reasons in the world to make up for it, but I am sorry."

I took in the apology, the remorse in his tone, and tried to let it soothe me in a way I hadn't yet allowed. Was there a point in going back? Rehashing the why's and demanding answers? There would never be anything he could say that would make it make sense. Why his thirst for success took precedence over being a decent dad or husband.

"How is your heart?"

His eyes widened with a quick flare.

"The doctor says I'll be fine. Although I do have high cholesterol and need to watch what I eat. Hence this." He pointed his fork to his lunch with a frown. Chicken. Broccoli. Brown rice. It looked like the kind of meal guys ate who only cared about growing muscles from weights in the gym and not real life.

"It looks miserable." No one could survive on broccoli and chicken, even if it looked well-seasoned.

I cut off a chunk of steak and scraped it off my fork and onto his plate. "A little won't kill you, will it?"

"Depends," he said and winked at me before smiling. "Is that your plan?"

We had issues as deep as the Grand Canyon, that couldn't be denied. "No. I don't want that."

"Good."

He chewed his steak and then managed to shock the hell out of me by going back to Mom. "I was loyal to her."

My fork froze in front of my mouth. "What?"

"When I was on the road. I know the stereotype. The whole 'a woman in every city kind of thing' athletes get saddled with. I just want you to know that, or Jennifer, in case she ever wondered. I loved her, and I was loyal. I was just a shitty, very selfish man."

I'd wondered. Was that why he didn't care about us? Other

women? Maybe better families he saw provided him with more excitement. Or maybe mistresses with sons...

"It helps actually," I admitted. "Thank you."

Ryann's text said she wouldn't use the card I slipped her in Calgary, but she didn't refuse the one I handed her in Edmonton or in Vancouver, either. I figured, every time she had the card in her hands it was a battle to do what she wanted versus what she thought she should do. I wasn't used to being outplayed, but she was definitely holding her own.

Since she was worried about her job—I'd looked into it. Nowhere in the staff's manual or player's code of conduct mentioned anything about players dating staff not being allowed.

So she wouldn't lose her job—but was she truly more worried about that? Or was her hesitation rooted in not wanting to disappoint a father she wasn't quite so sure she even liked?

Time would tell, and since I'd already waited four months—I could wait longer.

Like right now, for example, when most of the team and at least half of the staff who traveled with us were currently in the hotel's bar, having a drink after dinner with the replay of our game highlights and others we'd missed on ESPN on multiple televisions all over the bar, she was there, laughing with Callie as the two of them tossed back a shot of tequila.

I was mesmerized. The flick of her tongue as she licked her wrist. The swallow of her throat as she took the shot and didn't cringe in the least. The puff of her pink lips I so desperately wanted to taste again as she sucked on the lime.

She threw her head back and laughed, playfully pushed at Callie's shoulder and shook her head *no* to whatever Callie said, nodding so seriously, and turned to the bartender.

Another set of shots appeared, quickly followed by a glass of water and Ryann mouthed *thank you* to the bartender before they repeated the shot, and I was glued to her movements from my spot at the table with Dominick and Kane like the pathetic stalker I was becoming whenever Ryann was in my vicinity.

But screw this.

She'd avoided me long enough and what could happen in a crowded bar? The coaches were long since gone, mostly likely tucked away in Vik's suite strategy planning for our next game in Vancouver.

She and Callie, abandoning their shots and grabbing their waters, weaved through the bar until they ended up at a high-top table with Ryder and Calix, which gave me a chance to make my move.

"Anyone need a refill?"

Dominick shook his water back and forth, ice clinking. "I'm good. Heading upstairs soon, anyway." He'd come down to the bar after he FaceTimed Ben, his soon-to-be stepson, before Ben went to bed. I had no doubt he and his fiancée Holly would have a completely different kind of call when he got back to his room.

"I'm good too," Kane said. "Heading up soon myself." He scanned the bar and smirked. "Keep an eye on the young ones tonight, would you? Like Calix?"

Right. Because the smirk didn't give away he was not talking about the player at all, but the woman standing next to him.

"Will do, captain." I was not one to defy his orders after all.

After heading to the bar and switching out my own beer for a fresh water, I grabbed a second one and surprisingly enough, when I reached the table where Ryann was with Ryder and Calix, she didn't flee.

"Here." I slipped the water in front of her. "Not roofied, I promise."

"Well that's reassuring," she muttered, and flashed me a wink.

"What are you three talking about?"

"Sex," Ryder stated, blank face and looking like he needed a good punch to the jaw.

"What?"

Calix laughed. "We were not talking about sex."

Ryann nudged my shoulder. "I was asking them about what life is really like with all the traveling, and how long it takes to adjust to it."

"And I happened to mention that the lack of sex completely sucks," Ryder threw in. "So we *were* talking about sex."

"Just you, Bromann." Calix slapped his shoulder. "Just you."

"And you?" He was the newest guy on our team. The youngest. It wouldn't surprise me if he was hooking up left and right.

"No way. I'm with Bromann on this one. I'm fucking exhausted every day right now."

The mid-season burnout. He'd played in the minor league professional teams, so he knew what it was like, but there was no doubt the stress of being a rookie was taking its toll.

"So, no sex," Ryann said, and I was pretty sure a blush was blooming on her cheeks. "And you're exhausted all the time. This job keeps sounding better and better."

Calix laughed. "It's worth it to hang out with us handsome guys, though, isn't it?"

Ryann's eyes slid in my direction and the blush darkened. "I suppose you're not all half-bad."

"But we are not always good either."

"Nice move," Ryder faux whispered and Ryann chuckled.

"Stop it. You promised not to bring it up," she said to him.

Ryder shrugged, finished his beer, and slapped the table. "So I lied. Come on, rookie, you need to buy me a round."

"What? Why do I have to?" But Ryder had already hooked his arm around Calix's neck and was dragging him to the bar.

"Hey, I'll go with," Callie said with a smirk that said we hadn't hidden much—or maybe Ryann had told her more than I would have thought she had. "The rookie can buy me a birthday shot, too."

"What?" Calix pouted, but relented, mumbling something about how badly he was going to haze the next rookie.

"That was not smooth," Ryann muttered, grinning at me after she turned back from watching Ryder shove Calix to the bar. "I would think players like you would have more game."

I waggled a finger in the air. "Let's not get started. You know very well exactly how much game I have."

"Maybe." She ran her finger along the rim of her water glass. "Or maybe I was just desperate that night. Would have found any man decent enough after the shitshow I'd had with my dad."

A fire, hot and unexpected, rushed through me at the thought. That she did not think of me like I had thought of her. Then I imagined her taking home another man. Any man who would do, and a growl slipped past my lips. "You are lying."

"Am I?" She brought her glass to her lips, giving me a look that dared me to defy her. To test her.

Or possibly—to throw her down on my bed this time and grab her wrists. Fuck her until she took it back. Until she knew I was the only man who would ever please her that well again.

"Yes." I nodded confidently and leaned on the table, forearms resting on it so I was close enough to her I could inhale the scent of her soft, feminine perfume. "Because you are blushing, and I bet you are turned on right now thinking of all the things we did together, and you and I both know you don't have the conversation, the connection we did, if all you're looking for is a random dick to get you off. Now tell me I'm lying."

Her grin wiped away. "No. You're not lying. It's just—"

"The job. I know, and I understand, but then maybe don't tease me about it either? Because I am trying to give you what you want from me, but you do not need to make it more difficult."

"You're right." Her voice was soft. Tinged with regret. "I'm sorry since I'm the one who drew the line. I'll be more careful."

"Thank you. Now tell me. How is your first road trip going? We are not too difficult, no?"

"Exhausting. Callie warned me, but I definitely have a lot more respect for not only the game but your lives, too. It's hard, isn't it?"

"It is worth every minute of it." I meant it. Hockey wasn't an easy life. It involved many sacrifices as soon as you started, and for most kids, that was around the time you started school. But yes, there was sacrifice. Early mornings. Late nights. Traveling.

"I should get to my room," she said, and her regret was heavier now.

But I liked she didn't want to walk away from me.

"I will walk you."

She opened her mouth to object, I could practically see it brimming on the tip of her tongue, so I lifted my hands in a placating gesture.

"To make sure you get there safe. That is all."

"Okay then."

I said goodbye to the guys as we headed out of the bar. Joey and André, our backup goalie, boarded with us and as they stepped off, didn't think anything of it when I said I was getting Ryann to her room.

They were good guys. They would have offered to do the same if it was not me.

I deserved a medal for keeping my hands to myself once we were alone and as she led me down the hall to her room. She stopped outside of it and pulled a key out of the pocket of her jeans.

"Thank you, Alix."

"You do not have to thank me for anything."

"No?"

"No." I slipped the keycard from her hand, slid it into her lock and opened her door. The move blocked her entrance to her own room and as I handed her back her key, I leaned down until my mouth was at her jaw, her ear.

Surprise made her shiver, or maybe something else better.

"Do not thank me when I am having a hard time breaking my promise of just being friends with you. I will wait for the day when you think the risk is worth it, but that does not mean I do not plan on helping you get there faster."

Her hand pressed to my chest where my heart was racing beneath my simple black T-shirt I'd thrown on once we returned to the hotel.

"You're asking a lot from me," she whispered, her voice thick with desire.

"And I will make every moment worth it. I promise you." I pressed my lips to the hinge of her jaw, breathed in her scent until I was certain I would never forget it and stepped back so she could get into her room. "Sleep well, sunshine. I'll see you in the morning."

WE PULLED into the hotel in Seattle after a delayed take-off with barely enough time to grab our rooms, get settled, and get back on the bus to head to the arena for a practice. Tomorrow's game would be tough but being given the day to practice and get a feel for the ice would be good for all of us.

Bonus, it was our last game on this long trip and it didn't have to be said to know we were all tired, sore, missing wives and girlfriends and kids back home that we were antsy, as well as exhausted.

These parts of the trip were always the hardest and even if we'd won all the games so far, we needed a win tomorrow to head back home ready to play again almost immediately. I had a slight headache from the late night last night, more from exhaustion than alcohol, but Ryann looked much worse—albeit still beautiful.

"Too much tequila?" I asked as I handed her my card. "You look tired."

"Thanks for the compliment." She squinted and scrunched up her nose. "And yes. Callie could talk a polar bear into needing a trip to the desert."

I snorted. "I have ways to help with hangovers."

She rolled her eyes, slipped the envelope into the folder she always carried and blushed, immediately looking away from me. "I bet you do."

Her tone implied innuendo I was very much in favor of.

"Medicine. Massages. Orange juice. Acupressure.... What were you thinking of?"

That blush that was so endearing came forth on the apple of her cheeks. "Sure. That's what you meant. I believe you." She scanned the lobby area, checked who was around. Coach LaMonde was headed our way and her voice quickly dropped along with her eyes to her iPad. "Are you hanging out with the guys tonight?"

"No." I tapped her iPad screen to get her attention. "I'm staying in."

She nodded once, turned her attention to Coach LaMonde. "Hi there, Jay. Here are your room keys."

"Thank you, Ryann. Halvrick." He glanced at me. "Don't be late for the bus."

"Never, sir." I grinned shamelessly.

"Liar," he quipped back and headed toward the elevator.

So I had a habit of running late. To games. Practices... whatever. He hadn't noticed I'd been better at being on time this trip, and that was mostly due to the woman in front of me.

"See you later?" I asked Ryann once we were alone again.

Because this hotel was smaller, the coaches had the top floor while we were smack dab in the middle.

She chewed on her bottom lip. It wasn't an automatic no, but as I watched her struggle, I realized I didn't want that.

I wanted her to come to me when she was ready. Willing. Not second-guessing anything or worried about being caught.

We had time for that.

With my keycard still in her hand, I tugged it out of her grip.

"I'm going to take that."

Surprise lit up her blue eyes and her lips parted. "Why?"

"Because you're unsure. And that's close enough to a no for me. There will be other days." Other hotels. "But what are your plans for today?"

"You have practice."

"Yeah, but then we have the night off. Maybe we can go grab dinner?"

That worry line returned and my fingers itched to smooth it away. Take away all her fears.

"There's an Italian restaurant I like north of here. Should be far enough away from the hotel where no one will see us. I could meet you there? Around seven?"

"You're sure?"

"Of finally being able to enjoy a meal with you? Absolutely."

She glanced down at her now blackened iPad screen like she expected it to be a magic eight ball. "Okay." She lifted her head, blue eyes met mine and it looked like excitement was winning out over her nerves. "Seven."

SIXTEEN

RYANN

Typical for what I knew of Seattle this time of year, the sky was overcast and dreary. An almost constant drizzle wet my North Face coat. At forty degrees, it felt colder due to the rain and the wetness in the air.

Perhaps it was because I was raised in the desert, where sunshine abounded the majority of the year, but for as charming as Seattle was and as much as I'd loved patrolling the streets and taking a trip to the top of the Space Needle earlier, I couldn't fathom why anyone would want to live with weather that would cause constant misery.

Since the guys didn't have a game until tomorrow afternoon, I had today off while they were at the arena doing a light skate, so I'd spent the day wandering Seattle. I caught fish being thrown in the Pikes Peak Market. Explored the history of rock and roll museum, MoPOP, and saw the foggy rain from the top of the Space Needle before heading back to the hotel, warming up, and getting ready for dinner, where Alix and I agreed to meet. I'd breathed a sigh of relief when I pulled up on Google Maps. North of the hotel by several miles, like Alix said in Fremont, there was hardly a chance anyone would see us together.

On my way, I popped into a nearby cookie shop and grabbed a four-pack of their extra large cookies, all different flavors, to enjoy later.

"Ryann?"

I jumped at the sound of my name as I stepped out of the bakery and back onto the street's narrow sidewalks.

No one should know where I was, and that I recognized that voice sent a chill through me. I turned to the owner of that voice.

"Vik," I said, and caught his lips tightening. "What are you doing here?"

He smiled, the tightness of me calling him by his first name, something he clearly didn't like, vanishing. "I love this area."

My dad liked an artsy, bohemian area of the city? I couldn't imagine the straight-laced, selfish man I'd always known to enjoy anything about the dilapidated buildings with spray painted art all over the crumbling brick walls.

"You do?" My voice rose in surprise. He had to be lying. There was no way he liked any of this. Had he... followed me?

"Yes. I found this Italian restaurant two years ago and stop in every time we're in the city when I have a chance."

"Italian?" The word lodged in my throat and came out garbled. I covered it with a fake cough. "That's, oh... okay."

"Care to join me?" He rocked on his heels, hands shoved into his suit pants. The only tell he was nervous around me.

I'd once enjoyed that look on his face, really any time I could knock him off his confident little perch. There was no joy in it then.

Nerves knitted themselves together, making my skin tight like a shrunken sweater, and I didn't have a good reason to say no.

"Um. Yeah. I was actually—"

"Coach?" Alix's wide eyes shot to me as he rounded the corner, thankfully spying Vik before he noticed me and then his own face paled. "Hey, Coach." He walked to us, adjusting much quicker than I had to Vik's presence. "Fancy seeing you here. What are you doing out?"

Vik turned in pleasant surprise. "Alix. Good to see you. I happened to run into my daughter and I'm trying to talk her into joining me for a meal."

"Oh. Well, that's... that is good." He gave me a quick, wide-eyed look before facing Vik.

"Where were you headed?"

"Oh. Um." Alix scratched his head. "I heard Portofino's was good. Thought I'd check it out."

"Excellent." My dad slapped his hand to Alix's shoulder, jolting him. "Then you can join me too. And maybe having someone else around will convince Ryann to have dinner with us, too?"

Oh God. He'd done it again. Somehow, my dad was slick enough to throw me under the bus. Did he do these things intentionally or was he so full of himself, it simply came naturally to him?

"If you want a dinner with your daughter, I do not have to interfere." Alix stepped back, ready to leave, but since Vik was looking at me, waiting for my answer, he didn't see Alix's eyes, the question in them asking me what in the hell we were supposed to do.

Like I freaking knew. I was upset with Vik enough already. Dinner with him sounded horrific.

"Sure," I mumbled, because there was no getting out of this now, not without making Vik look bad in front of his players. I really needed to try harder to keep my professional life and personal life separate. So far, I was royally messing it all up. "It's okay. Dinner would be nice."

"Excellent." Dad gave Alix another shake of his shoulder before letting go. "This will be good, then. You can get to know the team a little better, and we can talk."

This was not excellent.

It was going to be torture.

Alix's expression said the same as mine, but we dutifully followed Vik inside Portofino's. I was blasted with heat from the restaurant and the enticing scent of tomato sauces and garlic and seasonings, but I couldn't drag up any excitement for dinner.

There was too much dread curdling in my gut.

"So, have you two had much time to get to know each other?"

Vik asked the question with a bottle of beer in one hand and his other elbow on the table. We'd ordered. We hadn't said anything else and if there was an awkward meter at the table, it would be alerting at maximum levels.

Sitting across from the girl I'd wanted to spend the day alone with while she made stilted conversation with a man she couldn't stand and one I respected was the worst way to enjoy an Italian meal.

"Um. No." Ryann brushed her hands over her lap, no doubt smoothing out the cloth napkin draping her thighs. "We've talked, but I couldn't say I know any of the guys that well, yet."

Points to Ryann for not blushing as red as this restaurant's marinara sauce.

"Come on, Coach. You know we're busy when we're on the road, focused on the next game." If there was one thing that could distract the man, it was hockey. "I tried to get some guys to come eat with me, but they were all watching film and working out."

"And why weren't you watching film?" Coach asked, and while

he wasn't exactly disappointed, I knew I had his attention. *Why was I out eating dinner when the team was working?*

"I will when I get back. I could not resist the call of authentic Italian. Hard to find as good as it is back home, and Portofino's owner is from Turin, Italy. It is only a few hours from my home. I had to check it out."

"Where are you from?" Ryann asked. Points to her for asking it like she was genuinely curious.

But this could maybe work, too. We could get to know each other with her father as a chaperone, ask all the questions we didn't yet know.

"Just outside of Geneva, Switzerland."

Her smile was soft, innocent. Still made my dick take notice which was not a good thing sitting so close to her father. Add in I couldn't touch her and it was downright painful.

"It must be beautiful there. How long have you been in the States?"

"We drafted Alix from the European leagues seven years ago. You were, what?" Coach turned to me. "Twenty? Nineteen? Just a kid."

"Twenty." I cleared my throat and forced my attention on Coach so he didn't see the lust I was certain shone like the sunshine all over me. "It was a few months before my twenty-first birthday. I will never forget coming here, alone in a hotel in a new country for the first time."

"Ah. Yes. And then you stayed with Marvin?"

"Marvin Hanz. Yes. Good man." I glanced at Ryann, who was understandably lost in the conversation. "He was the captain at the time. Retired a year later, but after I stayed at the hotel for a couple of weeks, he brought me into his home. Married. Two kids. It was an experience, to say the least, to go from my home with only a sister to that. But it was good."

"Is that common?" Ryann asked. "To move in with other teammates?"

"Sometimes."

Our server appeared at the table and slid salads and fresh, warm, bread, still steaming, onto the table.

After we requested drink refills, Vik continued. "Sometimes older guys on the team will bring new, young ones like Arlo or Callix into their homes to get them used to the team quicker. Helps them feel bonded. Other times they stay at the hotel, like where you are staying."

"You're at the Sunset?" I asked, and Ryann's grin was almost too telling.

"Yes. While I get settled. The move and job happened so fast I didn't have time to get an apartment first."

"Where are you looking?"

She laughed, glanced at her dad, and shrugged. "I have no idea where to start. I want to be close to work, away from the Strip, but I would love to be able to have someplace where I could walk for shopping and food too."

"You should reach out to Joey Taylor. His wife Gabby runs a hair salon and spa that's on the main level of some condos or apartments. Maybe there could be something to rent there. A lot of wives have started getting their hair done there though and I know there are restaurants and some clothing stores. Nearby grocery store."

"Thank you." She tore off a small piece of bread. "I'll ask Joey for her information."

I shrugged. "You're a part of the team. It's what we do."

"And if you want me to go with you," Vik said, and I'd almost forgotten he was sitting next to us. "I'm happy to help. Check things out."

Ryann's jaw worked back and forth, and she took a sip of her wine. "Thanks, Vik. I'll let you know."

Next to me, the man tensed. He either didn't like that she didn't jump at his offer or the use of his first name, but from what I now know of their history, he hadn't done much to earn the moniker *Dad*.

Although it probably irritated him more to have her use his first name around me. That could spark questions. Not like I'd ask them.

Plates were cleared, our dinners brought out. Ryann asked me more about Switzerland, mundane, simple questions she mostly knew the answer to but she was also making it clear she didn't have much to say to her father. As I answered them, I could feel his irritation at being ignored simmering off him.

We were halfway through our meals when there was a lull in conversation, and Vik filled it.

"How are your sisters?" He twirled spaghetti around his fork and glanced at Ryann.

Whatever irritation he'd been feeling spiked in a sharp, heavy wave as I met her eyes. "You should know. You talked to them."

"If I upset them, that was not my intention."

"Of course it wasn't. Because you were thinking of—" She snapped her mouth closed. Glanced at me. Back to her father. "Never mind. This isn't the time or the place, but I asked you to give me and both of them time, and now they're pissed you're reaching out before I could smooth the water. That wasn't cool."

"I didn't—"

"You did," Ryann snapped, interrupting him. "And you deserve whatever they said, but they don't deserve to be blindsided, so back off."

"Ryann." Her name was a warning on his lips and my own frustration grew.

Vik was a good coach. A tough man, but I'd always respected his knowledge of the game. Personal issues aside, he knew how to create and inspire a winning team. What I did not want to get in the middle of were family issues I had no business being involved in.

"I mean it," she all but hissed. "You can't do this and then have them think I'm in the middle of it. It's not cool. To me or them."

His lips pressed together, and his cheeks turned a scorching, heated red. A quick glance at me, and his chest unpuffed as he forced himself to settle.

"Understood. I'm sorry if I overstepped. My offer to help you with the apartment stands, though. Okay?"

"All right."

His phone rang, lighting up with Jay LaMonde's name on the screen and he excused himself, pushing back his chair. "I need to take this."

I waited until he was outside, phone to his ear, before I turned to Ryann.

"You okay? With all of this?"

The conversation, our planned dinner interruption.

"No." She stabbed at a piece of her ravioli. "I'm not okay with any of this. And listen... tonight was too close. This is exactly what I was afraid of, and now you're learning crap about my family Vik would hate that you knew. I just—"

"Don't," I cut her off, and if I could reach across the table and take her hand in mine, I would. But who knew how long Vik would be gone. "So we have to be more careful. Maybe not be together out on the road, or at least alone. But that does not mean this can't happen at all."

"He is an overprotective and intrusive jerk without having any reason to be either. But if he finds out you and I..."

"Sorry about that," Vik said, and I'd been looking so hard into Ryann's pained expression I'd missed him returning.

I jerked back in my seat, too fast and too hard, and he gave us both a questioning look.

"It's no problem." I grinned up at him.

"And I am sorry," he said, ignoring me and still standing. "But I need to get back to the hotel. I'll pay the bill if you two are still eating. LaMonde needs me."

The way he said *needs* had me giving him my full attention. "Is everything okay?"

Vik brushed his hand over his forehead. "Yeah, we have some things we've been working on that he needs my help with."

He frowned, and that didn't sit well with me, either. Our defense had been strong this whole road trip.

"Do you need to go?" Ryann asked me. Yeah. Probably, it'd be the right thing to do. But leave her alone?

"Don't worry about it." Vik pulled out his card from his wallet. "Stay here. Finish. Make sure Ryann gets back to the hotel safely, okay?"

Well, since I had his blessing and all...

"Sure, Coach." I glanced at Ryann. "If that's okay with you? You can head back..."

"That would be fine." She flashed a timid smile, one she probably never gave her dad. "Thanks, Vik. For dinner."

"Yeah." He gave her the credit card and ran his hand over his head again. "See you tomorrow at the bus. Get some sleep tonight."

He left, and once he was gone, Ryann leaned forward. "Do you think everything is really okay? With Jay?"

"I think so. Who knows... trade deadline is coming up. Maybe they're working on things in that regard." Something as a player, I wouldn't get word of until a locker was empty or a new one was filled.

"If we need to go, I can take this back to my room with me."

"No." I shook off the worries about Jay. There wasn't anything I could do about it tonight.

There'd be a time to find out that information, but this moment wasn't it.

"I think, since we might not know how many dinners out we'll get, we should enjoy this one as long as we can."

Ryann's worry lines softened, and she rested back against her chair. "You sure?"

"Sure I want to spend some time with the most beautiful woman I have ever met? Yes, I am sure of that."

I took a sip of my club soda and lime and dug back into my lasagna. We requested fresh bread, enjoyed our meal and split an order of cannoli.

All of it made to perfection. Light, freshly made pasta as thin as my mami used to make with spices I was certain they didn't sell in America even if the names were the same. The food was incredible.

The company even better.

Too soon, we were in the Uber, headed back to the hotel, and after a couple glasses of wine, my limbs were loose and my body warm. Not too much where I'd feel it tomorrow, but the perfect amount of alcohol to enjoy with dinner and company. Next to me, Ryann must have felt similar because she relaxed into me, her side pressed to mine and her head on my shoulder. My arm was behind us, although I'd wanted to take hers in mine, hold her.

I'd settle for draping my arm around her. For now.

"We're almost there," I told her.

She'd gone quiet, almost too quiet.

"I don't want to go to the hotel. To go back to pretending I don't want to be with you like this all the time."

Victory rushed through me at her admission.

She tilted her head back. A sleepy smile curled up the edges of her lips, grabbing my attention right before her tongue slid out, slid along her lower lip.

"You are making it very hard to not kiss you right now."

I'd promised we'd be friends, and I'd already broken it once. The other night when I walked her to her room.

"Maybe I want you to."

Her admission came on a breeze, so quiet I could barely hear it and we were so close I was hearing her breathing.

"Ryann—"

"I have spent too long wanting attention and notice from

someone who doesn't deserve it. Maybe now that I've found someone worthy of it, someone I want, I don't want to push that away."

A groan rumbled deep in my chest and my hand slid to her cheek. "What about just being friends?"

"Maybe we can be more if you give me time?"

I had all the time in the world for her.

"Time then." I leaned in and brushed my lips over hers. She gasped at the first touch of my skin on hers and sank deeper against me. "I can give you that."

I kissed her slowly, aware of the flickers of our Uber driver's attention on us in the rearview and despite how desperately I ached to push my tongue in her mouth, dig my fingers against her scalp and kiss her the way I desired, I pulled back before I lost control.

Before our Uber driver got a show he hadn't paid for.

"Maybe," she whispered, a beautiful flush creeping onto her cheeks, "when we return to Vegas, you could come over?"

I would be there as fast as my Lamborghini could take me.

The game was intense. Tied after two periods, the floor beneath my feet seemed to rattle from the roar and chaos of the crowd. We were watching in the staff lounge area, a beautiful ninety-four-inch projection screen displayed on the wall large enough when I stood close to the screen, the men seemed life-sized.

"I wish we could be out there."

I turned to Callie and found her reclining in one of the leather massage chairs. Her chest shook and wiggled as the chair pulsed and kneaded her shoulders, and the Kindle she was reading on wobbled back and forth.

"You'll get your chance. Besides, wouldn't your dad give you tickets to the home games if you wanted them?"

"Probably. But they'd probably be in the owner's box or something like that and I don't want to sit there."

"So ask him for different ones."

Asking Vik for anything, even if it was tickets to the game, made me gag. "No thanks."

Callie chuckled and went back to her book as the team retook the ice for the third period.

I'd pay money to be a fly on the wall of their locker room, to hear how Vik coached, how he treated them and talked to them. It'd been years since I was so invested in the team, and I had no doubt my current excitement had everything to do with Alix having two of his team's three goals, and an assist on the goal made by Arlo.

Joey took the face-off against Seattle and quickly gained control of the puck, passing it to Arlo, who quickly lost it in a scuffle near the edge of the boards. Seattle got the puck, passing it up the ice. It was a race between one of their players and Alix to get it, and neither could reach it before it was called for icing, and brought back.

"If you stand that close, your eyes will go blurry."

I laughed and took a step away from the screen.

"Why are you so invested in this game? You haven't seemed to care about any yet."

There were too many people in the room to tell Callie why I couldn't take my eyes off number ten's jersey as he flew across the ice. He slammed into a Seattle player, both of them hitting the boards as they fought for the puck. The arena roared as Seattle's player came away with the puck and then was just as quickly lost again as Dominick Masters flew into the player, taking him right off his feet.

Whistles were blown, and the crowd roared as Dominick skated straight to the penalty box.

The game continued, Seattle failing to score on the power play. I didn't bother answering Callie. She'd gone back to the book, not really seeming to care about my interest, and there was no way to explain it.

But last night? Sitting next to Alix, tucked under his arm in the warmth of the Uber and inhaling his sandalwood scent, I'd started to want things. Being around him made me want to take risks I normally wouldn't, wanted me to reach for my own path. To finally let go of trying to gain approval from a man who, so far, seemed incapable of giving it.

The more I was around Alix, the more I wanted him. To get to know him in every way, both inside a bedroom and outside of one, too.

And tonight, we'd be back home in Las Vegas. Sure, we'd be exhausted, and maybe he'd be too tired, but as I watched him take a shot at the goal that barely missed, the goalie having to stretch impossibly wide to snag it with his skates, and it bounced away from Alix, I decided two things.

I was going to start living for me.

And I wanted to get to know Alix more while I did.

THE PLANE WAS quiet and dark. Most, if not all, of the players had slipped noise-canceling headphones over their ears before they boarded. My limbs were exhausted, and I was counting down the hours until I could settle back in Las Vegas and readjust before doing this exact same thing next week. And the week after.

I sighed, tried not to think of all the travel still ahead of me, all the grunt work and checking names off lists, and pulled up my phone.

Alix gave me a little smirk and a hello as he boarded the plane, but he'd quickly taken a window seat halfway back next to Callix.

You played a really great game tonight.

I pulled up sudoku on my phone and hit the daily challenge on the app while I waited to see if he'd text back. I had the aisle seat next to Paul Schaffer, one of the members of our medical staff, who had fallen asleep before we pulled out of the gate, so I wasn't worried about anyone seeing my texts.

You watched?

I pressed my lips together to hide my smile. Paul might not see my texts, but if Callie, or heaven forbid Vik, saw me having too much fun playing sudoku, there'd be questions I wouldn't want asked.

I watched you more than the game. And I did a lot of thinking about that kiss last night.

I imagined him grinning at the text, sleepy blue eyes flashing with surprise. It was usually Alix that started any flirting and me putting a stop to it, but I'd opened myself up wide last night. Been vulnerable.

It was time to keep pushing.

I want to do that again. And more. And soon.

My place? After we get home?

I held my breath while I waited for his reply. We wouldn't get in until midnight.

Three black dots appeared. Vanished. Reappeared and once they vanished a second time, my heart sank to my lap.

Maybe I'd gone too far. Tonight wasn't the right night. He was trying to let me down...

My phone vibrated, and I prepared myself for excuses and reasons and a gentle, "another night" when my jaw almost hit my screen in surprise.

Trying to figure out a way to sound cool, and say yes, and I just sound like an idiot so yes. Absolutely yes.

A grin split my face, and I tapped my finger on the screen.

I'll meet you at my hotel room then. Enjoy your flight.

Difficult to do when I'm now hard, thinking of all the things I will do to you when we get there. Thankful Callix is sleeping. He does not need to see that.

I don't want anyone but me seeing that.

Same. Get some rest, Ryann. You're going to need it.

Two quick knocks on the hotel door at Sunset Resort and it opened. I hadn't wasted a minute in following Ryann out to the parking lot, suitcases flung over my shoulder and in my hand once our flight landed. She was still dressed in her black, ass-hugging flared leggings and her Vipers shirt she'd worn to the game. As much as I loved seeing her wearing my team's logo across her plump, perfect breasts, I couldn't wait to see her without anything on at all.

"You were fast." She laughed and stepped back.

The door slammed behind me, and my hands were at her waist. "That is the only time you will say that to me tonight."

She laughed again, a beautiful laugh that sounded like a song, a siren sent to lure me in forever and never let me out of her clutches.

I silenced her sexy laughter with a kiss. She tasted like strawberries. Watermelon. Something fruity was on her lips as I slid mine against hers, and as she opened her mouth, she tasted like freshness and life and joy and all the things I'd ever wanted since my mother's death and I escaped the confines of my father's rules and expectations.

"Perfection," I whispered against her mouth, tugging the hem of her shirt out of her waistband. "But I know there is more to see. More lovely, exquisite places I need to see."

"Yes," she huffed against my mouth and stepped back farther into her hotel room. I slammed my mouth to hers, cupped the back of her head, and wrapped her in my arms at her lower back. I kicked out of my dress shoes as we moved backward, bodies entwined, until we reached the bed.

I wanted to devour every inch of her. It'd been far too long since I'd used my hand and pleasured myself with the memory of Ryann's body against mine, the way I felt that first moment I'd slid inside her all those months ago. Now she was here, and all the things I imagined I could do.

I forced myself to pull back. To slow down. It didn't matter that she seemed as greedy as me, as needy as I felt to strip each other out of our clothes and get to the best part.

"Are you sure?" I still had to ask. I'd wanted this since the moment I knew she was back in town, but it hadn't been that easy for her.

"One hundred percent." She pressed her mouth to mine, climbed up onto the bed so she was on her knees, arching her back to kiss me. Her hands went to my waistband and she tugged my shirt out of it.

My hands slid into her hair, gripping her head and tilting her so I could take the kiss deeper, control the speed as she undid the buttons on my shirt with frenzied tugs and pulls. Every brush of her fingers against me electrified my skin until I'd had enough.

Screw slow. Maybe she would call me fast one more time tonight, but then again, we had all night for slow.

I bent down and grabbed her hips. Before she could react, I lifted her and tossed her back onto the bed. Removing my shirt while she brushed hair off her face, she was laughing, shimmying out of her sweatshirt while I flicked the buckle at my belt.

"That was unnecessary," she chuckled, and her sweatshirt flung to the floor.

"I disagree. I was going to slow this down, but we can do slow next time."

"Next time?" Blond brows arched in wonder and her hands went to her waistband of her pants. Which would not do.

I'd waited months to be able to unwrap her like a present. Climbing onto the bed, I settled my knees outside of hers. "Please tell me you remember how many times you came the last time we were together."

"Pretty sure I lost count."

My hands covered hers and I slipped my fingers beneath her waistband. She jolted as my skin met hers and her tongue peeked out, swiping along her bottom lip. Heaven. The feel of her was heaven, and as much as I wanted to see what I was revealing as I began tugging down her pants and underwear together, the rapturous look on her face held me captive.

This woman just *did* something to me, spoke to the deepest parts of me, and I did not care if the road ahead would be difficult.

If she could agree to be mine, I would already be a winner. Soon, dressed in her bra, that I would quickly be removing as well, Ryann laid on the bed, panting, flinching at every contact of my hands roaming her sides, down her thighs. My thumbs brushed inward, staying away from her sex and when I bent down and tugged at the satin of her black bra, her hands wrapped around my wrists.

"This is not the fast I had in mind," she whispered, as I lapped my tongue over her pebbled nipple. A moan quickly followed, and her back bowed off the bed as I sucked harder. This was what I had never forgotten.

Ryann was responsive, liked the brief sting of pain, and her hands digging into my wrists told me she liked giving it back too.

"Please. More. I need you." As she begged so sweetly, she loosened her grip and slid her hand down her body.

And oh *yes*. Because I had a feeling I could watch that for *hours* on end without growing bored.

"Do you think I'm going to sit here and let you take care of yourself when I've been dying to be inside of you again?"

"Move faster," she demanded, and her eyes rolled as she must have reached her sex. I bent down, huffed a laugh at her throat and I thrust my tongue into her mouth while her hand moved between us. Occasionally, her knuckles brushed over my dick, hard and confined in my pants, and when she was close, when little gasps and rasps and moans were slipping from her throat into mine, I pulled off her, kissed down her body. her fingers worked her clit and I sat back on my knees, running my hands along her thighs.

"Alix. Please. I need you."

I pressed a finger inside of her, harshly, added a second, all while her hand was still at her clit and I shook my head. "Keep working your fingers, Ryann."

"I want—"

"My dick. I know. And I promise you I'm going to spend the rest of the night inside of you, tasting you, eating you, but give me this one. Let me see how perfect you are for me when you come from my fingers alone."

"Shit." Her entire body shivered. Her thighs widened and the glistening wetness soaking my fingers had me letting loose my own groan. My dick jumped, demanded to be a part of this, but he could wait.

This moment was mine.

The moment Ryann shattered beneath me, as we both took care of her together.

She came quietly at first, biting on her tongue while her thighs trembled with the force of it and I crooked my fingers, thrust them hard and deep inside of her, pulled them out slowly. My other hand went to her lower stomach and pressed down, creating more friction and tightness and as soon as my fingers ran against her rigid flesh inside, she came, clamping her free hand into the bed beneath her, and her slickness wetting both of our fingers.

So damn perfect and gorgeous.

As she came down, I climbed off the bed long enough to ditch my pants and roll on a condom. Sheathed and desperate and ready for her, I slid back between her legs, pushing my hands beneath her back to unclasp her bra.

"I do not know if I can keep up with you," she laughed, shaking her head. Her eyes twinkled with contentment that only came from excellent orgasms and as I removed her bra and added it to the pile of clothes on the floor, I bent down and rushed my lips over her swollen ones.

"If you need a break—"

She cocked one of her legs behind me, pulling me closer. "Don't even think of finishing that sentence. Ruin me, Alix. I'll enjoy every minute."

Ruin her. Please. "I will only ever take care of you exactly how you deserved to be treasured."

As I spoke, my hand gripped my shaft and I slid in slowly, gave her time to adjust. I took the leg she had wrapped around me and pushed it out, opening her up, allowing her to take me deeper.

"Holy shit. You are so *good* at this."

I laughed, enamored with her openness, her humor, and the way her body sucked me into her wet, pulsing heat. I watched every moment of our joining, until I was fully seated inside of her and then I reminded her exactly how *good* at this I was.

"YOU HAVE GOT to be kidding me," I groaned, careful to be quiet and fully aware of the woman I spent the night with considering she was draped all over me.

But the ringtone coming from my phone was one I never ignored. Given the time difference, communicating was already difficult.

A quick half-opened glare at the clock made me bite back a curse that would risk waking up Ryann.

I answered as it rang again and quietly cursed my sister. "It is too early, Arya."

"I'm sorry. I'm sorry to call so early but it is important."

In all my years in America, I'd taken to speaking English most of the time. Arya though, had little practice and with her crying, it made it more difficult for her.

"Qu'est-ce que c'est?" *What is it?*

"*Papa.*"

Our father had used to be a kind, patient man. I vaguely recalled moments of his laughter and playing games with us and family trips where he would hold my mother's hand while carrying Arya on his other hip. Then she became sick, and he turned into a robot who only cared about success and money and power. And even though I was an adult then, he'd begun hating that I played a game for a living. That I needed to get serious. At first, I thought he worried because I was away from home so much, and he worried about my safety.

He had not let it go in five years, and Arya has now carried the weight of his control.

There were days, like that moment, listening to my sister weep and tell me in French how horrible our father was being, how she didn't want to marry Enrich, the man he forced her to become engaged to, and how mean Enrich was to her, how he was just like Dad and only wanted money and would only marry her so he could follow in our father's footsteps, I began to think Father was right.

It was time for me to stop playing games and be a man who could help protect his sister.

I could not do that from here.

Next to me, Ryann shifted in bed. Crap. I'd forgotten she was there, so alerted by the early phone call.

"Une minute," I told my sister and covered my phone to glance at Ryann. She was lying on her side, one hand propped beneath her cheek, the other on the bed, stretched out toward me. She'd probably rested her hand against my hip or stomach while we slept, but she was still sleeping. Still unbothered by my voice.

It was early, though, and I did not wish to wake her.

"Donne moi une minute." *Give me a minute*, I repeated and hurried out of bed.

"Tu dormais," Arya whispered.

"Bien sûr." *Of course* I was sleeping, but it wasn't unlike her to totally forget the nine-hour time change.

I was also whispering, something else Arya caught because there was normally no need for me to lower my voice or tell her to give me a minute when I could easily put her on speaker while I threw clothes on.

"Ooohhh," she whispered right back, and at least her realization had temporarily blocked the tears. "A girlfriend?"

"No." I peeked back into the room and quietly closed the door.

Ryann was sleeping and hopefully she'd stay that way while I dealt with my own slice of my family drama.

Outside in the hotel hallway, I had no idea where to go. The elevator and stairs would lose the call. Given the twelfth floor, I was not taking the stairs anyway. Thankfully, the hallway was long and empty. I started walking.

"A friend," I told her.

"Hmph. I would like a friend. And not one named Enrich. Please, Alix. Tell me how to get out of this." She spoke quickly, more panicked now. "He is not nice. An imbecile. I told Father if he forced me to go through with this, I would leave, and now I can not find my passport or my birth certificate to get a new one. I think he hid it."

Of course he did. "What do you need me to do, Arya?"

"Come home."

"What?"

I pulled to a stop and rested my back along the wall outside the elevator bank I'd found myself in. In all the years she'd struggled with Dad on her own, she'd never asked this of me.

And I wasn't sure I could deny her.

"Come home, Alix. If you do what Dad wishes, I will not have to do this."

"I'm in the middle of a season," I reminded her, although she knew.

I hadn't seen Arya since last summer. Two weeks back home was enough and I'd returned to Vegas earlier than planned for the sole sake of escaping my father's constant disappointed expression. Arya had always been in my corner since Mom died. She knew how much this meant to me, how there was no way I would return home.

"Maybe Dad is right," she said, and for the first time, there was steel in her voice.

"What?"

"Dad. Maybe he is right. You do not have many years left anyway, no? What is so wrong with leaving now? You have done all you said you wanted. Why must you stay?"

"Because I am happy here, Arya."

"Is it the girl?"

"No." Not entirely. I'd been happy here, and yeah… Ryann was currently making me happier, but there was no guarantee with her. "Not completely, anyway."

"I will be miserable forever if you stay. We will marry by fall, and you are my only chance to get out of this. But fine. Continue to think only of yourself. It is what you're good at."

She hung up before I could respond or formulate a simple thought.

I stared at my phone, the bank of elevators and collapsed my back to the wall. My head hit it with a thump, and I closed my eyes and scrubbed a hand down my face.

It was too early for all of this, but I had always promised my mom I would take care of Arya. I would look out for her.

Instead, maybe she had a point. I'd made it to the pros. I played for a decade in the NHL and helped multiple teams bring home the Stanley Cup. I had done everything I truly set out to accomplish for myself outside a few personal goals left of making it to the top ten highest scorers.

Was that one goal worth Arya being forced into a marriage she didn't want?

I shoved off the wall. I needed to skate. To lift weights and clear my head.

What I did not need to do was return to the room with the woman still sleeping—the one woman I could see myself with forever, and get drawn back into her when she still had not changed her mind that we could not date.

What was I doing?

Throwing away my family? My promise to my mom and being selfish... all for now, maybe a woman who would never choose me?

Was I willing to banish my sister to a lifetime of misery for, potentially a few months or weeks of pleasure?

I woke up to the click of the hotel room door and Alix's heavy sigh.

"What is it?" I asked, and it was so early my eyes felt like sand-paper covered my eyelids. "It's early."

He held up his phone. "My sister called. I stepped out to take it."

"Oh. How'd that go?" I brushed hair off my cheeks and sat up, glanced at the clock. Barely five thirty in the morning. I double-blinked to make sure I was reading the clock clearly. "Is she okay?"

We'd talked a little about his sister and his life in Switzerland. Most times I brought it up, he changed the subject. He rested against the corner by the closet and ran a hand down his face.

"She's fine. But I should go."

"Go?"

"Yeah. I have things to do today."

"At five thirty in the morning." There was something off. The way he wouldn't look at me, the tone of his voice. "What's going on?"

"Nothing. I just... I need to think."

A whip of cool air stole the air from my lungs. "About what?"

He shook his head and bent down to grab his shoes. "Nothing. It is nothing. I just... I need to go."

I now knew exactly how he felt the day last fall I kicked him out of the room. If he felt half as confused as I currently did, his head must have been spinning.

"You're leaving. After last night."

After I finally let him be with me. After I finally broke down. He'd spent weeks pursuing me, and now...

Wow.

"I'm not leaving because of last night, Ryann. I just need to think."

"About us."

"There is an *us* now?"

I gasped, shocked at how cruel he could sound. He cursed. Stood and grabbed his wallet and keys. "I did not mean it like that. And I am sorry, but yes, partly, I need to think about us. And other things with my family."

Things he was in no hurry to tell me about.

I might have daddy issues a mile long, but I was also stubborn, and there was no way I would allow him to see how much his words hurt.

How much seeing him in such a hurry to get away from me hurt. "Fine then. Have a good day."

I walked past him toward the bathroom and slid the door shut as he said my name.

"Ryann. Do not be mad."

I flipped on the sink, hoping the rushing water would clue him in to the fact I was done.

"You have things to do. Don't let me keep you," I called out.

I hadn't locked the door. He could have come in, pushed the conversation. Instead, there was a quiet thump on the door. "We will talk later."

Sure we would.

I stayed silent until the hotel door slammed behind him and splashed water over my face.

I was a fool. An absolute fool to invite him into my room.

It was definitely not how I envisioned the morning after going, but maybe, like last time—there were too many things, complications keeping us apart.

CONSIDERING my early morning wake-up I was determined to get over, I accomplished an immense list of to-do items.

Most of them done before Gabby Taylor's salon, "Elite Salon and Spa," opened, and thankfully, since I called as soon as it did, she was the one who answered.

Turned out she didn't know much other than to give me the number for the leasing company, but I was able to book an appointment for my hair next week. So, a win-win for me. And as we chatted, she said, "Anyone connected with the team is always welcome, and if there's anything else you need, don't be afraid to reach out. Joey's mentioned you in passing."

"He has?" I swallowed the thickness in my throat. What would he have known? He was at the bar that night, but I couldn't remember if he'd made it to the dance floor.

"Oh, yes, nothing big." She must have registered my surprise. "He only mentioned Vik's daughter was working with the team. Said he was glad to see the man reaching out to his family for once."

I couldn't hide my snort. Reaching out to his family?

Sure... if me begging was an effort on his part, we could call it that.

"Stepped on some toes there, didn't I?" Yet she didn't sound all that bothered or embarrassed by it. Which made me like her a little bit more.

"It's okay. My father and I have a difficult relationship and that's the nicest way I can put it. But I am thankful for the opportunity to be working with the team."

Gabby laughed, and it almost felt like she'd read between the lines in a heartbeat.

"All right, Ryann. Cool name, by the way, love it. But my first client is here, so I'll see you next week. Let me know if you get a viewing on the building, otherwise I can try to make a call, too."

"Will do. Thanks again for fitting me in."

I hadn't had time to get my hair done before I left Reno, and my extensions were in dire need of a touch-up. I was already late scheduling the appointment to get them re-tied and I hadn't at all accounted for the stress hotel showers would put on my hair, or how busy I'd be with all the traveling. Fortunately for me, Gabby didn't tend to schedule clients on days her husband had home games so she could go to most of them, but there was a day next week she said she'd make the exception.

Everyone's kindness was starting to throw me for a loop. I might have judged most athletes and their families based on my own dad's handling of his. Not that I didn't think I had a reason for the preconceived notions, but so far, most of the guys on the team had come across as way kinder than I could have predicted, and the way they talked about their wives or girlfriends or children even was endearing.

In fact, with as much time as I'd spent around them in the last couple of weeks, I hadn't overheard a single comment from any man that would be considered typical *locker room talk*.

Which was almost a bummer.

If Alix and his friends could be the stereotypical athletes with egos for days and women in every state, neglecting their wives and children for the sake of more zeros in their salary and admiration with peers, it'd be easier to keep my heart out of whatever it was we were doing.

If he could keep being the guy he was earlier, it would make my attempts to keep us friends a lot easier.

OUTSIDE OF ALIX leaving the way he did, the rest of my day worked out perfectly.

Not only did the leasing company return my call immediately, but they were also open for showings, and bonus, they not only had condos for sale, but also for rent. I had no idea how long I'd be in Vegas, or how much time I could spend long-term around my father so renting was definitely my preference, but I enjoyed the idea that if I ended up loving my job and my life there, I could someday have the option to purchase.

At the very least, I needed to get out of my hotel room and into a place with a halfway decent kitchen. A bathroom where I didn't knock my elbows on walls and the door every time I turned around would be an added bonus.

"Ryann Boucher. Thanks for meeting me so quickly." I held out my hand toward the leasing agent, dressed in a pair of relaxed, dark gray dress pants and a black dress shirt, buttoned up to his throat and sleeves rolled up and pushed to his elbows.

Aiden Miller looked a little wrinkly in both his dress and with his messy auburn hair and had a kind smile with bright green eyes almost too large for his face.

"Aiden. It's great to meet you, and I'm not going to act like your name doesn't ring a bell. I'm a big Vipers fan."

"Aren't we all." I flashed him a smile and pulled back my hand. *This* was something I wasn't used to. Being recognized or having people assume they knew who I was based on a name wasn't the most comfortable feeling.

At least in Reno, I had the benefit of distance and ability to claim ignorance even if it was a lie.

Considering I now worked for the team, I couldn't exactly spit on the floor at the mention of my father's—name.

"Good team this year," he said, and it felt more like conversation than an overzealous fan as he led me toward the elevator banks. "I only get to a game or two a year, but I try to stay on top of them. Them and the Raiders."

"They're definitely hoping to bring back the Stanley Cup." As far as hockey went, I knew the game. I could rattle off stats and where we were in standings and exactly what the coach hoped for the team, what they were working on and what their potential trade plans and hopes were before the trade deadline in March, but I wasn't exactly going to spill anything to Aiden.

We stepped into the elevator as he handed me a folder with the building's information in it.

"Inside are floor plans for the units we have available to lease, along with their monthly rent. After a year lease, we do accommodate shorter leasing arrangements if necessary. You've mentioned you were looking for a one or two-bedroom apartment, so I'll take you to go see those first, but we do have a one-bedroom with an office if you'd want to consider that."

I kept the folder closed. "What's the difference?"

"Two bedrooms have two bathrooms. The one plus office has one, and the door to the office is a glass French door, so less privacy, but it does have a closet, technically making it a bedroom."

Not ideal, but it could work depending on the price range. Aiden sent me their website when I called this morning, but I didn't have time to look at it.

There was still a chance all of this could be out of my price range, but like Alix had mentioned, the area had a lot of potential. There was a wine bar, a brewery across the parking lot. Dry cleaners and hair salon, not to mention an ethnic grocery store along with a regular, smaller box chain a block away. Other services and shops and restaurants, including fast food sandwich and coffee shops, also sprinkled throughout the still-growing area on the ground floor.

A ton of potential indeed.

All of that convenience could skyrocket the rent right out of my price range.

The elevator stopped on the ninth floor, and I glanced at Aiden with surprise.

"Top floor," he confirmed, a small twist of his lips. "Thought we'd start at the rooftop and go back in and warm up."

"The rooftop? Oh wow. That'd be nice."

"Green area. There's a small, gated area for dogs to make taking them outside more convenient. There are lounge chairs, a grilling area. Most of the residents in this building so far have been younger professionals, maybe recently married, and they use the roof frequently, even if it's for a few drinks late at night to see the city view."

"Well, that'd make up for all the cement and sand."

We stepped out, and the cooler air made me shiver, despite my long sleeve shirt and vest. There were couches and chairs meant for lounging. Coffee tables in the middle of sitting areas with rocks in the center of them, probably for fire pits. A covered area offered an escape from the sun and the fenced-in area for dogs, based on the sign, would be ample enough if I was ever brave enough to try to take care of anyone more than myself.

"In the summer, we bring in misting fans where those heated lanterns currently are." He gestured to a half-dozen heat lamps hovering close to the sitting areas and at a corner of the small dog park. "The mist helps keep you cool in the summer heat, so regardless of whether it's winter or summer, you should be comfortable up here."

"This is… great. Really. And the view is fantastic." There was desert and rocks in the distance, overlooking single-family homes and townhomes, office buildings with fewer floors so the view of the red rocks was unobstructed.

"The developers planned for this area to be higher than surrounding for the view alone. It's a nice selling feature when most apartments are crammed in with views of the building next door outside their windows."

No kidding. I'd already crossed off a dozen apartment complexes for that same reason.

A cool breeze kicked up and I shivered, holding the folder to my chest to fight it off.

Aiden must have noticed because he started heading back to the door. "Come on. I'll show you a few of the units available."

"Wonderful. Thanks."

We toured two two-bedroom apartments, one on a higher floor with a view of the parking lot and restaurants, the other on a lower floor with the same view I'd appreciated on the roof.

The one bedroom with the office sold me though. Not just for the view, but the kitchen had an island instead of a bar, and while it was a smaller living room, it was still feasible. I'd rarely have company, but I could make do with a pull-out in the office for extra sleeping if Hayden or Braylen came to visit. Maybe a second one in the living room in case my whole family ever came. The final selling point was the fact it was a corner unit with a balcony that wrapped around the building, entrances to it from the living room and the bedroom. On the seventh floor, and on the opposite of the street, the car noise would be less and as soon as I'd stepped out, I'd already envisioned a small sitting area for morning coffee or to cuddle up with a book after dinner while the sun set.

"How much do you require for a deposit?" I turned to Aiden, who stayed in the doorway of the living room.

He laughed. "Let's go fill out some paperwork."

I still hadn't checked the price. Who cared?

I'd go over budget for the view, the conveniences, the style, and the space.

It was perfect.

I set my phone down and grinned at Callie across the way. Bright and early Tuesday morning, no human should have smiled as large as mine beamed. "That was the condo complex. I can move in this weekend!"

Callie threw her arms up in the air. "That's awesome. You totally lucked out."

Surprisingly, and much to my delight. While the condo I loved was out of my desired price range, it was still feasible. That it was empty, all the better. A week's extra rent was worth the price to pay to be able to finally get out of the hotel room and be able to finally make a place a home. Which meant I had a lot of work to do.

"Oh my gosh. I'll need to go shopping." I hadn't even considered. "There's an IKEA here, right? Because I need *everything,* down to silverware organizers. The works."

Callie threw her head back and laughed. "Of course there is. But you better look into renting a moving truck or something if you head there. Sounds like you're going to need it."

"On it. And thanks. My mom was happy, but I know my family is still nervous I'm here, so thanks for being excited with me."

"Happy employees are better employees," she teased me with a wink. After a few short weeks of working with Callie, I learned she was rarely serious outside of job duties. "You should tell your dad."

"Ugh. Thanks for bursting my happy balloon." I poked my tongue out at her.

"Sorry."

"It's nothing. I suppose I should tell him, though. At least so they know the hotel room will be opening up."

With the trade deadline less than two months away and the whispers I'd heard about potential trades in the works, he'd need it.

"Right." She rolled her eyes. "Because Vik would only care about the room being available. Not your welfare."

I shot her a doubtful look that said it all.

In an uncharacteristic moment of seriousness, Callie tilted her head to one side. "I know you two barely have a relationship, but have you considered the fact he's trying? And that he cares even if he's been shitty at showing it? He did offer to go look at apartments with you, didn't he?"

"I'm trying not to get my hopes up."

"Understandable. But opening the door an inch wide wouldn't hurt too much, would it?"

She was right. I knew she was. I also knew Vik *was* trying. He didn't have to try to have lunch with me. He didn't have to pay for my dinner the other night. And he didn't have to offer to help me find a place. He was doing all the right little things to show his effort.

None of it negated the last twenty-three years of my life, but at some point, didn't I have to accept his attempts to heal the breach as true desire to want to get to know me if we had any chance?

"I'll go talk to him."

"Thatta girl. Now shoo...." She opened her office door and waved me out like an annoying fly. "I've got work to do. Hotel rooms to confirm, yada yada."

I rolled my eyes and did as I was told.

Which meant a few minutes later, I was once again standing in front of Susan as she pressed the button to my dad's office to let him know I was there to see him.

Except this time, he didn't send me in like I was an employee. His tinny voice came through the phone as he said, "Great. I'll come get her."

And then he was at the door to his office, opening it. Smiling at me, even if it was timid. "Hi there. What brings you to see me today?"

He stepped back and gave me room to enter his office. "I found a place to live."

"Oh." His smile fell, and wow. Callie had been right. He'd actually wanted to help me.

Then it reappeared as he closed his office door, the disappointment quickly washed away. "Well, that's great. Good news for sure. I bet you're looking forward to getting out of the hotel."

"I am."

We were in Texas tomorrow and Thursday. They had home games this weekend and then on Tuesday before we flew out for North Carolina. He could help Saturday, or maybe Monday, early Tuesday if he had the time. Unless he chose work over his family which was always the risk.

Since Callie was right once, maybe she was right about me too. So I nudged my foot at the metaphorical door between us, nudged it open an inch, and asked, "I can move in this weekend. I was wondering if you'd be free to help me? After I go buy some things?"

His shoulders fell with relief. "I'd like that. I'd like that very much."

Well. Hell.

I pictured Callie's *told you so* smile in my mind and found myself smiling back at Vik. "Good. I'd like that, too." And since I'd already opened the door an inch, I went for two. "Any chance you're good at putting together IKEA furniture?"

MY EXCITED BUBBLE was popped the moment I reached my floor at work, and Alix was standing right outside the elevator.

"Hey." I hadn't seen him or heard from him since his rapid-fire exit Saturday morning, but he didn't seem nearly as surprised as me.

"I was looking for you."

"I was upstairs with my dad. Talking to him." I rocked back on my heels. We weren't quite friends. Definitely not dating, but my excitement over the condo couldn't be contained. "I found a place to live. Those condos by Gabby you told me about."

His face lit up, and a broad smile stretched his face. "That's great."

"Yeah. So, thanks for the tip. I'm grateful."

"When do you move?"

"This weekend. I asked for preference since we'll be on the road the next two weekends."

Whether it was my reminder of work, my rambling, or the distance he was keeping between us, Alix nervously shuffled to the side and ran a hand through his short blond locks.

"I would like to explain what happened last weekend."

I was still aware of where we were, even if it seemed he wasn't, but fortunately, it was lunchtime and the floor was mostly empty. I wasn't willing to let this go, even as much as I wanted to pretend it didn't happen.

"You said you needed time. What else is there to explain?"

"Perhaps I need to enjoy the most of the time I am given instead of worrying about it."

"Cryptic." And not helpful. I took a step back and put space between us for both him and me. Him, because he asked for space. Me, because my fingers burned to touch him. To soothe him through whatever suddenly troubled him.

"I had a difficult call, from my sister. Maybe... maybe I can help you shop and tell you about it then?"

It was an offer I should turn down. But this close to him, it was difficult to remember all the reasons why I should stay away. "Maybe we were just a mistake." My throat ached as the words fell out, and Alix's eyes widened in surprise.

"We are not a mistake. We are... complicated." He tripped over the word like he didn't want to let it loose into the atmosphere, and I couldn't blame him. "Let me take you out for dinner. Or drinks or coffee or whatever, so I can explain. Please?"

It was the please that made me waver. "When?"

"Tonight. We can do it at the hotel again if you'd like."

If he thought that made it easier so I could run upstairs if necessary after, he was wrong. I had enough memories of Alix in that place.

"Somewhere else."

"Ryann?" I turned, and Callie was there, iPad in her hand with a notebook and pen. Shit. We had a meeting for our trip to Texas.

"Be right there," I said to her and turned back to Alix. "I need to get back to work."

"I'll text you."

I went to walk around him, and he stopped me with my name falling from his lips with a hoarse whisper and my heart squeezed. "Yes?"

"I am very sorry about Saturday. It would not happen again, given the chance."

A chance I wanted to give him as much as I wanted to save myself from.

My father's constant disappointment had the ability to hurt me.

Alix Halvrick had the power to destroy me if I let him, and I wasn't sure I was ready to hand that over to him quite yet. Not after how much he'd already hurt me.

"I'll answer the text," I told him. "See you later."

"Yes. You will."

WE WERE SEATED at a back corner table in a no-frills sports bar where hockey and basketball games were playing on the dozen televisions hanging on one wall on the opposite side from where we sat. It was also far off the Strip and several miles from where both of us lived. If he planned a more clandestine meeting, I had no idea how he'd accomplish it but from my perspective, this was perfect. We were practically in the dark, but the ambiance was casual and inviting. The room pulsed with quiet conversations, couples and families. There was no way anyone would recognize Alix, despite the sports atmosphere, mostly due to the hat he had pulled low down over his eyes. The darkness shaded most of his face, and even I barely recognized him when I arrived. I wasn't sure if he planned the restaurant and the exact table for that purpose, but it helped, and I let him know as soon as I slid into my padded booth seat across from him.

"I am simply glad you agreed to join me."

Neither of us touched our menus, but I reached for the drink menu near the wall at the same time Alix did which he easily gave up.

"You can have it," I said and slid it back to him. I didn't need a drink even if my nerves whispered it'd help me chill out.

We didn't have time to say anything before our server arrived and we both asked for waters, plus a Heineken for Alix, and I threw in an order of chips and queso. After I talked with Alix at the office, I'd barely managed to eat anything. I was two seconds away from my stomach announcing to the restaurant how hungry I was.

Alix's gaze was heavy, bearing down on me as I avoided him and scanned the menu but saw nothing. He'd been the one to ask for space, and then this meeting, so until he said what he needed to,

I was pretending the menu full of burgers and sandwiches was the most important thing I'd ever read.

"I have a complicated family," he finally said, and I glanced up to see his eyes shifting back and forth. "It was always good growing up, even if my father was distant—although not as bad as yours."

He tried to smirk, but it fell flat. I wasn't getting into who had the worst dad competition.

"Anyway. My father is the president of a bank in Geneva. His father was the president of the same bank."

I sat back in my seat, understanding a little of what was coming. "And your father wants you to become the next president of his bank."

"It is not something I had ever wanted, and it was okay, because when our mom was alive, she was able to keep my father in agreement with my love of hockey." He swallowed and cleared his throat.

"When did she die?"

"Six years ago. Almost. Cancer, and it came fast, unnoticed until it was too late. A brain tumor, and she showed no signs until it spread enough there was nothing to be done."

"I'm so sorry."

"Thank you." He blinked, blue eyes filled with sadness. "I was here, already playing, and am fortunate enough she held on until I could get there, spend time with her before she passed."

I fought between reaching out to hold his hand, comfort him, and giving him the space he requested. The moment was broken when our server returned. We ordered, sipped our drinks, and Alix drank his beer much faster than normal.

Once our server left, Alix sighed and wiped a hand across his mouth. "It was not an easy time, and I think in my father's grief, he became more rooted in what he could do to keep his children safe. Which meant the pressure for me to return home and follow in his footsteps became worse. And at the time, Arya was still a teenager. Only seventeen." He chuckled, but there was no happiness in it.

"She is now the same age I was when our mother died, and she has had six years of living with very strict rules, very specific expectations."

"That must be hard for her."

"Arya is... she is spoiled. Has always been. I will not lie, we grew up with wealth, went to the best private schools and after my mom died, Arya was sent to a boarding school in Germany because my father did not think he could raise a daughter. She is... yes, she is spoiled but sweet, and she is stuck between wanting to please our father and wanting her freedom, but she has not yet learned the confidence to fight for what she wants."

Another heavy sigh and it seemed like he was only just getting started on his story, even though he'd already said so much.

"What's going on, Alix?"

"That phone call the other morning?"

"Yes." I would never forget the aftermath of it.

"She called because since Mom's death, my father has been putting more pressure on me to return home. Arya has always supported me, but that morning, she begged me to return home. Father has her engaged to a man who I do not think is a very good man, but he is working his way up through the bank, and my father likes him. He says if I don't return home and learn and take over someday, that Arya will have to marry this man."

A cold pulse rolled off Alix.

"Father has taken Arya's passport, so she cannot leave. And she is stuck. She begged me to help her, and the only way I can do that is to go home. To quit and leave."

That chilled pulse became an ice storm in my veins, making my skin prickle.

"She wants you to just walk away from what you love?"

"If not, she will be miserable and maybe married to a man who will not treat her right." He finished his beer in three large swallows, clanking the glass to the heavy wood table top. "I have had the privilege of playing the game I have loved since I was a young child, and I have reached almost every goal I have set for myself. And yet, when I am with you, I am happier than I have ever been."

Whoa. "Alix..."

"What am I to do, Ryann? Stay and be selfish or take care of my sister?" His jaw worked back and forth, and when he spoke again, his voice was thick. "What would our mom want me to do?"

I was speechless. He couldn't stay here for me. And there was no way he could just walk away from hockey. Not now. Not when he was still one of the best.

"She's asking you to choose between your happiness and hers." It was an impossible choice, and yet he was a good guy. If push came to shove, Alix would choose his family above himself, but that didn't mean it was the right choice. "I'm not sure that's fair if she's not willing to fight for herself. Is there any other way? Can you just bring her here for a while until she figures out her next plan?"

"Not without a passport."

"There has to be a way to get a new one. People lose theirs all the time."

"Perhaps, but that all depends on how strong she wants to be and how tight my father's leash is on her."

I reached across the table and took his hand in mine before I could stop myself. He was hurting, and frustrated, and all but admitted how happy I made him. I couldn't sit across from him and watch him struggle and do nothing.

"We'll figure it out, Alix. There has to be a way to make everyone happy."

"Perhaps," he repeated, but he flipped his hand over beneath mine so our palms met and locked his fingers with mine. "I am torn, and I am worried about the position on my team if your father finds out we have been together if you do not tell him first. I want my sister happy, but I want her to fight for it on her own, too, like you said. I am stuck between a lot of options with no guarantees, and I do not like those risks."

I jerked my hand out of his hold, but he tightened his fingers around mine.

"That sounds like an ultimatum to me."

"It is not, it is me explaining why I left on Saturday even though I wanted to spend all day with you. Arya made me feel selfish, and I do not like her thinking that of me, and... well... until Friday, you had said we could only be friends. I can give you time, Ryann... but I do not know how much more I can give. That is just me being honest."

I knew that. It still felt like an ultimatum. If I said no to anything further with him, would I be the reason then he gave up what he loved for his sister?

If I said yes... would he turn his back on her?

There were no easy answers. No good options. And like he didn't weigh the decision on his shoulders, I hated him settling it on mine as well.

"What do we do?" I asked, and slowly tugged my hand from his with a small amount of resistance.

A shadow fell over our table, queso and chips were delivered, and we sat back in our booths to make room for our appetizer.

"We eat." Alix grinned like he hadn't dumped a bucket of heaviness straight into our laps. "And then you tell me about this apartment of yours you got."

My grin shook, along with my hands as I reached for a chip. He'd told me why he left, where his mind was at, and now the ball was in my court—or the puck was in my rink—whichever.

AIDEN GRINNED and dropped the condo's keys into my waiting and trembling palm. "Welcome home."

"Thank you so much." The metal was cool to the touch and yet my heart was still heated and thumping wildly with excitement.

My first place. That I was renting on my own.

Look out world, I was finally adulting and everything, including going IKEA shopping tomorrow so, at a minimum, I could set up a bed and get out of the hotel.

The resort was gorgeous, and I loved everything about it, but after three long weeks in a tiny little room, I was almost climbing the walls at night. The tiny fitness center and restaurants could only keep a girl happy for so long, and now I had my own home, ready to be furnished.

Along with a shopping date with Alix in the morning.

My phone rang as I said goodbye to Aiden, grinned like a fool with bubbling-over excitement and I dug it out of my jacket pocket.

It was Hayden, and with the time difference it had to be around midnight wherever she was, if not later.

"Hey, sis. What's up? Isn't it the middle of the night there?"

"Almost, but I wanted to catch you before I boarded another plane."

Well, that explained it. She was no stranger to red-eye flights.

"Where to this time?"

She yawned and through it, said, "I'm actually headed your way for a bit. Thought I'd stop by and see how you're doing before I head to Sedona."

"I'd love that. When will you be here?"

"This weekend sometime? I have a quick stop to make on the East Coast so I'll be there for a day or two first."

"Oh." If I wasn't holding the phone, I'd be clapping my hands. "That's great! I move into my new apartment this weekend, so you can see it."

"Sounds good. Text me the address and I'll let you know when I'll be there when it gets closer."

"All right. See you soon, sis."

"See ya, baby sis."

I stuck my tongue out at her even though she couldn't see me and we said our goodbyes as she yawned again.

Once I ended the call, I fell back against the pillows on my bed.

My sister was coming.

I'd just left Gabby's salon and my extensions were fixed up, making me feel great on its own.

And I had the keys to my very first, living on my own like an adult, condo.

If I could figure out what to do with Alix and Vik—everything would be perfect.

Tomorrow, Alix was going to IKEA with me. He'd offered at dinner the other night, said he could help me drive the U-Haul and was a great shopping buddy. It was his attempt to move past what happened on Saturday and since I was currently in limbo myself, I figured maybe some time together in a neutral place could help me figure everything out.

I wanted Alix.

I didn't want to piss my dad off.

And now, I didn't want Alix having to choose between me and his sister.

Complicated. We were definitely complicated. And the secrets we were keeping might just be the end of me.

"This one. I think." Ryann tapped her newly painted light blue fingertip to her mouth, frowned, and glanced back to the other couch she was debating between. Which was different than the third one she also really liked.

We'd been in IKEA for forty-five minutes and hadn't yet moved beyond the living room furniture area. Considering we were just entering the maze, it was possible I wouldn't be out of the store to make it to my game tomorrow.

"I think." She shook her head. "No. Wait... I like..."

"This one." I plopped down on the one she kept coming back to. It was a pull-out like she wanted. With one end that had a chaise lounge with storage underneath. I kicked my feet up on the chaise lounge and threw my arms to the back of my couch. "Come sit. I will show you how perfect it is."

"Alix—"

"No. Come on." I patted the cushion next to me and with a roll of her eyes, she sat down next to me. Rigid. Back straight, like she attended the boarding school I did and was being reprimanded by a fierce and holy nun. I tugged her shoulder until she fell back against me.

"Hey!"

"See?" Grabbing her shoulder, I held her to me and rested the side of my head against hers. "This is cozy. Soft. Perfect for watching movies cuddling up," I leaned in and whispered. "Or pulling the couch out and fucking, and ignoring the movie altogether."

I should have shut up. But this close to Ryann, it was difficult to remember the burst of pain that speared through me at my sister's words the other day. Of all the times to try to manipulate me into returning home, it couldn't come at a worse time. And even more frustrating, I hadn't been able to get a hold of her since. It wasn't like Arya to play the cold shoulder game and it definitely wasn't like her to convince me to move back home when she knew how much I despised the idea of it. Something had to be going on with her, and until I knew more, I was trying to push it out of my mind.

Ryann froze before she laughed again and shoved herself off me and the couch. "Stop this. I need to be serious."

"And if we don't move out of this section in two minutes, we might just have to move you into the store."

She scrunched her nose up at me and then fiddled with her hair, pulling it up off her back before letting it fall. She'd had it done yesterday. Mentioned something about extensions and a new color and whatever went over my head. All I knew was she was beautiful. Color in her hair or not.

"Do you really think so?"

I kicked my feet to the floor and rested my hands on my knees. "It is a couch. What does it matter?"

Pushing up, I watched as her eyes roamed all of them to the dining tables we hadn't even explored yet. Chairs and ottomans and everything else we still needed to see.

"It's my first place. I want it to be right. To fit me." Hesitant, nervous blue eyes fluttered in my direction. "That probably sounds stupid."

"It does not." She wanted her condo to make her feel like her home. That I understood well. "I understand, but we do not have all day."

"You're right." With resolution, she nodded and scribbled down the item number of the couch I was just on.

"You sure? This one?"

"Yep. You sold me with the movie night story." She started walking away and glanced back at me over her shoulder. "The not watching it part."

Ah... that little...

If we weren't in the store, I'd tackle her right back to the couch and show her all the ways we could *not watch* a movie together.

Learning from the living room fiasco, whenever Ryann debated too long and my stomach was so hungry I was at risk of it eating itself before we checked out, I created sexy little images for her to help her speed things along.

It got tricky when we came to the dressers—but fortunately, she chose the one I could bend her over and not the one where I'd have to throw her to the top and feast on her while standing.

That move would be tricky, even for me.

By the time we finally reached the bottom floor, she was tossing utensils and organizers and bath towels and small rugs into the cart like she was in a race to get out of there.

"In a hurry?" I asked, leaning in to whisper in her ear.

She responded with a quick inhale and rubbed her lips together. "Maybe. It's possible I don't know what piece of furniture to put together first."

Tossing metal measuring cups and spoons into her cart, she wheeled around the corner and looked at dishes.

"We can do takeout tonight. You can deal with the rest later."

She still needed lamps. Rugs. Dishes. Silverware. In truth, she needed all the small things, but screw it.

Amazon had overnight delivery for most essentials these days.

We could online shop after we put together her bed.

Or the couch.

After all, our possibilities were endless.

———

"THERE IS a ton of shit in here." We were at the back of the U-Haul after loading everything up with the help of three IKEA employees.

It was a wonder that she hadn't gone over her credit card limit and that everything she requested furniture-wise was in stock.

"Don't call my furniture shit."

"My apologies. There is a ton of new sex furniture in here."

Ryann laughed and shoved her hip against mine. "You're insufferable."

"If that means adorable and perfect, then yes."

She shook her head, still laughing. "No, it means crazy and out of touch with reality."

"Huh." I frowned. "That does not seem like me at all."

With a heave, I slammed the U-Haul's door shut, and said a silent word of thanks for not crushing anything before locking it up.

"We do have a small problem." Ryann glanced at the back of the truck and then at me.

"What's that?" In my head, we had many.

"We just had three men help us load everything."

"And?"

"And my condo is on the seventh floor. With an elevator. How are we going to get everything into my apartment?"

She nibbled her fingernail and cringed.

"Leave that to me."

I was already pulling out my phone. No doubt Kane would help, and Emmersyn had asked me more than once when she'd get to meet Ryann.

Plus there was Ryder. He had no social life from what I knew.

Dominick and Joey and hell... all the guys were great. I could have the entire team meeting us at her place and we'd be done in ten minutes.

Which meant we'd have time to build her bed before we broke it in.

"Who are you calling?"

"Not calling. Sending out a group SOS text to Kane and some of the other guys for help."

If worry had a look, it'd be Ryann's face. "Trust me. They won't say anything and they'll be happy to do it."

"All right." That fingernail ended up between her teeth again. "If you're sure."

"I'm always sure." I shrugged. "Mostly I am always right, too."

Pretty sure she muttered *"insufferable asshole"* as she headed to the passenger door.

"WOW. THAT SOS TEXT REALLY WORKED."

I scanned the parking lot where Kane and Emmersyn were standing outside his car. Next to them were Ryder, Joey, and Callix.

Exactly like I predicted. "Perhaps someday soon you will start believing I am right more than I am wrong."

Next to me, Ryann laughed, but it was tense as the guys started heading our way, Emmersyn with more of a bounce to her step than usual.

"That's Emmersyn," I told her. "Kane's wife. She's good people and she's been excited to meet you. They're the neighbors with the hot tub."

"Thanks for the warning she'd be coming."

"I didn't know, but I'm not surprised. But I promise you'll like her."

Emmersyn flashed a wide, happy smile in my direction and headed toward Ryann's side of the van.

"Might as well get out and meet her before she drags you out of the van."

Wide, blue eyes hit mine. "She'd do that?"

Hell no. Emmersyn was too sweet. "No. She would rather smother you in a hug."

Her fist knocked on Ryann's door and as Ryann opened it, Emmersyn pulled it open the rest of the way.

"Hi. I'm Emmersyn. Sorry if I scared you, but I've been waiting for Alix to bring you around."

Ryann introduced herself and held out her hand. Emmersyn took one look at it and laughed.

She proved me right and pulled Ryann in for a hug and the poor girl had not even climbed out of the moving truck.

"Emm. How about you let Ryann get out before you assault her."

"Ignore him," Ryann said, grinning back at me as Emmersyn apologized and stepped back. "It's fine. All good."

"Great." Emmersyn clapped her hands. "We'll let the guys do all the heavy work. I've already ordered pizza and wings and a salad for dinner when they're done."

While Emmersyn took care of Ryann, I hopped out of the truck and opened the back.

The door banged open as the guys reached me at the back.

"Holy shit," Kane muttered. "You weren't kidding."

I shrugged. "She needed everything. I told you."

"We can count this as our weightlifting workout for the day, right?" Callix asked.

"We can." I punched him in the shoulder and he flinched. "You need more work."

Joey laughed and clapped his hands together. "Let's get the job done and then we'll talk. Probably depends on how much pizza you eat, rookie."

"I don't even know why I pretend to like you assholes," Callix muttered.

"Aww." Kane pounded his fist to his chest. "That hurts me right in the heart. Truly."

Callix shoved him.

I shoved them both. Sometimes we were overgrown children. I could recognize it.

"Come on, assholes. I want to get this inside before the sun goes down."

"It's three in the afternoon," Kane said.

He clearly didn't know yet how jam-packed the U-Haul was. "I know."

TWENTY-THREE

RYANN

I stared at my living room, stocked full with boxes so high there wasn't even an inch to open one and start getting anything built. Surprisingly, it only took an hour and a half to get everything unloaded from the U-Haul and up to my place. Thank goodness they had multiple elevators because the men had paired off and each claimed an elevator as soon as they started unloading everything.

At least my bed and mattress, still in boxes, were in my bedroom. I could get those things done and since my dad had offered, Monday he was going to come and spend the day helping me with the rest.

By then, I should have most of the rest of the small things purchased, but with the pile of cardboard in front of me—it all seemed daunting.

"Food!" Kane shouted, and at once, every man left in my condo, let out an animalistic groan—like they hadn't eaten in weeks instead of mere hours.

"Yes. I don't even care how much I'll have to work out to work this off." Garrett patted his stomach and shoved his way past Joey. He toppled into a stack of boxes, almost knocking one on top over.

"Whoa." Callix grabbed him and settled the box.

At least it hadn't crashed. Returning broken IKEA furniture would be a pain in the ass.

"Quick question," Alix said, scanning the stacks of furniture that needed to be built.

"What's that?" Joey asked, flipping open a pizza box before moving it to the counter and opening another.

"Does anyone have any tools?"

He settled his hands on his hips.

"I think they usually come with everything you need, right?" Joey glanced at Kane who shrugged.

"Uh, no," Callix said. "You'll still need a screwdriver. Probably more than one."

"Damn." I guess I would have to go back to the store.

"Hold up." Joey picked up his phone. "Let me call Gabby. She might have some stuff in her salon."

"Thank goodness," I said and yawned. I was a natural-born shopper and hadn't even done any of the heavy lifting, but after hours in IKEA and watching the men work, I desperately needed that bed together.

Hell, maybe today I could just sleep on the mattress on the floor. Except we'd left IKEA before I'd bought sheets.

"It's all right," I said when Joey hung up and got Gabby's voice mail. He was starting to text her when I stopped him. "I need to make a Target run anyway."

"You sure?"

"I'm sure."

"For what?" Alix asked.

"You pulled me out of IKEA before I could buy sheets."

"I did not pull you anywhere."

Not physically—but with all the innuendo he'd been tossing around faster than he slapped pucks, my head had been spinning by the time we reached that area of the store. Hell, at that point, had I even tried to get sheets, I probably would have bought the wrong size anyway.

"Come on." Emmersyn grabbed her purse and snagged keys from Kane's pocket. "I'm always up for a Target run. And with everything you need, maybe we should take the U-Haul again."

This woman.

Alix had been right. She wasn't only sweet, but she was funny.

"Don't even think about it," Kane warned, thick black brows tugging together. "You're not getting that moving truck anywhere close to a Target."

"Truck needs to be returned today," Alix said and I was pretty sure Emmersyn pouted.

"That's fine. The Escalade should be big enough."

"Heaven help me," Kane muttered.

Emmersyn grabbed my hand and tugged me out of the condo. "Have fun putting the furniture together without us! We'll be back with a screwdriver and sheets. Maybe some pillows."

"What is it with women and pillows?" It came from one of the men right before the door closed, so I had no clue who asked.

"You don't need to come with me if you're busy."

"Nonsense." Emmersyn tapped the button to call the elevator. "I have nothing else to do today and I wasn't joking. I really do need more pillows for the couch. Valentine's Day ones and spring ones. Kane thinks the gray ones that came with the couch are sufficient, but he doesn't understand."

Men. They really didn't.

Two hours later, we were checking out of Target. Me with sheets and plates and coffee mugs and drinking glasses and some other basics I needed.

Emmersyn—with two carts full of pillows.

I was loading up my items onto the belt when I realized...

"Oh shit." I glanced back at Emmersyn. "Do you know what we forgot to get?"

Her brows scrunched together in thought right before she broke out in a laugh. "A screwdriver."

"A screwdriver," I confirmed.

WE RETURNED with a tool kit that included a half-dozen different screwdrivers, both a socket and Allen wrench set, and a cordless drill. Sure, Alix's face had scrunched up when he saw the pretty pink color all the tools came in, but after all the food was eaten and Kane and Emmersyn cleared out, it only took us two hours to assemble the bed frame.

By that time, I'd done the laundry, washed my new sheets so they were ready to be put on the bed as soon as the frame was assembled.

It was a simple, gray upholstered platform bed frame with four storage drawers beneath, which I planned to use for storing extra bedding for the pull-out couch and additional linens and bed pillows.

Exhaustion settled into my bones, making me yawn as I settled the final pillow over to the far side of the bed where Alix stood, hands on his hips. We worked well together while putting together the bed and I had enough experience building furniture with my sisters, Mom, and even Paul, I knew that wasn't always a sure thing.

"Tired?"

"Pretty sure my arms won't work tomorrow." I shook them out. I hadn't even done the heavy lifting. "How are you doing?"

He glanced at the bed to me, blue eyes darkening in a way that made me not so tired at all anymore. "Wanting to use this bed for everything but sleeping and not sure if it's smart."

"You're probably right." The smart thing to do would be to take a step back. Stay friends. Regroup in a few weeks once he had more clarity about his sister, for sure.

Except my hands went to the hem of my shirt.

"I should probably go then."

I lifted my shirt and tossed it to the floor. Alix's eyes widened in a way that was more comical and his hands fell to his sides. "Ryann—"

I shrugged. "Who said I wanted to be smart?"

"I don't want to hurt you."

"And I don't want to hurt you." Because there was more going on than just his sister. I was still keeping this from Vik and if I was truly open to having some kind of relationship with him, keeping lies and secrets didn't sit well with me.

"Tonight," Alix claimed, and he stalked around the bed with the grace he moved on skates, managing to ignore the pile of Styrofoam and boxes and plastic bags and tools without glancing at them.

"For now," I agreed.

His hand slid behind me, and the heat from his palm on my flesh evaporated any fears.

How could something that felt so *right* end up being wrong for either of us?

I barely managed to breathe out his name before his chest pressed to mine, his other hand slid up to my neck and then his lips were on me. No time for teasing. No tempting and there were definitely no casual caresses.

He took my mouth like I wanted him to take my body. Hard. Fast. Alix devoured me with the impatience of a man who had waited far too long and was too damn desperate to hold himself back.

"I really wish we had time to put together that dresser," he murmured, skating his lips down my throat and over my collarbone while my hands pushed down his pants. "I have been thinking of you bent over it, your ass on display since we saw it in the store."

"Next time," I rasped, slipping my hand into his boxers. The evidence of his arousal was hard, thick, and pulsed in my hand as his groan filled the empty space in my room as I wrapped my hand around him and tugged.

His mouth returned to mine, his hands to the clasp of my bra and soon we had shredded our remaining clothes, and he was pulling me down to the bed, rolling us so he was on top and skimming his mouth down my body, over my breasts and biting my nipples as he moved farther south.

I was aching, hot and needy for every single touch he gave, and relishing every scrape of his flesh against mine from his calloused hands and teeth. He spread my legs, and dove in, no preamble and no teasing before he took my sex and speared his tongue deep inside of me.

"Oh." My back bowed off the bed. My fingers dug into my newly bought and washed duvet cover, and my heels dug into the mattress. "So good."

He grunted his agreement, too worked up with what he was doing to me and that only made me wetter, more needy for him. He brought me to the edge quickly, so fast my heart was racing and I was fearful it wouldn't slow before he pulled back, making me wail in frustration.

"I was so close," I whimpered, hating the desperation in my voice but loving the glazed, dark look in his eyes.

"I know." He pushed two fingers deep inside me, and dragged them out slowly, brushing over the most sensitive parts of me until I was breathless, arching into him.

"Finish me."

"When I feel like it." He'd never looked so evil or so joyful at the way he dragged out my orgasm. His finger rolled over my clit, making me gasp in both pain and pleasure.

I was so sensitive. And every time my hips rolled and tried to take instead of wait for him, I swore the jerk slowed down and teased me a little bit more.

"Please," I begged and wrapped my hand around his wrist. "Please, Alix."

He smirked before he bent over, but instead of going where I was aching for him, he pressed gentle, playful kisses to my stomach, up to my breasts before adding a third finger at the same time he sucked a nipple into his mouth. The pain of the stretch was nothing compared to the ache in my core and I groaned out of measure and frustration, before he laughed against my skin.

"Because you asked so nicely," he whispered, and then sank down to my center and slid his tongue over my clit with expert precision.

I came, crying out his name and cursing and thanking God. White hot pleasure blinded me behind my lids and my body rolled from one orgasm into two. Hell, maybe three. It seemed to last forever before Alix was dragging his fingers out of me, moving up my body, bathing my body with his kisses and affection until he was looking down over me with the same lust-filled expression I knew I'd had only moments ago.

"Condom," he whispered as he kissed my cheek, and I was pretty sure if he left this bed for even a second, I would be passed out when he returned.

"Pill. I'm religious about them. They're in my purse if you want to see, and an alarm on my phone to remind me."

I'd had a scare once in college, too many days sleeping too late in a row that had terrified me of permanent consequences before I was ready from then on. To say I was anal about taking my protection at the exact same time every single day was an understatement.

"Are you sure?" His bottom lip slid between his lips, and I brought my thumb up to release it. "I'm clean."

"I wouldn't have offered it if I didn't trust you."

"Fuck," he groaned and slammed his mouth to mine. "You will feel so damn good. I already know it."

If I were willing to bet on who this would feel better for, I was pretty sure I'd win the house. As it was, he was reaching down, wrapping his hand around his thick length. The tip of him pressed against me, stealing all thoughts except for *yes* when he bent over me, eyes so serious and jaw clenched tight.

"Are you sure?"

I nodded, licked my bottom lip, and as he pressed inside of me, his head fell back. The most illicit groan I'd ever heard fell from his lips. His corded throat and muscles appeared while he gritted his teeth together, and I fought against my eyes closing, wanting to experience every beautiful moment of this—of *us*—in order to watch him chase his own pleasure.

"Shit," I gasped as he thrust into me, and I expected him to wait, to give me a moment, like he did before with tenderness, but there was none of that left in him. Only raw, carnal need, and as he began to move, he shattered every expectation I had of Alix as this kind, patient guy.

He'd banked it and was currently unleashing it on me in the most delicious and feral of ways and when we were done, when we'd finally sated ourselves, we were drenched in sweat, and I had his orgasm splattered all over my stomach.

"I'll clean you up," he whispered, back to the sweet and tender Alix. I now didn't know who I liked more.

"No." I grabbed his hand as he went to climb off me. "Shower with me."

"There is no possible way I could resist."

TWENTY-FOUR
RYANN

"Oh shit." *Shit, shit, shit.* Of course this was how my day would start. I scrambled off the bed and grabbed my phone I'd dropped to the floor when my text alerts for Hayden started pinging off the freaking hook. I'd read the first text and my internal panic-mode alert activated.

I must have woken up Alix because he was shoving to his side, wiping sleep from his eyes with his free hand.

"What is it?" His voice sounded like last night's sexcapades, thick and gravelly and so damn sexy I forgot what I was doing for a second.

"Nothing. It's nothing."

I shoved my hair away from my face and tossed my phone to the bed and tried to remember how to freaking *breathe*. This was not how I wanted them to meet, and now it was unavoidable. She was going to be here in *minutes*.

Loved my sister to death, but she tended to forget that some of us needed more than a two-minute preparation to be graced with her presence.

On the bed, still looking rumpled and sexy, Alix chuckled.

"This is not typically the reaction I get after spending a night with a woman, you know?"

"It's... my sister is here." I glanced at the bedroom door and back to him. "She doesn't know you're here. Or that—"

"She's *here?* Now?" His head whipped toward the door.

"No. Not now, *now,* but she will be, in minutes."

Alix laid back in the bed and stretched like he had all the time to preen himself. He didn't seem too bothered by the fact he was meeting the craziest sister of the three of us.

"Alix." There was regret in my tone, he noticed. Of course he did.

"Wow. Okay." His brows tugged together and he shoved off the covers. "I should probably get dressed then, huh?"

"No. Crap, but yes. I'm sorry. It's not, it's not you, Alix. Hayden knows about you. I told her, but with my dad coming later..."

My phone pinged again, and I grabbed it off the bed, and holy crap. Could this day start off any more manic or panic-attack-inducing? My eyes flew to Alix on a gasp. "My dad is on his way, too."

Wide, worried blue eyes met mine.

Being here while he met my sister was one thing, my dad another.

"Right. I need to get moving."

And I hated, *hated* the look on his face and the slump of his shoulders.

"Shit. I'm sorry. Again." I tugged on the sweatshirt I'd worn yesterday. My suitcase was shoved somewhere in my closet to make way for the IKEA explosion taking place in my home. "Hayden and my dad together will be bad enough. I thought he'd wait until I called. We hadn't agreed on a time."

Alix pulled his T-shirt over his head. "Maybe he is excited you asked for help. That is a good thing."

"Yeah, until World War Three breaks out in my brand new

condo." I tried to smile, but it was forced. "At least there isn't furniture for them to break."

"Right."

Okay, so we weren't in the mood for jokes today. Got it.

My phone rang again, and I threw my hair off my shoulder to cool down. *Hayden,* I mouthed to Alix on my way out.

"I'm here. Going to let me up or let me stand out here like a moron forever?"

Dramatic was my sister.

"Forever if you keep up the sass when you woke me up," I teased. Because she might be dramatic and live in her own world but I loved her more than life itself. "Come on in. I'll buzz you up."

When I turned around, Alix was standing there, dressed, socks in one hand, reaching for his shoes at the front door. "You do not want me to see Hayden again."

"I don't think that's fair, and you know this is complicated." I went to him and put my hands on his chest, hoping the weight of my hands on him would help. I could see I was hurting him, but deep down, he had to understand.

"Of course it is."

"You'd love Hayden if you had time to get to know her. But I didn't want it to happen like this."

A breath fell from him, and his heart rate beneath my palms slowed. "I get it."

A rapid knock hit my door, and I attempted a smile that felt too forced. "I guess you will, though."

I turned, took the few steps to my door and as soon as I opened it, two tanned arms and a face that looked so much like mine threw themselves at me. Hayden wrapped around me with so much force she knocked me back a step and thank God for Alix who was there, his hand at my lower back, stopping me from toppling over.

"It's so good to see you and this place is amazing!" She shook me back and forth, giving me whiplash, and I tried to extricate myself from her grip, fully aware of the man at my back she hadn't yet noticed, but she clung tighter.

I relented and hugged her back. "You too—"

"Oh." Her grin stretched ear to ear, and she pulled back. "Well hello again, Viper." Her manic grin turned to me and she finally released me from her death grip. "And he's here… so early.… Look at you, sister."

"He has a name," I teased and grabbed her hand. "Hayden. Alix."

Hayden's gaze trailed all over Alix, scanning him, taking his measurements. "Huh. I expected more muscles."

I knew her well enough to know she liked what she saw but wouldn't in any way admit it.

I punched her shoulder and laughed. "Be nice."

Before Alix could say anything, even a simple hello, she shrugged. "Still working out those daddy issues, I see?"

"Don't be such a brat."

"It is okay." Alix held out his hand for Hayden. There was a smirk on his face telling me whatever Hayden dished out, he could take. He lived with thirty men in a locker room, for crying out loud. They were much worse.

"It's nice to see you again. Your sister told me you were charming." The look he gave me made my knees wobble. "I did not know you were a liar, Ryann."

Hayden gasped, and I choked on my own laugh.

"Oh. I might like you." She let go of Alix's hand. "You're all right, I guess, outside your chosen profession."

"Obviously. And I should go before the next Boucher arrives, yes?"

Hayden's brows arched. "*Vik* is coming?"

I cringed. "I asked for his help putting together all the furniture, and I didn't know what day you were coming because you were supposed to call me."

"Huh. I thought I did. My bad." Hayden shrugged like it was no big deal.

"Right." I loved my sister to death, but thinking of others wasn't her strongest suit. Especially when she was traveling. I blamed the constant time zone changes for scrambling her sensitivity and thoughtfulness.

"Walk me out?" Alix asked, his hand moving to rest at my lower back.

"Of course." To my sister, I said, "And you stay here. I want to talk to you."

She flipped her hand in the air. "If it's about dear old dad, don't bother. I might need to go to a casino for the day."

I ignored it. It wasn't my fault she showed up unannounced and my dad was doing the same. Pointing out how similar they were in their thoughtlessness of others probably wouldn't be good timing.

"Come on." Alix took my hand and tugged me toward my front door. Outside, once it had shut, he cupped my cheeks in his warm palms.

There was a look I didn't like on his face, nor did I like I was the one who put it there.

"I'm sorry."

"At some point, you will have to tell him."

"I know."

"And I said I would be patient, but that does not mean I can do this forever. I understand why you are torn, but do not forget he is a man I respect as well."

I knew that too, and I let my acknowledgment spread across my face, because it wasn't an ultimatum, but someday it could become one, and with everything rocky with my dad, I wasn't so sure which one I'd choose.

His respect?

Or Alix's love—if that's even what this was, but I definitely knew I hated sending him away like this.

"I need more time," I admitted and hated the sadness tugging down his typical smile.

"I know." He leaned in, brushed his lips over mine and that simple touch of him settled me, warmed me. It had me rocking into him, reaching for him, but he ended the kiss and stepped back before I could. "Enjoy your visit with your sister. And Vik today."

"I'll try."

It'd be harder now, sending him away like this but there wasn't time to fix it either.

"Call me later?"

"Of course." I rolled to my toes and kissed him again before he walked away, and then he was pressing the button to the elevator and Hayden was opening my door behind me.

"Talk," she demanded. "And fast."

Alix lifted a hand and waved goodbye, and I did the same before I had to face a completely different kind of conversation.

As soon as the door shut behind me, Hayden's hands were on her hips. "That man is a delicious little snack, isn't he?"

"Trust me." I snorted. "There is nothing little about him."

Hayden barked out a laugh and threw her arm over my shoulders. Yanking me to her side, she ruffled the hair on the top of my head. "Look at you, my goodie little two-shoes becoming a spicy little thing."

I shoved my hip into her side, throwing her off me. "Enough with the baby crap. What do you think of my new place?"

She wrinkled her nose. "Looks boxy."

Hayden was a certified dork. Had to be. "That's because the living room is filled with boxes, you moron."

"Ah... of course. I didn't see them at first."

I rolled my eyes and headed to my kitchen. "Do you need coffee or anything?"

"No thanks. I had some at the hotel."

"You're staying at a hotel?" I hadn't even considered that she showed up without luggage, but Hayden knew how to travel light.

"Travel points. Free suite. And I figured you'd be unpacking and everything."

"Right." I slipped a coffee pod into my new coffee maker and started brewing. "Because you wouldn't want to help or anything."

"If I hurt a finger, I can't do my job." She wiggled her index finger and mimed clicking a camera, made a *click, click* noise out of the side of her mouth to drive her point home.

"Of course. We wouldn't want that."

She rested elbows on the island countertop opposite me. "My flight got in late last night and I didn't want to bother you. That's why I went to the hotel."

"And you didn't bother texting until this morning when you were already on your way?"

"I like the element of surprise."

Of course she did. She just forgot not everyone did.

Another thing she and Vik had in common I wouldn't mention.

Hayden tilted her head to the side, smiling as I inhaled my caramel-flavored coffee and took my first sip. I'd really dealt with too much already to not have caffeine in me yet.

"So, you like this hockey guy, you're hiding it from Vik, and you're apparently growing so close with him he's coming over today?"

"I wouldn't say we're close."

"No?"

"He offered to help, Hayden. I didn't say no, and trust me, we've had as many arguments as we have decent conversations since I've been here."

"Good."

"Good that we're arguing?"

"Good that you're making him work for it." Her hands tapped a nervous rhythm on the marble counter. "What's he like?"

"Selfish. Bossy."

"Ahh. All the things we already knew."

"I think he's a man who, for whatever reason, never learned

how to think of others, but I see him trying, even if he screws it up and throws us backward. I didn't take the job to become close with Vik, Hayden. I took the job because I needed one."

"You're lying, and maybe it's not to me, but it's definitely to yourself."

"I'm not."

She shook her head and pushed her lips to one side. "Out of all of us, you're the one who always wanted him around, Ryann. I'm looking out for you, whether you like the way I'm doing it or not. Vik is going to hurt you—either from just being him..." She nodded her head in the direction of my front door. "Or once he finds out about that."

Irritation spiked, and I set my coffee down, fully aware of my knuckles aching from my tight grip on the mug. "Consider your warning received."

She wasn't right. She couldn't be.

I couldn't have taken this job, spent all this time around Vik because I was hoping he'd someday still love me, did I? He'd made it clear back before Christmas he didn't.

At least, he didn't love me in any way I wanted to be on the receiving end of.

"He's probably going to be here soon," I told her.

She pushed away from the counter. "Then that's my cue to split. Call me when you're done and I'll get dinner and bring it over. I'm assuming you're not up for a night on the Strip after you spend all day clearing out these boxes."

I'd probably be exhausted. Climbing back into my bed after the way my day started already sounded like the best idea.

"I'll call you. But... would you be willing... to see him?"

I felt the weight of her sigh from across the counter. "Drinks, *maybe,* but that's all I'll give him and you'll be the best buffer in the world or I'm cutting you out of my life forever."

The offer was better than I could have anticipated. "Deal."

I held out my hand, two fingers—index and middle extended—in the secret handshake we agreed on when we were kids.

Hayden took it, tapped her same two fingers to my palm before hooking our pinkies together. "Deal, but I admit right now you're a pain in my ass."

"It pays to be the baby sometimes."

My head hasn't been right since I walked out of Ryann's condo. Not quite true. My head hasn't been quite right since September when I was kicked out of a hotel room by the same woman as soon as she found out I was a hockey player. I should have known then that my ass was in trouble. I never claimed to be a smart guy.

I understood. I understood why Ryann rushed me out of her condo today like my ass was on fire. I understood why she didn't want me there with her sister, and definitely not with her dad. But playing the part of the dirty little secret, the guy she only seemed to want when it was convenient didn't feel right either.

I didn't treat women that way, and being on the receiving end was starting to suck.

It wasn't true. But I couldn't keep the thoughts from spinning into a vortex while I was in the gym, lifting weights in Joey's pool house either. It was where I'd come after leaving Ryann's, needing to work off some steam and since we didn't have practice, I figured I'd use his indoor hockey flooring in his pool house to work off steam and adrenaline and frustration and get my head on straight.

Lucky for me, Joey let us use this place whenever we wanted. Normally he joined, but today he'd said he and Gabby had a late night and needed sleep, so he'd join me once he woke up. I'd had two hours of working out, skating, spending some time swimming laps outside as quietly as I could, and returning to the weight room before he entered.

"You've been here for hours. What's up?"

He had dark circles under his eyes and his dark hair was disheveled. I lowered the dumbbells I was lifting.

"Maybe I should be asking you that? What's going on?"

"Nothing." He covered his mouth while he yawned and then brought one of his arms out in front of him, pulling it across his body with his other to stretch out. "Just a long night."

"You and Gabby okay?"

"Never better. But you didn't come here to talk about my wife..." He arched a brow... "Unless you did, which means we might have some problems."

"Needed a workout and didn't want to drive all the way to the arena."

"Right," he huffed and settled near me and continued stretching. "Ryann getting all settled?"

"Coach is there today helping her put furniture together."

"Ah." He let it linger in a way that didn't make me entirely comfortable.

"What?"

"Nothing, but I'm guessing now I know why you're here looking like you are."

"How am I looking?"

"Like you're in a mess and don't know how to fix it. Trust me, pretty sure that's what I looked like when I woke up married to Gabby."

"You fixed it though."

"Things seem to have a way of working out the way you want them to when they're supposed to."

Wise words.

I let them settle and dropped my weights and moved closer to him to stretch. I'd put my body through the wringer this morning and was at risk of overdoing it if I didn't stop.

"Gabby thought she was sweet. Said she did her hair the other day before the move."

"Yeah. She told me."

"So are you two a thing or not?"

"Don't know." I was on my back and pulled a leg over my hip to my other side, bending it. My back cracked and tension released.

"Explains why you're here then."

"Maybe let's talk about why you look like you haven't slept in days instead, yeah?"

He grunted, which I figured was a no. "Braxton's been playing better."

"How did I know that'd get you to change the topic?" I laughed.

Joey reached out and slapped my shoulder. "I get it, I'm pushing, but I can't say I'm not worried. If Coach finds out before you or his daughter tell him, I'm guessing he's not the kind of guy who would let that slide, regardless of how good of a father he is. Plus, how would he react to Ryann?"

"Trust me. All things we have already considered. And I am glad, too, that Braxton is playing better. His loss would hurt."

Joey chuckled and dropped to the mat to stretch out his legs. "Now I know how the topic change felt to you."

"It is true though."

Braxton was a good friend and his wife, Sophie, was always taking in women who joined girlfriend or wife status. They were great people. Friendly.

"I know. I'm hoping he makes it through trade deadlines. Anyone else you think is a concern?"

As the talk moved to hockey, I was grateful. It was exactly what I needed. Joey and I discussed everyone, because truly no one was safe when it came to trades. Guys with years left on their contracts could still be traded if management felt like they'd served their purpose. Being at the top of the division helped mean we were safer, but at any moment, things could change.

Yet that was why I loved the game. The constant shifting. The constant moving for what was best long term. Which also made me less frustrated with Ryann.

If we could keep her father from finding out about us—whatever we were doing—until after trade deadline, I would be safer. Which meant I might need to apologize for my behavior this morning and put my own hurt feelings on the back burner.

<hr>

"YOU COULD JUST WAIT until the off-season."

That would be the end of June if we made it to the championship like we wanted. Five more months of not having Ryann with me. I had already waited so long.

"As helpful as that is, Emmersyn, I rather hate the thought of it." Waiting until March was bad enough.

"If she's not ready to stand up to her dad, you might not have a choice." She sipped her wine, making too much sense.

I hadn't intended to spill my guts to her after Kane and I got back from Joey's. Emmersyn knew me though, and after countless times checking my phone and then my watch, asked me what was up. So I was currently, two drinks in, while Kane cooked Emmersyn and me dinner, grumbling about how I finally found the girl I wanted—and how messed up everything absolutely was.

I hadn't even brought up Arya—who was still ignoring my phone calls. A full week of not answering me, texting, or returning a call, and I was getting worried. Enough I might actually need to call my father and talk with him, which was the last possible resort. But if she did not call me back soon, I might have to swallow my disdain for the controlling man and do it anyway. I wouldn't be surprised if he put Arya up to that phone call last week. She wasn't above being used, and if it got her out of her engagement, I could see her being willing—and then regretting it every day since. Until I could talk to her, though, I would not find any answers.

"We should go to Malley's tonight." We had the day off tomorrow and no game until Tuesday night. I could use the distraction.

Emmersyn groaned. "Nothing good comes from men who are upset about women going to drown their sorrows at Malley's."

I snorted. Could not be helped with the narrowed, snake-eyed glare she shot toward Kane.

"It was one bad night."

"Where I had to take your shoes off because you were too wasted to walk straight."

"I remember," he muttered and grinned at me. "Vaguely."

"So that is a no?"

"Hell no," he replied. "I'm always up for Malley's. Emmersyn can be our driver."

She held up a finger. "One, who says I want to go?" Another finger was added to the first. "Two, why do I have to drive?" Another finger... "And three, what time do we leave?"

Kane wrapped his hand around the back of her neck and pulled her in for a quick kiss. Averting my eyes was the gentlemanly thing to do, but instead I made kissy noises, earning a middle finger from Kane with his free hand.

"Nine," I said.

"And you'll see if Ryann wants to come with?" Emmersyn asked. "She can. It's not like the entire team doesn't already know what's going on."

I doubted she would, but there was always the chance that after spending the day with her dad, she might need a drink or twelve herself.

"I'll ask her."

For all the issues I had with Vik, it was easy to see why he was so respected as a coach. He was not the tallest man in the world, or the largest, but his presence and confidence as soon as he stepped into my condo, scanned it, and found it satisfying based on the quick nod of his head, was enough to consume the space with his attitude alone.

He was a man who commanded attention and worked like he spent a lifetime assembling furniture. Not that it was a difficult task, but within only a few minutes of his arrival, he not only had a game plan formed, he'd begun issuing orders as if I was a peon and not his daughter.

I let that irritation go, because even though he'd arrived far earlier than I planned, I'd had enough time to not only get ready but ensure any lingering evidence of what Alix and I had done in my bedroom and shower was long gone. I also let it go because after staring at the mountainous pile of cardboard in my living room once I was alone, the task was entirely overwhelming if I'd had to do it myself.

So I'd let him boss me around for a little while in order to get my condo feeling like a home. And boss he did—but five hours later, after only stopping for a sub sandwich I'd run out and procured for us downstairs—my living room was entirely put together except for the blank space on my TV stand where my television would go once I had time to go get a couple of them.

By the time dinner rolled around, my dresser was put together in my bedroom, I'd unpacked my suitcases and had the drawers filled. I'd finished another couple loads of laundry, washing towels, and the extra sheets I bought.

Vik was finishing up putting together the smallest side tables out in the living room before he stood, scanned the room, and did that confirming head nod thing again.

"Looks good. It's a nice place."

"Nicer because of your help." I was in the kitchen, unloading the dishes I'd bought. "Thank you."

"Happy to help." His eyes scanned the view outside before returning to me. "I mean that. It means a lot to me that you gave me this chance, that you asked."

He cleared his throat like he was uncomfortable with the admission, the vulnerability, and I fought my rising emotion.

He wasn't a perfect man. He wasn't even a great father. But I had to admit he'd been trying to have *some* sort of relationship with me, and he hadn't truly messed it up yet.

Which was probably why I didn't push open the door between us another inch but kicked it wide open. "Hayden is in town."

He couldn't hide the surprise on his face. "She is?"

"Stopped by this morning."

"How... how is she?"

"A pain in the ass," I admitted, because after showing up this morning, she most assuredly was.

"Oh." Like he wasn't so sure he enjoyed my description of her. "Do you see her often?"

"Every couple of months. More when she takes time off work to recoup."

He nodded like he understood. Heck, I'd only gone on one

long trip with the team, so maybe he did. "That's good. Good you three are so close."

I bit back the retort I might have tossed out a few weeks ago. *We'd had to be because we were all we had.* He'd shown up today when I needed him. I could let it slide this one time.

"They're my best friends. Always will be."

A small smile appeared and then vanished. "It bothers me, more than I think you would know that I was not around enough to see that." He held up a hand to stop me from speaking, not like I could form words anyway. "I know that's my fault, but I regret it. Truly."

"It's nice to hear, but I didn't bring Hayden up to make you share your regrets and guilt."

"No?"

It could have been a tease. I wasn't quite sure. He probably wouldn't blame me if I'd done it for that purpose.

"No. I told her we might go do dinner when we're done here. She said she *might* be willing to meet up with us for a drink after."

"Oh." Relief and surprise flew across his face. "That would be great. I'd like that, if she's willing."

"Just don't be surprised if she guts you when you walk away from her either."

"Message received." A gleam hit his eyes. He thought I was joking.

Too bad I wasn't. Hayden could be brutally vicious when needed, even if that dagger might only be in her words.

I didn't *actually* think she'd stab Vik, but when it came to Hayden, it was really anyone's guess.

SINCE HAYDEN HAD TOLD me she'd be on the Strip hitting up casinos and exploring, in case she decided to join us for drinks, Vik and

I got a table at a Mexican restaurant that overlooked the canal in the Venetian Hotel. It was casual, which worked for me since neither of us were dressed up fancy, given the day we had. I'd mentioned Hayden happened to love margaritas on the drive to the Strip, so I figured Vik picked this place in hopes of enticing her to come for that drink.

As soon as we were seated, I sent Hayden a text.

We're at Canonita's in the Venetian if you're interested in that drink.

Hayden's reply came faster than I expected. ***Don't hold it against me if my margarita ends up in his face.***

Lie. Hayden would never throw away a good margarita, but considering I'd felt like that more than once or twice, I wasn't one to judge. **Deal.**

We'll see.

She'd either come or she wouldn't, and I wouldn't put pressure on her. My sisters didn't understand my need to have any kind of relationship with my dad, but I thought Hayden might be cracking a little bit. Asking me what he was like today told me she was at least curious.

I also figured she wouldn't show up too early, so we had some time.

"Hayden." I flashed my screen at Vik and tucked it into my purse. "I wanted to let her know where we were in case she decides to come."

"Good. Thank you."

He didn't say anything else about her, and even while we ordered our first round of drinks and appetizers, he didn't mention Hayden or my sisters. Or my mom. Instead, he kept the questions to my college experience and what my ultimate goal was in majoring in sports marketing.

All easy questions, all surface level, but I appreciated the attempt to really get to know me and not pry information from me about my family, something he'd done before which always ended us up frustrated with each other.

Everything was going well, so well, that once we'd ordered our food and were halfway through our second basket of chips and salsa, I considered Alix's position earlier.

Vik had told me not to date one of his players, but just like I didn't hide things from Alix, I also didn't want to hide things from Vik.

What kind of relationship could I hope to have with either man in my life if I wasn't being honest—either with them or myself.

What was the worst they could do? I already knew there wasn't anything in the employee handbook about us dating. Dad wouldn't trade Alix. I had no doubt about that. He was having a stellar season and even if Vik took this personally and wanted to get rid of him, he'd have to sell it to management.

I doubted they'd go along with it.

Still, it was a risk, one that had a ball of nerves gathering in my stomach.

"There's something I'd like to talk to you about."

"Oh?" Vik's eyes widened and something caught his attention behind me because his jaw dropped.

"What—?"

"Oh. Chips!" Hayden said and was at our table. "I'm just in time!"

What the hell? I texted her twenty minutes ago. "What are you doing here?"

She sent me a look that could freeze oceans. "I was invited. Wasn't I?"

"Of course." Vik stood and tossed his napkin on the table. "Hayden. It's good to see you."

His hands trembled as he stood there, waiting for Hayden's next move. Couldn't blame the guy. She was smiling, but it was more serial killer smile than daughter happy to see her sperm donor.

"We'll see about that." Hayden slid into the chair next to me and pulled my margarita toward her.

"Sure. Help yourself."

"Thanks, sis." She smacked her lips together. "So much better than the dirty martini I had earlier."

She was still smiling. And Vik was slowly lowering himself back into the chair, gaze bouncing between both of his daughters as if he was on uneven footing. Couldn't blame him. Hayden was making *me* nervous.

"Why am I not surprised?"

"You know how much I love them. Besides, what do I always say?" She snagged a chip and popped it into her mouth.

"If it's not a little filthy, it's not worth doing," I muttered.

Vik's cheeks flushed, and he was at a loss for words. Couldn't blame him for that either.

Hayden lacked tact, had a protective streak longer than the Great Wall of China, and currently had her fierce little smile set on Vik.

For the first time ever, I felt a little sorry for him.

"WELL THAT WAS FUN." Hayden swayed on her feet, and I grabbed her bicep to steady her.

If fun was eating a bowl of chili, being thrown on the teacup ride at Disney World, and not let off until you spewed that chili on yourself and everyone around you—yeah, dinner was a freaking blast.

She didn't let Vik relax for a single second and he was still visibly shaken. Had to hand it to her though, even I hadn't been able to knock him off his feet in all the arguments we'd had so far, but that wasn't exactly what I was hoping for dinner or when she agreed for drinks.

It was possible, though, I'd misread Hayden's lack of interest in our father incorrectly, because this wasn't a girl who didn't care at all that her father once walked away.

She *despised* him, and now I was left wondering if the reason she always traveled and was never in one place long enough to get close to anyone was because of him.

Not that I was bringing that up.

I didn't want a margarita in my lap, either.

"Do you girls need a ride home?"

"Nope." Hayden popped the *p*. "I have more exploring to do. Perhaps I'll do what Ryann did back in September."

"Hayden—" I warned.

"What did Hayden do?" Vik asked.

Hayden's crazy grin slid in my direction. If she told him, I'd kill her. Or not talk to her for two weeks. "It's just too bad we didn't know you still cared about us back then, Vik, or maybe you'd know. Toodles!" She spun on her heel, fingers in the air, and walked away like she hadn't just almost thrown me under the bus—again, how similar they were.

Or that she hadn't just made a dinner with Vik a complete failure.

"I'm sorry," I muttered because while I didn't need to apologize for my sister's behavior, that still wasn't how I wanted dinner to go.

"You were right. She hates me, and I don't blame her, but maybe makes me appreciate how easy you've gone on me."

I hadn't thought I'd been easy on him at all, but compared to Hayden's antics, which I would be talking to her about because even that parting shot was more vicious than she usually was.

"I'm not sure whether that's a good thing or not," I admitted to him.

Vik glanced up at the dark sky and sighed. "Do you need a ride home?"

"I think I'll take an Uber." The day had been long and exhausting and nothing, outside of my furniture now being assembled, went right. At least there was that. I had a couch to go home to and wallow on if I so chose.

"You sure?"

"I think maybe we've had enough family time for one day."

He laughed, looked back down the street and worry knotted his thick brows together. "Will she be okay? About what she said about you and September, it's not my business, but—"

"She can take care of herself."

I wasn't touching September with a steel-enforced ten-foot pole.

"I'll stay with you until your Uber gets here then."

Since standing alone on the Strip on a Saturday night didn't thrill me, I agreed, and a few minutes later, my Uber was there and Vik was holding my door open for me as I slid inside.

"Despite what happened at dinner, I had a good time with you today. At least before."

A smile lit up his face making him almost unrecognizable to me. "Good. Me too. Get home safe."

"Will do."

I was halfway home before I called Alix. Screw going home alone and wallowing, I needed something to take my mind off that clusterfuck of a dinner and talking to Hayden now would do neither of us any good. But the last thing I wanted was to be alone, replaying tonight's disaster in my head.

Besides, maybe it'd help things with Alix if I told him I tried to talk to Vik about us. I certainly hadn't handled many things right, but maybe I could start making up for it.

My phone rang as I was locking up my house. Since Emmersyn said there was no way she was staying fully sober tonight, we agreed to order an Uber and it was due to arrive in a few minutes. I planned on waiting outside in our almost connecting driveways for it.

Ryann's name showed on the screen, and I almost dropped the phone in such a hurry to unlock it. "Hey. How was your day?"

"Are you doing anything? Like right now?"

Panic laced her tone, instantly igniting my own. "Are you okay? Where are you?"

"I'm in an Uber, headed home. Dinner was a disaster and I don't really want to talk about it but I don't want to go home and be alone, and I'm sorry for calling so late, because I know this morning didn't go well, but there's no one I can call and—"

"Hey, hey. Calm down, Ryann. It is okay. I don't mind." I was thrilled she called me. "I am home but heading out. The guys and I and some of their wives or girlfriends are going to Malley's for a few drinks tonight. Why don't you meet us there?"

Silence slammed through the line.

"They already know about you," I reminded her, making sure

my tone was gentle. She sounded like a woman ready to crack. "And I think Gabby is coming. I know Emmersyn is."

"What's the address?"

Not a yes or no, but I gave it to her, and she repeated it to the Uber driver. "He says it'll be fifteen minutes."

"We will be there in less than that."

The bar wasn't far away and a white minivan, our Uber, was coming down the street. "Do you want to talk on the way?"

"No." She sniffed, and so help me, if Vik made her cry or hurt her, I wasn't sure I could hold back from letting him know how disappointed in him I was. Not that he would care what I thought.

"I'll be okay. I need a few minutes to calm down anyway."

"Okay. If you change your mind, call me."

Emmersyn and Kane stepped out of their townhome next to mine and we headed to the end of the driveway where the Uber was pulling to a stop.

"I will. And Alix?"

"Yes?"

"Thank you."

"Anytime, Ryann. We will see you soon."

Emmersyn's brows rose. Smiling, she leaned closer to my phone and shouted, "Hey Ryann! Can't wait to see you again!"

"Tell her I'll see her soon," Ryann said, and I was pretty sure she was now smiling.

Good.

I hope she would do it more after she worked out whatever happened with her father.

"I'M GLAD I CALLED. This is exactly the kind of night I needed."

"Yeah?" I had refrained from too much physical touch with my teammates around, but we were currently sitting at a booth where

I'd taken the seat next to her. Close to us, Kane and Joey were playing pool while Gabby and Emmersyn played darts. Dominick and Arlo and Callix were sitting at a high-top table on the other side of the pool table, and every once in a while, one of their loud laughs grabbed everyone's attention. Braxton and Sophie were hanging out with Holly in the booth behind us.

Odd to see Dominick smiling and laughing so much. After playing with him for several years before Holly walked into his life, it was still unsettling to see the former grumpy man so happy.

"Do you want to talk about what happened yet?"

She huffed and spun her beer bottle around in her hands. "Hayden happened."

My brows must have furrowed because she reached over and pressed her fingertip between my brows, rubbing gently. "I do not know what that means."

"It means I love my sister to death. She's one of the best humans I've ever met, but she's also a tornado. She shows up out of nowhere, wreaks havoc, and then flits away to her next location, leaving destruction in her wake."

I could see this from the brief moments I spent with her.

"She told me this morning she'd be willing to have a drink with Vik, so I texted her when we were at dinner. She showed up and then... God, Alix, she was a bitch to him. He was so shaken when we left *I* felt sorry for him."

She shook her head and blinked slowly. She must have been tired, and it did not seem like her drinks were helping her relax at all.

"What did she say?"

"Everything. She showed up, and when he said it was good to see her, she got all catty and sneered *'Is it?'* Sat down, and then every time he asked her a question, she started every sentence with, 'well if you'd ever called before, you'd know...' or 'like I tell Mom since we talk all the time...' And he was trying, and kept trying. Kept acting like he deserved every arrow she flung at him and I'm not saying he doesn't deserve a hard time. He gets to answer those hard questions if he wants a relationship with us, but man... she was *harsh*. And by the end of it, which I had to end because it seemed he was going to just sit there and let her treat him like gum on her shoe, he looked so broken."

"I am sorry you had to see that. Perhaps they should have met in private."

"If they would have been in private, I'm not so sure Hayden wouldn't be looking at murder charges right now."

So, it was really that bad.

"Where is she now?"

"Hayden? Who knows." She shrugged and took a drink. "She took off down the Strip with a '*toodles*,' a vague mention that she might do what I did back in September, and vanished."

"She brought *us* up?"

"Not specifically, but she seemed so on edge it almost looked like she was going to, and I was just so mad and so shaken. I don't understand why she'd be willing to have a drink with him for me, only to be that mean and horrible."

"Maybe she did not know how she would act herself."

"Maybe," Ryann muttered around the mouth of her bottle. "That would make sense. I imagine she spent all day alone, thinking about all the things she wanted to say to him, and it bubbled over. But God, it was bad."

I draped my arm behind her and massaged the back of her neck with my hand. "I guess you will see then how much Vik means it when he says he wants a relationship with you girls. If he is scared away at this first hurdle, that will tell you much."

"You're right." Her head fell to my shoulder and I inhaled the soft, minty scent of her shampoo.

I'd used it last night and all day I caught faint whiffs of eucalyptus and bergamot. It smelled better on her.

I let her rest against me, pressing my lips to her temple when it seemed no one was looking. It did not matter to me, but I knew it would bother Ryann.

"Enough talk." She pushed off me and faced me, hands on my thigh. As soon as she touched me, heat spread to where it should not be spreading given our circumstance and the company. "We should do something fun. Get my mind off this wretched day."

"I can think of a hundred ways to take your mind off the day."

"Really? One hundred?" She laughed and leaned in and kissed my chin before scooting back.

She did not even glance to see if anyone was watching. Progress of the best kind.

"One hundred and one, I think, yes. Should we try them?"

She scooted backward until she was on her feet at the edge of the booth. "Only if one of them involves me kicking your ass in pool."

"I think maybe we should bet on whose ass is going to get kicked."

She made a guffaw sound and tossed her blonde hair. I trailed my gaze over every move she made, hoping she was letting go of her night. She came to me when she needed someone... that would be enough.

We waited until the girls were done playing and I racked the balls. We had both just grabbed our cues when a thunderous sound came from the bar.

Every head jerked in the direction.

Joey stood on the bar, stomping his feet. Behind him, his manager and current bartender, Bonnie, wore an annoyed expression like a badge of honor.

Joey cupped his hands around his mouth like he hadn't already gained our attention. "Everyone hold up. I got something to say!"

"Oh dear God," Gabby said close by. "I told him not to make a scene."

"A scene?" Emmersyn asked. "About what?"

Gabby wore a secret smile and kept her gaze on her husband. "You'll see."

"My beautiful wife." Joey squatted on the bar and held out his hand. "Come here, please."

She headed toward him, and Ryann moved closer to me, so close, that whiff of eucalyptus almost made me groan and bury my nose in her hair.

"What's this about?" She tipped her head back and up at me as she asked.

"No clue."

Joey squatted on the bar, and Gabby, who was never shy or embarrassed, pressed one hand to her cheek and then her stomach before she let it fall to her side.

"No way," Emmersyn whispered. "No fucking way."

"No way what?" I asked.

She rolled her eyes at me, and Ryann rolled her lips together.

"There is no way you know what's going on," I said to her, right as Joey reached out and took his wife's hand in his and kissed her knuckles.

"I bet I do."

I rolled my eyes. She could not.

"You all know Gabby and I had a rather *different* start to our marriage. You've also all been with us since the beginning. You kicked our asses when you needed to and while Garrett and Lizzie aren't here tonight, you know we were there to witness their beautiful boys come into the world which was also the last day Gabby and I were apart."

A hush fell over the bar, but Emmersyn and Ryann shot each other gleeful looks.

I was missing something.

Something only a woman could figure out.

Which meant—*oh...*

"So it is my pleasure tonight, with most of the team and our closest friends here, to tell you that Gabby and I are having a baby!"

"No way!"

"Yes!"

"Congratulations!"

Shouts rang out. More congratulations and the small bar with only a smattering of locals who couldn't be bothered to care enough about us—which was the way we liked it—rattled and shook with the noise.

"Drinks!" Callix shouted, cupping his hands around his mouth like Joey had done. "Drinks on the house!"

"No way! We don't give anything away for free here!" Joey stood and hopped off the bar, pulling Gabby into his arms.

That explained his exhaustion earlier today. Morning sickness, perhaps?

"Oh come on!" the kid shouted back. He pushed out his bottom lip into a pout and Dom shoved him in the shoulder.

"Only if you're buying," Joey shouted back.

"Spoilsport," Gabby teased him. "They're happy for us."

"Fine." He kissed his wife's temple and something in my heart squeezed. "One round on the house for everyone, but only one!"

Another round of applause and cheers shook the small bar. Joey and Gabby pressed their foreheads together, happy, sweet, and content smiles on their faces while Joey whispered something to Gabby that made her tear up.

That was what I wanted. That connection and the happiness and pure joy you knew came from more than friendship and lust and good sex. It was soul deep, what they had.

Ryann leaned into me, pressed the side of her body against mine and my arm draped around her body, hand settling at her hip. "They look so happy. I really liked her when she did my hair. She's good people."

"Two of the best. They deserve all the good things."

Eventually, as the team surrounded them and the girls hugged

Gabby and rubbed hands on a belly that was not showing anything, we met up with them. Ryann gave Gabby a timid hug while I shook Joey's hand.

"Congratulations. This is good news. Worthy of a little free booze."

"Right." Gabby rolled her eyes. "Like Joey isn't paying for every drink here."

He shrugged and tugged his wife tight to his side. "Can't have the bar losing money. It goes to the kids."

"Kids?" Ryann asked.

"We host a youth baseball league in the summer." I zoned out while Joey explained why he bought the bar to Ryann and enjoyed the moment of her relaxed next to me.

When they were pulled away, Ryann did the same. I would have hated it, but she had a soft smile on her face. "You have good friends. Good teammates."

"I will not leave them." It was not the time to discuss Arya, or anything else, but I couldn't stop myself. She had to know. I *wanted* her to know.

Her smile turned soft and she pressed her hand to my cheek. "Tonight, before Hayden showed up, I wanted to tell Vik about you."

"Did you?"

"No. She interrupted, and then I was thankful because I hadn't talked to you first. But would that be okay? Tonight was a mess, but I realized that if I want a relationship with you *and* him, in whatever way I can, I don't want it built on lies and secrets and hiding things. Not anymore."

Something in my chest released, like a valve that had been pinched and was finally set free. "I am okay with that. Whenever you are ready, and I am glad that you are considering it, so yes, tell your dad. And as far as Arya, we will figure it out, too."

"Good." She glanced around the bar, but I only had eyes for

Ryann. I only ever had eyes for her and I hope she knew that. "I should go home."

"Alone?"

"I don't want that, but it's been a long day, and I want to talk to Hayden tomorrow before she leaves town. Plus, I still have more things to unpack."

"I understand." Screw where we were. She was with me in more ways than one and for the first time, I truly had hope we could figure everything out. "We will figure the rest out later, no?"

"We will."

I waited outside with her until her Uber came, kissed her like I wanted to when no one was watching before the driver showed, and sent her home.

I might have been going home alone that night, but I felt less lonely than I ever had before.

We would figure things out.

I would accept no other option.

TWENTY-EIGHT
ALIX

I was not a violent man, but if my father were to be standing in front of me, I was not so sure my fist would not end up breaking his nose. I paced the hotel room in North Carolina, where we were getting set to play before heading down the Florida coast to play in Miami, back up to Tampa Bay before returning home.

Game nights in North Carolina were always some of the best games, and while we both wanted to win, there was a friendly rivalry due to Joey's older brothers, Jude and Jason, being on the Ice Kings team. Typically, I would be with the team, eating lunch, prepping on how to beat them.

Instead, I was stuck in my room, listening to my father speak to me as if I was still a thirteen-year-old teenager and craved his attention.

"Tell me where she is," I stopped him mid-rant of reminding me of my need to fulfill my familial duties as if we controlled a crime organization instead of a bank.

After Ryann left on Saturday night, I had spent the last three days trying to call Arya again and still had no response.

"I sent her on a holiday." His words were wrapped in arrogant confidence. Typical for Conrad.

"Without her phone?"

"What she and Enrich choose to do with their time is not my concern. Perhaps if she is not answering your call, it is because you have hurt her feelings. You know how women are."

Ahh, a conversation where he did not miss a chance to show how sexist he was. Women as in fragile, unimportant, *emotional*. How horrific. Heaven forbid they be better at expressing theirs than most men.

"Do you have her phone?"

"It is none of your concern."

Yes. He did. My jerk of a father sent his daughter away with a man she could not stand. There had been more than simple frustration in Arya's which did not thrill me that she had no way to contact anyone if she did need help.

"Fine. Have a good night, Father." I ended the call and tossed my phone to the bed. I needed to push this to the side, get focused on the game, but as the afternoon wore on, I found myself unable to. I had showered. Tried to sleep. After giving up on all of it, I was still late to the bus.

Ryann's shoulders slumped with relief as I hurried to the bus at the back entrance of the hotel. "We almost had to send someone to your room to make sure you were alive."

"If it would have been you, we would still be there." I smirked, and she shook her head in the way that told me I was being adorable and she liked it.

"You okay?"

"Called my father to see if he knows where Arya is. Said he sent her on holiday with Enrich and I'm pretty sure he kept her phone."

"That's bizarre. If he's trying to use her to get you home, you'd think he'd want you to be able to reach her."

"It is a mess, and I have no idea what to do."

"Halvrick!" Coach Vik shouted from the door on the bus. "Get your ass on board."

"Yes, sir." I glanced at Ryann. "Later?"

"We'll see." Her bottom lip landed between her teeth. "Depends on how you play."

Only Ryann could get my mind off Arya and looking toward the future in a span of seconds.

I boarded the bus, and she followed quickly after. Ducking into a seat across from Joey, I slid my headphones on. His foot tapped a frantic beat, and I reached over and punched his thigh.

"Ow. What the fuck?"

"You are nervous to play your brothers? Still afraid they are better?"

"Please. I've kicked Jude's ass in speed drills every summer since I was eighteen, and Jason's so damn old now I can't believe he hasn't retired yet. We all know I'm the better Taylor."

Jason had to be nearing thirty-five, maybe older, so Joey wasn't wrong. "Are you using me for practicing your trash-talk?"

"No." His knee bounced wildly. "I'm nervous that Gabby is going to be home alone for the next week and she's been feeling like utter shit. Lizzie will check on her, and I know Sophie and Holly will, too. But I hate I'm missing this."

Joey had been married before and as far back as I could remember talked about how badly he wanted kids. After his divorce, he later realized his ex-wife kept putting off having children, not because she wasn't ready, but because she didn't want any. I was surprised Joey and Gabby waited as long as they did to start their family, but Gabby's reasoning of wanting the salon stable first made sense. Needless to say, they'd both been through enough.

"I am happy for you. You and Gabby will be great parents."

"Thanks." He gripped his headphones draped around his neck. "It's thrilling and terrifying at the same time, and we've only known for four weeks. Not sure how men survive this."

"Because they have good women keeping them sane."

He chuckled. "Yeah. Probably right. Thank God I have the best of them."

It seemed to be what he needed, and he slid his headphones back onto his ears, his legs calmed. I leaned back in my own chair and closed my eyes. The trip to the arena was short, but I'd at least helped a teammate.

Now I needed to take care of myself.

All too soon, we were in the halls of the arena, shortly after a warm-up skate and staying loose and limber. Some of the men were on leather couches, watching movies on their phones or listening to music. Garrett and Arlo were on the stationary bikes, keeping their legs warmed up.

I joined Braxton, Kane, and Dominick in the hallway, where they were kicking a soccer ball around.

"Anyone seen Joey?" I hadn't seen him since we left the ice after the skate.

"Calling Gabby. Making sure she's okay, which she *is*, because he's already called her three times today," Kane said.

Dom chuckled and kicked the ball my way. "Last time he talked to her, she said she was going to chop off his balls if he called again."

"So he'll be ball-less soon," I finished.

Joey rounded the corner and Dom smirked. "Not that Joey ever had big balls to begin with."

"I heard that!" he called out and slid his phone into his pocket. "Happy to compare them whenever you're man enough, Dom."

"The only person who needs to see my balls is Holly, and trust me, she's plenty pleased with the size of *all* of me."

This was what I needed, why I loved my team. It was the banter and friendship and family we had built over years of struggles and victories. It was the closeness I had never had, and especially not since Mom died.

Soon, I lost myself in game preparations, centering myself, and by the time we took the ice and the "Star Spangled Banner" was playing to a fully packed arena in Charlotte, worries of Arya and my father had been nicely shelved in a box in the back of my locker. I could carry them later.

THE RACE WAS ON. Tied after the first period, the Ice Kings rushed out onto the rink for the second period like someone had lit their balls on fire. We were all having a hard time keeping up with them, which made sense. They were usually one of the top teams in their conference, and we were the best in ours. It made sense the game would be tough, and throw in the family drama, and it was tougher.

Which meant as I chased Jason Taylor down right as he snagged the puck from Joey, I couldn't resist egging him on. "Aren't you too old to be out here? Joey tells me you've been needing a cane after games." I hustled and slapped his stick with mine to try to get him to lose control of the puck. "Retiring soon, right? Headed for an old folk's ho—"

A flash of blue slammed me into the boards and Jude was there. "Leave him alone."

A laugh burst from me as we grappled on the boards. "Awww... is the man too old to fight himself?"

Jude was grinning and then slammed into me, pushing me harder into his brother and the boards behind him. "Oomph. Fuck, Joey."

"Get moving, you slow asshole," Joey called and skated off.

I shoved Jude off me and took off, racing with him and continued to throw our shots—both with the puck and our mouths at each other for the remaining ten minutes.

The game was brutal and loud and obnoxious and by the time it was over, the Ice Kings won—by one, with Mikah Lutzgo scoring the final goal with twenty seconds left on the clock.

The buzzer was still going off, celebration for the Ice Kings on the ice as we slapped gloves. "Flying out tonight or staying here?"

"Flying out," I told Mikah.

"That is too bad, mate."

We met years ago when I was first on the team and we had an overnight stay in Charlotte. Joey's whole family showed, along with most of the Ice Kings where we met up at a bar that was now owned by one of their player's wives, Gigi, after her dad retired.

"Next time. Good game." I punched his glove and almost lost my skates when Jason shoved me as I reached him.

"How's that for old?"

"Don't know, did you touch me?" I brushed my shoulder. "Felt like one of Garrett's twins punching me. Getting weak, old man."

He shoved me again, slapping my helmet and laughing. "Someday, you'll be big and strong just like me, Halvrick."

"Maybe. But you will never be as cute as I am."

I skated off the ice and into the locker room where our crew was already working, piling our skates and jerseys and gear into the laundry bins as quickly as we stripped them off.

Our crew deserved medals. Every game, without fail, our shit was always clean and ready to go, sitting exactly how we wanted it in our cubbies. Down to the socks, and regardless of location, they never messed a thing up.

"All right. Listen up!" Coach shouted, cupping his hands around his mouth. "I got something to say."

We'd lost, had fun doing it, but a loss was still a loss and Vik would be pissed.

The locker room quieted and when he didn't start shouting immediately, but put his hands on his hips and glanced at a couple of the other coaches, an eerie sensation filled the room.

Coach was *never* quiet after a loss.

"I got some news to share, and I was hoping to wait until we returned home, but that's not gonna work out, so I figured I'd get it done now."

Coach ran a hand over the top of his head and dropped his arms to his hips, crossed them in front of him. A glance at Coach

LaMonde, and back to us. In all the years I'd played for the team, I'd never seen him look so uncomfortable.

"Wisconsin's head coach got canned tonight."

"What?" Shouts of disbelief and some not surprised carried across the room. It was no secret Wisconsin's team had been struggling the last couple of years and this season was no different.

Coach lifted a hand, and our murmurs silenced. "Dave is a good man. A good coach and I know how hard that must be this close to the end of the season, but they've been looking for several weeks now for someone to step up and take his position. Someone to really be able to take the team and turn it around, make them more fierce on the ice. And unfortunately for us—"

"You're leaving?" The shout came from Braxton and holy shit.

I hadn't considered. I assumed he would never leave. That someday we would have to haul Coach's dead body off the ice.

But to turn around a team? Take someone last in the division to first? Of course Vik could do it.

"No." He threw his arm out into the air to silence the fear building. "I'm not going anywhere. You assholes are stuck with me for as long as I let you be. No. They've decided they need someone who can truly pick up their defense most of all. Someone with a proven track record. Which means...." He swung out his arm and Jay stepped toward him.

Oh *no*. My eyes instantly widened and I searched out Kane and Bromann. As the best defenders on our team, they'd be most shaken, even if Ryder was a newer addition to our team.

"Coach Jay LaMonde has accepted an offer, starting immediately, and he's going to be taking off to Wisconsin tonight to start getting his new team ready for their next game."

"No fucking way!" Dominick shouted, and he looked ready to burst. "I mean, this is awesome for you... but what the hell? *Now?* When we're playing so well?"

"I wouldn't do it if I didn't know you could handle this," Jay said. He swung his gaze through the entire locker room. "I'm sorry if it feels like I'm letting you down, but I want you to know that Vik and I have been in talks with our next head defense coach since whispers started. We're confident we'll get someone in full-time, but until then, I have every confidence that the other coaches and Michael Gravisk, our assistant defense coach, will be able to hold it together."

I was at a loss, as was most everyone else. We'd had very few coaching changes over the last few years due to our success, but who could fault the guy for wanting his own head coaching job?

"Congratulations," Joey finally said once the shock wore off. He was closest to LaMonde and wrapped him in a quick hug. "You'll do great things in Wisconsin. I mean, if anyone can turn Dominick into a halfway decent player, that says all the league needs to know about how good you are."

"Oh, fuck right off, Taylor," Dom shouted, but he was the next to come forward. He gave LaMonde another man-hug and the entire team fell into line.

This was a change. It was part of the game.

We'd adapt, we'd stick to our game plan, and LaMonde was right. Michael Gravisk was also a damn good coach. We had nothing to be concerned about because there was no way Vik would allow a coach to walk into our locker room if he wasn't one hundred percent they were just as good as LaMonde if not better.

TWENTY-NINE

RYANN

What a game. And a night. The loss sucked. Hearing that Coach LaMonde was leaving immediately threw a wrench in our typical ability to relax during the away games. Callie and I both went to work, coordinating with Wisconsin's team travel coordinator, Lyle, to get Jay on a flight as soon as possible, to the hotels they set up new players in and for their next quick stretch of away games up there.

Thank goodness he was single. There'd been word he'd been having quiet conversations with Wisconsin for several weeks now, so the position and move wasn't such a surprise to him. Apparently it came down to the timing, giving the Wisconsin coach some more time and a few more chances to get the team turned around and tonight they'd not only had enough of losing, but since they knew Jay was interested, pulled the trigger.

Both Callie and Lyle worked so seamlessly in coordinating the abrupt move for Jay, it was a wonder they didn't sort through a fiasco like this every week.

"Oh dear sweet Jesus, I'm so glad we don't," Callie groaned when I mentioned it to her. She closed her eyes and leaned her head back against the airplane's seat. "Tonight was *painful*. And that loss was a bummer."

"Yeah. Sucked all around for the guys for sure."

Most of them looked pretty dejected as they boarded the plane, even Alix barely managed to summon up a fist bump for me as I checked him onto the plane. Now we had to settle in for a two-hour flight down to Miami, arrive at the hotel around two o'clock in the morning by the time we unloaded and shuttled over. Every time I boarded a plane, I dreamed of a different position in marketing and it wasn't that I wasn't thankful for this job. I was. Extremely.

But I was quickly learning this constant travel lifestyle was not my thing. I'd leave that to Hayden—who had yet to call me back after that lovely parting salute she'd given over the weekend. Braylen, though, had called me and mentioned Hayden in passing, so I knew she'd left Las Vegas for Sedona, Arizona. It gave me some comfort to know she wasn't drunk or passed out in some seedy Las Vegas hotel.

I closed my eyes and was trying to rest through takeoff, fully aware my fingers were playing with the bracelet Alix had given me. The lavender infusion didn't seem to help me any, but I wore it every time we flew.

It had to be the most thoughtful gift anyone had ever given me —definitely any guy I dated. Which wasn't saying much since my last relationship was a six-month thing my sophomore year of college.

We were well past takeoff, the plane leveled out and the soft sounds of some of the guys snoring were the only sounds on the plane over the hum of the engine when my phone buzzed in my hand.

Tonight sucked. You should tell me a bedtime story to put me to sleep.

I grinned, made sure Callie was sleeping, or at least uninterested in my late-night text.

Sorry. You played well though except with that fight with the Taylors.

The announcers had talked about how physical this game could get, with the brothers on both teams and close friendships between the two.

Told Jason he was too damn old to still be playing and his baby bro didn't like that much. :-) Now about that story? Tell me something.

I couldn't pull a story out of the air for anything, at least not one that wasn't a children's bedtime story and I doubted that was what Alix was really looking for.

I have a scar in my hairline at my temple. When I was two, Hayden wanted my doll and I wouldn't give it to her and I was running away from her. She shoved me from behind and I slammed my forehead into the corner of a wall in our living room. Gave me eight stitches.

So she's always been a playful pain in the ass.

I chuckled softly. He wasn't wrong.

What else?

I thought you wanted to sleep.

Talking to you is better.

My heart fluttered and I had to resist the urge to stand, turn around and find him in the dark plane.

My mom makes the best chocolate chip and M&M cookies. She would always have them fresh, right out of the oven for us on Fridays after school. Besides those, we were never really allowed treats unless it was a birthday or holiday.

My mother once set our oven on fire when she tried to bake.

I fought a laugh and covered my mouth so it didn't burst free. Hopefully my shaking shoulders wouldn't wake up Callie.

Not a baker?

Phenomenal cook, but no. She always said she was too impatient to measure things exactly but she kept trying.

What was she like?

Happy. Klutzy. Was always running into doorways and tripping over her own two feet. She had a quiet laugh and proper manners and liked our house looking perfectly clean but never got mad when Arya and I made messes. I wouldn't be where I am today without her.

I'm sorry you lost her so soon.

She's not lost. She's with me every minute, every second of the day.

My eyes welled with tears. This wasn't supposed to be a sad conversation.

Arya got lost once when she and I walked to the park. I looked for her for what felt like forever and couldn't find her at all. And I didn't know what to do. Home was a mile away and I didn't want to leave so I kept walking around the park, peeking in stores nearby to see if she hid in one of them. I eventually found her in a patisserie, sitting on a barstool, eating a handful of brunsils—a cookie—and kicking her feet.

OMG. What did you do?

I told her mom was going to yell at her when I got her home and she laughed. Said, "Mom does not yell silly. She is too nice." The woman who owned the patisserie laughed and sent us on our way with a bag full of cookies.

Did your mom yell??

No, she thanked us for the cookies and asked us how the park was and never questioned it.

How old was Arya?

She was about four. How my mom thought we had the money for the cookies is still unknown. I was only eight or nine.

I sent him a laughing face emoji. **Braylen once used her babysitting money to buy me clothes from a garage sale because I'd told my mom I didn't have anything to wear. She came home with all boy clothes and forced me to wear them for a month.**

Why?

Because she said she'd always wanted a brother and I was as close to getting one as she'd ever have. For a year she walked around calling me "bro." And she was thirteen.

A big bully.

And a pain in my ass.

Our texts continued, one story after another about all the stupid and silly things we did and all too soon, our flight was landing, the guys were grumbling awake and we were rushed off to the charter bus and into their hotel rooms.

And when Alix slipped his keycard into my hand after I handed them to him, I didn't hesitate.

Twenty minutes after settling into my own room, I snuck into his and the conversations and stories continued—only with our bodies instead of our words.

There were still unknowns before us, but we found solace, even if temporarily, with each other.

MY MIND WAS RESTLESS. Slipping AirPods into my ears, I turned on my Focus App as I reviewed travel plans for March. It'd been almost a month since we were in Miami. Weeks of Alix and I still sneaking around my father. We slipped in and out of hotel rooms on the road and when we were home, we were holed up in either my apartment or his townhome. Some nights we spent with Kane and Emmersyn, having drinks in their hot tub while Kane prepared delicious meals the equivalent of a five-star restaurant. Other nights we laughed at Emmersyn's attempt to salvage whatever she'd attempted to make. Occasionally, I cooked for Alix in one of our places, and while I was enjoying learning how to cook, it surprised me when I realized he was better than me at it.

"Just because I don't like to cook for myself, doesn't mean I don't enjoy it," he'd said last week when I teased him about the steak he'd seared to perfection and served with garlic roasted mashed potatoes, asparagus, and a salad topped with cranberries and walnuts.

It was scrumptious and I sucked down every bite before we cleaned up his kitchen and then I showed him my appreciation for the wonderful meal by dropping to my knees and sucking down every drop of him.

I still had dinner or lunch with Vik on the road, and it was becoming harder to continue calling him Vik. Our relationship was bumpy, filled with potholes, and yet some days it felt like those potholes were on schedule to be filled. I'd even managed to speak about him with Braylen without her anger pulsing through the phone. She'd started asking me questions about him shortly after Hayden's sudden departure. She might not have liked the man, but Braylen was also less inclined to fly off the emotional handle, and apparently even she had felt dismayed at Hayden's behavior on Viktor's behalf.

"He's a completely worthless father, but no human deserves that sort of nastiness," she'd said one day and then finished with, "Tell me what he's like. As a man... or a coach."

Now that Callie trusted me to do the job while we were on the road, she and I were trading off away trips. It was helping my sleep and enjoyment of the job immensely and Callie was currently on a quick one-night trip with the team in Arizona. I was coordinating our next trip to the northeast where we'd play Buffalo, Boston, New York and down to DC for an eight-day trip, the first long trip I would be handling on my own.

On top of that, Kane's family was joining us at one of the games in Buffalo and required hotel rooms. Vik had requested I block off six other rooms at our hotel in D.C. and yet hadn't given me the names of who would be in them, making me curious as the trade deadline was approaching and the whispers of the new coach joining us soon. He could be holding those rooms for anyone.

Lizzie and Gabby had also decided to travel to Chicago to spend time with Garrett's parents for a game as soon as we returned from DC. They wouldn't need hotel rooms since Lizzie was planning on staying at her parents' house with the twins, and Gabby would stay at Joey's parents' house so they could spend a quick night together. Due to the travel and constant demands of the team, it wasn't frequent wives or children traveled to games, but it happened when there was family nearby and it was always an extra hurdle. Organizing separate flights for the wives since there wasn't usually room on the team plane. I needed to coordinate departures and arrivals with preferred airlines for the families as well as find extra rooms in the hotels. For Lizzie and Gabby, in order to make traveling easiest for them, I also pre-scheduled drivers to take them to and from hotels and to the arenas.

Which was what I was currently working on when my phone rang and my mom's name appeared on the screen.

A grin broke out as I answered her call. "Hey, Mom. What's going on?"

"Hey, sweetheart. I'm sorry to bug you at work, but I had a question for you." Like always, my mom's tone was soft and gentle and I had to turn up the volume to hear her properly.

"Sure. Hit me."

"The Vipers will be home on Saturday, correct?"

I practically had their schedule memorized by now. "Yep. They're playing Anaheim, why?"

"Paul and I thought we'd come down, maybe go to the game if we could get some tickets?"

My pen froze in mid-air and my jaw almost hit the desk. She wanted... "What?"

A soft, nervous laugh drifted through the phone. "You heard me. We've been talking, with Braylen and Blake, too. Based on how things are going with you and Vik, we thought, well, maybe it'd help Hayden some if she saw us getting along with him. She's been... distant, you know, since she saw him."

At least it wasn't just me she'd practically fully blown off.

Worry gnawed at my gut at the reminder. "Yeah, I know. How do you think coming here will help?"

"It might not, but I was hoping if she saw how I'd truly forgiven your father and moved on, and how we could all at minimum, be polite to each other, she might soften a little bit." A heavy, motherly sigh echoed in my ear. "I truly hadn't expected her to get so worked up over seeing him. It never occurred to me she had so much disdain or anger and pain still inside of her—"

"That's not your fault, Mom. It's hers."

"I know. But as her mom, it's now my job now to see to my girl and try to help mend her. So," she started, much more playfully. "Game on Saturday? And Paul and I can't wait to see what you've done with your place. But don't worry about us. We'll get a hotel somewhere."

The team still had rooms at the resort where I originally stayed. "I can probably find you some." If anything, they could stay at the hotel where Anaheim's players stay. They'd probably get a discount.

"No, no." She laughed. "You book enough hotel rooms for your job, don't worry about us. We'll take care of it, if you can take care of the tickets?"

I hadn't been to a home game yet and was now looking forward to it. Too bad I couldn't wear Alix's jersey like so many fans do. That'd throw him for a loop for sure.

"All right, all right. I'll see about tickets. Do you want me to let Vik know?"

"I'm sure he'd appreciate the heads up versus the surprise. If memory serves, Vik doesn't like surprises much."

It surprised *me* she could laugh while she said it. Like she truly felt no anger with the man who was barely a father to her children. But I heard her, and she was right. Vik was definitely a Type-A needed to know everything kind of guy.

***

"THEY'RE COMING? YOU'RE SURE?" I would have paid good money to see Vik's face when I made the phone call after their afternoon skate in Arizona, letting him know about Mom's phone call.

"Yes. Mom and Paul and Braylen and Blake. They'll be here for Saturday's game. The problem is it's sold out, even team tickets."

I'd spent hours checking earlier.

"Let me see what I can do. If anything, they can have a suite, I'm sure there will be one open and you might all be comfortable there."

"I don't think that's necessary."

"I'll take care of it." His tone broke no argument. "Okay. Well, this is a surprise, but not a bad one for once. And Braylen is okay with this?"

"I think they're hoping if Hayden can see the rest of us moving on, she might start letting go of some of that anger we didn't realize she held, so yeah, she's okay with it."

"To help her sister. Of course." There was sadness there, heavy in his words.

"Dad—" My mouth snapped closed as soon as it came out. "I didn't—"

"Mean it, yeah," he huffed, and I imagined him shaking his head, maybe scrubbing his head with his meaty palm. "I'm sure you didn't, but it was nice to hear regardless."

Oddly enough, it didn't feel *wrong*. Perhaps we'd both grown a lot in the last couple of months.

"I should let you get ready for the game, but I did mean it, Vik. Or Dad."

He chuckled, this time lighter. "Thank you, Ryann. That means a lot considering. And I'm looking forward to Saturday, maybe now more than ever. I'll let you know about the tickets."

"Sounds good."

We hung up, and the road ahead suddenly seemed a lot smoother.

Ryann opened her door, blonde hair thrown on top of her head, wisps flying out every which way. She was breathless with flushed cheeks, dressed in a hot pink sports bra and black, booty-hugging shorts.

Outside of the times I'd been with her naked, she'd never looked cuter, but that could have been partly because she looked adorable when she was nervous.

"Are you going to let me in or allow the pizza boxes to burn my palm?"

I held out the boxes and the small paper bag I brought as a surprise for her in my hand.

"Oh. Sorry! Come in, come in." She stepped back, and I kissed her lips, tasted sweat and cherries from her ChapStick on them and grinned.

The smell of bleach tickled my nose. "You're cleaning."

"Like a maniac which is silly since I just moved in and have been gone half the time, but I want everything to look perfect."

Her parents arrived tomorrow afternoon, giving them barely enough time to see her home, much less critique it before they would leave for the game. Not that I figured anyone in her family would do such a thing, but over the last month, despite the traveling we were doing, Ryann had added small touches to her place to make it feel more like her home. There was a green, potted plant in the corner of the living room, just inside the sliding doors to the patio that held a small sitting set where we often had our morning cup of coffee or a drink at night. She'd bought a few pieces of artwork to hang on her walls and added area rugs in front of her couch. There were books for decoration purposes only she found at thrift stores and removed the covers so the colors of the pale blue and green and cream matched the rest of her place. One had some wicker ball set on top which I did not understand at all, but she'd smiled prettily when she set it there so I'd told her it looked perfect.

"Hungry now? Or do you need to finish something up first?"

"I'm starving. But let me take a quick shower and wash my own stench off me first."

"I could help?" I wiggled my brows, and she shoved my chest. "If you help, the shower would be anything but quick."

"And?"

"Shut up." She laughed and gave me another shove before she hurried off to her room. While she was gone, I shoved the pizza boxes into the oven and set it on the *keep warm* function and then grabbed plates and silverware and marinara sauce from her fridge. Ryann liked her pizza heavy on the sauce, dipped and doused in marinara with every bite so I poured it into a small bowl and by the time she returned from the shower, dressed in similar shorts, these a pale pink and a gray sweatshirt with the Vipers logo splashed onto the center of her chest, I had the dinner table set and ready for her.

"Oh." Her eyes gleamed and a soft smile I wanted to kiss off her face appeared. "Thank you. You didn't have to do all of this."

"You've been working hard."

She huffed and ran a hand through her still-wet hair. "Right.

Because you've just been being a lazy ass, nothing to do, at all, lately."

Her hands went to her hair and she made quick work out of braiding the length of it before binding it off with a band she tugged off her wrist.

"Yes, yes. That is me. A lazy bum who does nothing but eat and play all day." I turned and went to the oven to remove the boxes. "If you're a very good girl, I will have a treat for you when you're done eating dinner."

"I'm always a good girl."

"Oh no, you are quite filthy, especially when you do that thing with your tongue I like so much."

"Shut up. You are in a *mood* today."

"Yes. A very good mood." It wasn't all about how I felt about her, either. The team, despite LaMonde's absence, was still raking in win after win. We struggled the first few games, more the loss of a great coach messing with our heads than anything else, but after those losses, Dom and Ryder had a defense guys-only night, along with the interim coach. Whatever they did or talked about that night worked, because we hadn't lost a game in two weeks.

If I could get a hold of Arya and ensure everything was okay, and if I could touch Ryann whenever I wanted—especially on the road—things would be perfect.

We would get there.

She saddled up to me in the kitchen and kissed my cheeks, rolling to her toes. "I will make sure your mood only improves later. Or wears you out."

"Ah. That is a promise I will hold you to."

"Good." She clapped her hands and rubbed them together. "Now, which box is mine?"

I flipped them both open. She wrinkled her nose at my chicken and bacon ranch pizza, and I could not stand the look of her pepperoni, mushroom, and jalapeño pizza. Not that I didn't like peppers. But on pizza, it seemed wrong. She felt the same way about the bacon I enjoyed on mine. Her bacon was only served with eggs. My jalapeños only belonged on a large plate of nachos.

Somehow, we still liked each other despite our vast differences.

We were halfway through our dinner, my pizza almost entirely eaten and Ryann still working on her third slice when she wiped her hands on her napkin and blotted the corners of her lips with it. "I was thinking, after my family leaves, I would tell my dad about us."

It was strange to hear her call Vik, Dad. Even stranger that it slid so easily off her tongue in the last few days.

"Are you sure?"

"I'm hoping he'll be in a good mood, at least, that's assuming Braylen doesn't freak out on him like Hayden did. But I think, yeah. Either way. He needs to know."

I reached out and took her hand in mine and squeezed. "I am ready when you are."

My phone rang, and I dug it out of my pocket. To my surprise, our old teammate's name Max flashed on the phone.

"It's Max," I told her. "I wouldn't take it, but I have not talked to him in a long time."

Months since we played in Los Angeles and Kane got shot by a literal psychopath and girlfriend-beater.

Ryann knew who he was, I talked about him frequently. "Answer it."

I did before I missed his call. "Hey, you and Kimmy sick and tired of Californians yet?"

He laughed. "Good to hear your voice, brother. Got some news for you."

"You and Kimmy are getting married?"

Ryann's eyes went wide and Max laughed again. "I wish. She still insists we can commit without the wedding and that's fine. I agree with her, I'm in no hurry to change her mind, but that's not why I'm calling."

"Okay..."

"I'm calling to see how it'd feel to start calling me Coach." His tone went serious. Nervous.

It took a second and my body burst out in goosebumps. "Are you kidding? Tell me you are not."

"Not joking. Shit, man, it's a fucking wild trip. Vik called earlier this week, and I don't know. I'm thinking..."

"You were loving college, yes?"

He'd quit hockey and the team before this season due to concussions and other injuries and in the fall went back to school in Los Angeles, where he moved to be with a woman he met over the summer. We'd all felt that loss, but once we accepted he was gone, Ryder slid right into his spot.

"I am. I am. I am glad I went back, and I will finish. Online courses as much as I can, at least. But when Vik called, I don't know, Alix. I miss it."

"Youth hockey not enough for you, then?"

I was grinning like a maniac and excitement had me pushing back from the table to pace Ryann's living room. I could feel her eyes on me, but this news... this was just the kind of excitement we'd need to finish the season on the best note.

"Yeah. I loved that, but if Dom can do it there, I figure I could still do it, maybe? I haven't worked out all the details yet. Kimmy and I have spent the last few days talking, and I'm considering it."

"You have to."

Having Max back as we head into playoffs? He was our leader. Our ridiculous teammate who could make everyone laugh and keep spirits high and when he left the team, he was one of the all-time highest-scoring defenders in the league and had the most blocks on goal. He was an *animal* on the ice, and every player would benefit from his presence.

"You have to do this," I repeated, already imagining our team. Their excitement. "Have you told anyone else? Called anyone?"

He was always closer to Kane than I.

"No. Actually, I haven't. I didn't want to get Kane's hopes up if

I said no, but I wanted your advice. And Joey's."

"He would say the same thing I am. You have to say yes, Max. This is... this is what we need to keep us going."

He was silent for a moment, and I imagined him scrubbing his dark hair, eyebrows knitted together with worry. He was probably fiddling with the new glasses he started wearing, too. "Kimmy's told me the same thing. She's already scheduling the Nevada Bar Exam."

Excitement churned and bubbled inside of me. This was *perfect.* "So, when will you start?"

He cleared his throat and laughed uncomfortably. "We're packing our bags now. I just, maybe, I've turned into a little shit. I needed to hear it was the right thing. We're planning on being there for the game this weekend, and then I'll officially start Monday."

I fell back against the wall, and a grin broke out so wide I shook my head. This was unbelievable. And wonderful. "You've already accepted."

"Yeah." And he still sounded nervous, but there was no need. "I'm nervous though. Making the switch."

"Ha. You always liked bossing us around. Now you will get paid to do only that. And no risk?"

"Not to my head, no, unless you assholes take a swipe at me."

"Fuck, Max. This is great news. I am excited. I have to keep it a secret?"

"Until Coach announces. At the game, I think. I want to talk to him more. Make sure Michael will be on board with staying."

"Gravisk will always do what is best for the team." And he was too young yet, too untried for a head coaching position. He was only an assistant defense coach for us for two years. He was good... Max would be better, even if he didn't have coaching experience. "And he will help you."

"Yeah. That's what he said, but shit. I might throw up."

We talked a few more minutes and I returned to the table,

Ryann now cleaning her plate. "I am sorry that took so long."

"It sounded like all good news." She beamed at me, hip resting on the counter, and it was her smile that said it all.

"You already knew."

"There were whispers in the office today, and we'd had to do some scheduling. Rooms to reserve without giving names but Max's name was mentioned. I wanted you to hear it from Vik, though."

"I am so happy. He was—is—the best kind of man. And teammate. He will be a great coach. And I am honored he called me. Do you know what this means?"

"What?"

"We need to go out and celebrate."

"Shouldn't you wait and do that with him once he gets there?"

"I want to go be happy with you tonight."

She glanced down at her outfit, lifted her head slowly back up. "I should probably go change then."

"Thank you." I pressed my hands to her cheeks and kissed her until she melted into me. "I am happy. And not just because of Max. But you—you make me happy, too."

"I'm glad." Her eyes were soft, cheeks flushed. For a moment I thought of changing my mind. We did not need to go out to celebrate, we just needed each other. But no, I wanted to do something fun. It had been awhile since I'd been out, normally too tired for much during the season.

"You make me happy, too, Alix. More than I expected."

"I am beyond all expectations." I rocked back on my heels and smirked.

She laughed that beautiful laugh of hers and slapped my chest. "I'll go change."

"Nothing fancy."

"Just something that will make you wish you never suggested we leave my bedroom and crave coming back to it."

Well, now that sounded like the perfect outfit.

"Hello?" I cleared my throat, and tried again, only to find my mouth just as dry and talking painful. Bright light made me squint my eyes as I checked the screen and frowned.

"Coach?"

"I am trying, very hard, to understand, and hoping you will explain to me, why I am currently staring at pictures of you and my daughter *kissing* at a roulette table last night." Fury vibrated in his voice, and it was too damn bad I had that fourth—or was it a fifth—shot of tequila because I was certain my brain was still swimming in it.

"Uh... what? What are you talking about?"

I moved my legs, tried to kick out from beneath the pile of covers and blankets and pillows on the bed and hit something hard.

"Oh. Ow," Ryann croaked and I flinched.

This had to be a dream. Right?

Because there was no way...

"Tell me that is not my daughter in bed with you right now, Halvrick."

"Fuck." I swiped a hand down my face. "Okay. I will tell you that is not your daughter."

That kick must have woken Ryann because her eyes peeled open. "What?" she mouthed and I shook my head.

"Now tell me the truth."

Goddamn, that sunshine was bright. We really should have shut the blinds before partaking in our at-home celebration when we returned from the Strip, some of it I vaguely recalled.

"Halvrick!"

I clung to my forehead with my free hand. "Shit! Stop screaming, Coach."

"Are you hungover?"

This was going from bad to worse quickly and I was not nearly clear headed enough to think straight.

"Um. Can I call you back?"

"No. You can get your ass to my office. Now!"

He barked the last command and the phone went silent. I turned to Ryann who looked as in pain as I felt.

"That was my dad," she whispered, voice as hoarse as my own. "How does he know?"

"He said something about a picture? I do not know. I was asleep when I answered and he started yelling. It's all... foggy."

"Shit." She flung off the covers and grabbed her phone. I took an inappropriate second and admired her breasts that were currently bearing the mark of my teeth before refocusing.

Now was definitely not the time to admire the marks I left on her body, so ravenous for her when we returned home because she'd been correct—the dress she put on made me want to throw her back into bed as soon as I saw her in it. Tight and skimpy and short and shiny, it had reminded me of the night we met.

So much changed since then—like this morning.

"There are pictures of us." She flashed her phone in my direction. "How? And why?"

"The better question is how Vik saw them so early."

"I don't know." She shrugged. "Wouldn't surprise me if he had

Google alerts for all of you, given the trouble I've heard you have given the team in the last couple of years."

She was teasing, but she was probably not wrong. This was not the first time pictures appeared, although last time it was a TikTok. And it was Joey and Gabby. Then there was Dominick's arrest making the news. So we were not perfect men. Good ones all the same in my mind, though. "Probably showed up on a WAGs site."

"WAGS?" She frowned. "Is that what I think it means?"

"Wives and girlfriends, yes."

Her fingers tapped quickly on her phone screen, another brow furrowed. I was both impressed how she was not as hungover as I was, and irritated that my head hurt so damn much.

"This site is dedicated solely to Las Vegas Vipers players and there are *dozens* of pictures on here, of the women. Do they know?"

"They know," I assured her. None of the women particularly liked it, but there were a lot of women who enjoyed the fantasy of being with a professional athlete, like our money and muscles somehow made us better men than the man they saw at the grocery store or dating site. Plus, puck bunnies, at least decent ones, tried to stay informed of who was single and who wasn't to target the men they could convince to take to bed.

"Well, shit. What'd he say?"

"He was upset. Very much so. And I need to get to his office."

"Now?" She glanced at her phone. "It's barely seven."

"Time does not wait for an upset father, Ryann."

I leaned in to kiss her, tried to make a joke out of this, but this was bad. Very bad. I moved to get out of bed, but her small, cool hand grabbed my forearm. "If you think you're going there without me you are absolutely, one hundred percent, dead wrong."

THE PICTURES WERE NOT HORRIBLE. At least she was not flung over my shoulder with her ass on display in any of them and we weren't stumbling drunk. All but one showed us standing next to the roulette table or sitting next to each other at slot machines. We could have been friends, except for the look in our eyes and the smile on our faces that proved a closer intimacy.

I could not be blamed for that. Ryann's dress and beauty was.

But there was one photo where Ryann had won five hundred dollars on a machine and I'd cupped her cheeks in my palms and kissed her. Our pressed-together lips were curled up at the edge into a grin, and you could tell we'd been laughing right before the picture was taken.

I should have worn a hat, and all of this could have been avoided, but I was also glad I did not.

The photo was so great, I downloaded it and several others.

We walked into Vik's office, Susan gone and the sight of her desk empty was strange, although only maniacs like Vik showed up to work on a Saturday before seven in the morning.

His door was also open, and before we walked through, Ryann reached out and squeezed my hand, clamped hers around mine. She was cold, but not nervous.

"Can you let me do the talking?"

"Only as long as he's respectful to you."

"Deal," she whispered, and we stepped across the threshold to his office to find Vik at the windows of his office that overlooked the practice arena.

The Zamboni was on it, circling and making it shine for what would probably be a long day of youth hockey.

Vik had either heard us, saw our reflections in the glass, or had somehow managed to grow a sixth sense for his daughter's presence because without taking his eyes off the ice below him, he said, "The one thing I requested of you was not to date one of my boys."

Ryann had not told me this, and I glanced down at her.

She shrugged. "And after I asked you if you said that to *all* the staff, you told me to forget it."

"So what... you did this to put me in my place?"

"Not everything is about you, Dad!" Amazing how it spilled off her tongue so easily now, especially in anger, but this was spiraling out of control, and quickly.

"Ryann." I squeezed her hand and tugged her back. This was not helping.

"And you?" Vik turned to me, venom in his eyes.

"I care about her, other than that, I am uncertain what you wish me to say."

"Say?" His eyes widened, large, blue eyes that reminded me so much of Ryann's I should have noticed it sooner. "For one, I expect you to get your hands off my daughter, and then end this."

"No." Ryann gripped my hand tighter. If she thought I was letting her go now anyway, she was dead wrong. "You do not get to tell either of us what to do when it comes to our relationship."

"Relationship?" He scoffed. "You've been here two months."

"I've cared about her since September."

"Shit," Ryann whispered and it took a second for what I said to sink in. To remember what Hayden had said right before she left the dinner from hell.

Shit was right.

"September," he repeated. Those scarily familiar eyes narrowed and bounced back and forth between us before his skin turned a pale shade of putrid before he rested his hands on his hips, turned back to the window. "Fucking September. I don't even want to know."

He was shaking his head, ran a hand over it. I looked to Ryann for guidance but she had her lips rolled together between her teeth and I was pretty sure she was hiding her laughter, at the very least, a smile.

Probably hard for a man to reconnect with his daughter *and* begin thinking of her sex life all in a short time span.

Softer, more guarded, he spun back to us and focused on Ryann. "Is that why you came to me for a job? Because... September?"

"No." She was blushing now, and I would never think the name of a month would become a term for sex, but there we were. "I saw you before."

"I see." He licked his lips. Paused. "When you came for the interview, you two were together...."

"We were not. And that was a coincidence," I jumped in. Ryann was beginning to look almost as uncomfortable as Vik. "She was crying and ran into me, I knocked her on her ass, and then I realized who I had run into and we were talking before you showed up. It was the best surprise I've ever had, though, and I will not feel bad about that."

"I see." He swallowed thickly. Probably the mention of the tears because he continued to soften.

"I am struggling right now, with being your father and knowing I haven't been a good one, but still wanting to protect you and keep you safe."

"I might respect that, but it's not your call. Even if you'd been the best father ever, I'm an adult and these are my choices."

"If I ask you both, again, to end it?"

Hell fucking no was *not* the answer he was looking for. "What is your hesitation?" I asked, instead. "With me. With her dating a player on your team. All the married men, or men in relationships are good men. Good husbands. Incredible fathers. You assume I will treat her like trash?"

I was starting to get offended. I was not like him. Would never be like him. I was not a bad man and I had not even been with a woman since I saw Ryann in September.

My question caught him off guard, and he struggled to answer. "I do not think you will treat her like trash."

"Then what is the problem?"

"Is it the traveling?" Ryann asked and Vik's face paled again.

"I do not want to even begin to think about what you two have done while we're traveling—while we're *working*."

Ryann scoffed, clearly unaffected by Vik's threat. "I have free time to use as I please and you know this. Do not begin to imply I have not been doing my job."

"I know. I didn't mean..."

"You never do, and yet you hurt me with your words all the same."

"I'm sorry. I'm trying to wrap my head around this. Your mom and sister are coming, meeting their men. That has been hard enough and then I woke up to this today. But be honest with me now."

"I have not been the one to lie," Ryann stated and even though she was being harsh, my respect for her grew, watching her hold her own in front of a man who continued to mess things up.

"Seattle. Dinner?"

Ryann smiled. "That was actually supposed to be our first date."

"I ruined it."

"You left early and paid for our meals," I cut in, "so it was not ruined."

That earned me a chuckle, and he seemed to be coming around. Maybe joking was not the right answer, but it was better than his scowls.

"Nice to know," he finally said.

"If it helps and is any consolation," I said, and this time I stepped forward. "After that first night, I looked for her. I wanted to get to know her more. Your daughter bewitched me from the first moment I saw her. Talk to the men, they know how upset I was when I went back to the hotel and she was checked out."

"The men know?"

"Some. We met the night we took Ryder out to get him closer to the team."

"Some team bonding event," Vik muttered. "You were with your sisters."

"Hayden and Braylen met Ryder and Kane briefly, and a couple others, so yeah. I knew some of them."

"And you kept this from me?" Vik's gaze swung back to me, hard and assessing.

"I like to think of it as protecting Ryann and the relationship she was trying to grow with you. I will not apologize for that. I will not apologize ever for protecting her. I *care* about her, sir. A lot."

"Same," Ryann said, smiling up at me with a softness in her eyes and a coloring on her cheeks that made my heart warm.

She turned back to her father. "We're together. I am sorry you found out this way. I had considered saying something the night Hayden met us for dinner, but her arrival ruined it, and so I was going to tell you after this weekend was over. I was tired of hiding it, hiding things from you."

"I see." He rubbed both his hands down his face and shook off whatever still plagued him. "I suppose, then, Alix, that this is the part where I tell you to make sure you treat her well, and if you bring her any harm, I'll have you shipped to a farm team in Fond-du-Lac, Saskatchewan?"

I wasn't sure where that was, but based on the threat, I assumed far north. Whether they had a hockey team there, farm or otherwise, probably wasn't the point. "The threat is unnecessary but received."

"Okay. Then, I am sorry for assuming the worst of you this morning. Both of you."

"Thank you." Ryan let go of my hand and stepped toward Vik. "I appreciate that."

"Good. And Alix?"

"Yes?"

"You have gone years calling me Coach. Do not start calling me sir, now."

I wouldn't be me if I didn't give him a hard time. "What about Dad?"

His expression turned to stone. "Don't even think about it."

Ryann shook her head, chuckling as she closed the space between them. "I should thank you that you care enough to be upset about this in the first place, but if we're going to have to have an adult relationship, you have to remember you weren't there for me when I was little. You have to accept my choices, treat me like you would any other adult in your life, okay?"

"I'll try," he finally said.

Ryann held out her arms, and her voice shook as she asked, "Can I, um... have a hug then?"

She shrugged, and I didn't have to imagine the sheepish, nervous look on her face as Vik appeared stunned at the request. I knew Ryann, knew what it meant for her to dare ask for this, or *want* it.

He then bent, and wrapped his arms around his daughter.

The move was stilted, his arms wooden, and it was over quick when Ryann stepped back.

"We will see you after the game, then?"

"Another round of family and difficult questions and moments. Can't wait," Vik said, lips twitching. "Go. Enjoy your day." To me, he glared. "Get rid of that hangover because if you aren't at one hundred and ten percent by tonight, you can expect punishment."

"Coach." I nodded. Held out my hand for Ryann.

It hadn't started well but had ended better than I figured it would.

Neither of us spoke until we were safely in the elevator before a smile broke out on her face. "At least now I can get a jersey with your name on it and wear it to the game tonight."

"Look at you, always seeing the sunny side of things."

"Bright side."

"Same thing."

I was jumping like a maniac as Paul's SUV pulled into my parking lot. Thank goodness for my sister's Snapchat location, allowing me to track their drive down here so I knew exactly when they arrived.

To say I was excited to see my family after months of being separated was a vast understatement. FaceTime calls and texts weren't nearly enough, and I hadn't realized how much I was truly missing them until my mom caught sight of me and her smile went wide and wild and she started clapping her hands, bouncing on her feet, like I was doing on the sidewalk outside my building in my Converse high tops.

Paul pulled into a parking spot and before he was able to turn off his vehicle or put it in park, both my mom and Braylen had thrown open the doors and were racing my way.

Four arms threw themselves around me and the floral scent of my mom's perfume and Braylen's minty shampoo invaded my nose, making my eyes burn with happiness.

"I missed you so much!" I screamed to both of them as we shrieked and bounced and swung back and forth. My sister and Mom were *here*. And damn, how I'd missed them.

We finally stepped back when the thumps of heavy male foot-steps arrived and Braylen was peeled off me.

"My turn," Blake said. "How's it going, sister? Hanging in there?"

He was six foot five and in finance and he always wore dress slacks with a dress shirt, properly tucked in and hair styled with gel that took longer than mine to get perfect, but he was Blake. The guy my sister married. I never thought I'd wanted a brother until he waltzed into our life.

"I'm good." I squeezed him back and was once again surrounded in large, muscled arms that had been holding me since I was a teenager, arms that had held me through my first heartbreak and celebrated my success.

Paul swung me in a circle, hand at the back of my head and one at my back. "How are you? We have missed you so damn much."

He sniffed, settled me on my feet and I wobbled a step as I moved back, scanned my family and their smiles and the love in their eyes. "I've never been better."

And it was true, especially after this morning and Vik's accep-tance—minus the threat given to Alix—of truly beginning to accept who I was.

At least he hadn't threatened to fire me or trade Alix.

"Come on in." I threaded my arm around my mom's and pulled her close to me. "Come inside, see my place, and I'll tell you all about it."

TRUE TO VIK'S PROMISE, he'd come through in a massive way for my family. Thankfully, we weren't in a suite, but he'd still gotten us all incredible seats in one of the club sections which include free gourmet food, and great drinks. We could eat inside the heated area or sit outside in a section for thirty people to watch the game. I'd lost interest in food as soon as Alix and the rest of the

Vipers took to the ice, but now that the first period was over and Alix had already scored a goal, I could breathe a bit easier. He showed no signs of being slow on his feet thanks to this morning's hangover, and he was playing as perfectly and seamlessly as he always did.

As soon as the buzzer went off, Braylen grabbed my hand and pulled me back toward the inside club area claiming the need for a fresh drink, which was a lie since she'd barreled rank her first one.

"Nervous?" I asked once we had our drinks and were away from the bar. The club area had several small bar-height tables where we'd snagged one to stand.

"No. I just wanted a moment alone with my sister."

"Please." I rolled my eyes. "You can admit you're nervous."

"Hard to be nervous to see a man you don't care about." She glanced to the left, lingered on nothing, and came back to me. "Fine. Nervous, I admit it, but that's stupid, right? Since I don't care about him?"

"I think you should figure that out before I get another surprise like Hayden's visit with him."

"Ugh. Fine. But Blake's been listening to me rant all week and I don't want to talk about it anymore. But yes, I want to see him. I want to see how he is with Mom, and I want to watch how he is with Paul mostly."

Given Vik's history of saying things he shouldn't, I wasn't entirely sure it would go well, but at least if he screwed up, we could leave. He'd gotten tickets for all of us to the family area after the game. Said it'd be more relaxing to be in the lounge room than in public. I couldn't fault him for that thought, at least.

"He's trying," I told her. "And he's not perfect about it by any means, but I do generally think he wants to be a part of our lives in whatever way we'll allow him. You get to set that boundary, Braylen. I can tell you I'm pretty sure he'll push that boundary, so know that."

"Why? Why is he like this?"

"He's a man who likes control, tries to regain it when he doesn't have it."

It was the best I could think of. Wasn't right or wrong, but after working near him for months, it just *was*.

She brought her drink to her lips. "That doesn't make me feel better."

"You get used to it. Or at least, I did. I no longer think he's the hateful man I used to, but he's far from perfect. Paul is still better," I assured her.

She grinned, shoulders fell. "That's because Paul kicks ass."

We clinked our glasses together, her rum and Coke, and my red wine. Paul came into our lives when we needed him and he'd earned every moment of our trust and our love and our kindness. It hadn't always been pretty, and we didn't make it easy on him, but it also hadn't taken us long to realize he loved our mother enough to stand against all of our attacks then the only person we were hurting was Mom.

Once we trusted he'd stay and be the kind of Dad we'd always wanted, his love was freely given, forgiving us for all of our nastiness. Said it didn't matter and he understood.

"How's Mom?"

She'd been quiet in the condo, sure she was excited to see my place and she complimented every inch of it and every tiny little decoration including the wicker ball Alix had laughed about, but she wasn't herself.

"She was quiet on the trip, but she's good. I think she's nervous to see Vik again, too, but I think she had her closure when she left him. We're the ones who never got that, and I think she realizes why we need it."

"She hasn't said anything? About me working for him?"

"No. Only that she hopes you're happy, and you are, right?"

"I am."

A knowing, soft smile stretched across her cheeks. "And I'm guessing that has nothing to do with Vik."

"Not a single bit of it. It's the job, the people, and yes, Alix. I'm happy there, finding myself and doing good work."

"Will Alix meet us tonight?"

We hadn't talked about it, but after this morning in Vik's office, I figured he wouldn't want me to go through this without him. "He will. I'm sure of it."

"Good. I'm glad you found him then."

"Me too."

———

BRAYLEN PACED THE LOUNGE ROOM. Blake stood with his back to the wall like a soldier, arms folded over his chest. His hardened look was in absolute opposition to his banker-boy outfit, but he tracked every one of Braylen's moves. I had no doubt he was preparing to unleash holy hell at the first wrong word from Vik. Mom's eyes were distant, and she'd done more than one lap around the room herself before smiling at me nervously, making her hands tremble. "Everything is so different than I remember."

I hadn't even considered. How many nights had she been in this room? Met with players? Snuggled one of their children or spoken with their wives? It was over a decade ago, but it felt like she was remembering every one of those moments that might have brought a smile to her face, but hadn't made her happy.

"I'm sorry, I didn't even think—"

"It is not yours and never has been yours to be sorry for. They weren't all bad memories, you know? We had good times. More before he started coaching, but any apologies that need to be given will not come from you."

The door opened and Alix stepped in. I went to him, but he met me halfway with a smile on his face.

"Great game, you."

"Nice shirt." He reached out and plucked at the Viper's sweatshirt. I'd decided not to go with his jersey for this game, there was enough going on.

Paul and Blake neared us, but Alix's eyes first meet Braylen's. "It is nice to see you again."

She scanned his outfit, a full suit minus the tie and the collar opened at his throat. She must have deemed him worthy of me, because she walked right up to Alix and hugged him. "You too. I've heard many great things about you."

Surprised, it took him a second to return it, while smiling at me the whole time. "Thank you."

Braylen stepped back. "But they all came from Hayden and she lies."

He laughed low and steady and he took my hand in his as I introduced him to Paul and Blake. Both were kind and respectful, not that I was surprised, and then I was introducing him to Mom.

"Mom. Alix."

"Jennifer." She smiled with her whole face and forewent the handshake to give him a hug. "It's lovely to finally meet you."

"You too. Ryann talks about all of you all the time."

"You played well tonight."

"Thank you. I appreciate that, and that all of you came. I know it's costing you a great deal."

"Yes, well... the waiting is sometimes the hardest part, but I do admit it's been a while since I enjoyed a hockey game. Thanks for making sure it was a good one."

"We won just for you." Alix winked, my mom laughed, and I leaned into his side.

"I'm sure you did." She patted his cheek like she'd known him for years and not moments, and soon, many of the other wives and girlfriends and women I'd met with children holding their hands or on their hips swarmed the room.

I turned to Alix. "Did you...."

"I asked them to wait a few minutes. Yes."

"Thank you."

They gathered up children and bags they'd left in the lounge to hurry off and find their men. The room was quieting down when the door opened.

Vik stood just inside the doorway, scanning the room, but it was not long before he found me. A smile broke out on his face, something I was still unused to seeing on him, and then he found my mom.

That smile froze, wobbled, and fell as Paul stepped close to my mom and took her hand in his.

The entire room seemed to freeze, even the babbling babies went silent. It was Braylen who moved first. She strolled up to Vik with the confidence she'd always had and didn't stop until she was in front of him.

"Vik." Her hands entwined together in front of her, the only tell she was nervous.

Vik looked ready to puke.

"Braylen. It is good to see you. Thank you so much for coming." She stepped to the side, and the pain on her face was clear. She wanted to rage but was controlling it, unlike Hayden who had let it fly from the onset. "I'd like you to meet my husband, Blake."

Blake was there, and he tugged his wife close to his side, offered Vik a nod. "Blake Hammond."

There was no offer of a handshake.

"Vik Boucher. Thank you, for loving Braylen as much as Ryann says you do."

It was the perfect thing to say, and all of their eyes came to me.

My mom had moved and was at my side. There was sadness on her face as Vik spoke quietly with Braylen and Blake before heading toward her. His steps were steeped with lead, and I must have aged five years before he finally stood in front of my mom for the first time since I was barely a teenager.

Paul was a strength at her back, Alix at my side.

"Jennifer. Thank you. I know this isn't easy for you to be here, and I appreciate it more than I can say."

Tears were in my mom's eyes making my heart ache but she forged through them and grinned. "Well, we both know words weren't always your strong suit."

It was a dig as much of a joke and put a small crack in the ice.

"Vik Boucher." He held out his hand toward Paul. "If Ryann has spoken much of Blake, she has told me more about you and how much they love you, how great you are for Jennifer. Thank you for being the perfect man they needed when I failed."

Paul's eyes clouded. I wasn't surprised. He was a man who wasn't afraid to show or express emotion. "It has been my honor, I assure you."

"And my greatest regret, so I am thankful they had you." A smile at my mom. "You raised lovely women, from what I've seen. I am truly sorry for allowing you to do it on your own, even when I was there."

My mom hiccupped. Paul stepped in and saved her from losing it completely, by talking about the game. It was simple, surface-level conversation that did not help the tension in the room, of everyone watching us, and it was over too soon when Vik glanced at all of us.

"I would like to talk more, maybe go somewhere for a drink, but I have asked my team to stick around. I have an announcement I need to make tonight while everyone is still here. Could you give me ten minutes? And then we can go somewhere?"

He focused mostly on Braylen, letting her choose. "I think I might like that."

"Good. Ryann, if you'd like to join Alix, I've said the families of players can be there, as well."

It was about Max. Had to be.

And after Alix's excitement last night, I couldn't wait to see how the entire team reacted.

THIRTY-THREE

ALIX

"You know what this is about?" Kane asked once we returned to the locker room. "Because you're grinning like a fool."

"Just wait."

I still couldn't believe Max hadn't called him, and yet wasn't surprised. Max would want to make an entrance. Since Ryann and I were the last to enter, Vik closed the door behind us.

"Listen up! I've already given you animals the post-game speech, and I thank you for sticking around so I can work on some other things."

He had the attention of the room except for one of the toddlers playing with a small car on the floor. Everyone else waited with bated breath.

"As you know, we miss Jay, but they had their first win last week since he took over so I called him and wished him well. I also let him know how well Michael here has been working, and we're adjusting."

Michael lifted his hand in the air in thanks.

"But I have more news." Next to me, Ryann vibrated with excitement. I could barely contain my own. As soon as Max walked into this locker room, the whole room was going to explode.

"I've been in talks with some men, some leaders, the other coaches and some former players to see who would work best to take over Jay's position. Management entrusted this call to me fully, although I've also gained their approval.

"So, hold on gentlemen, because you are going to love this." He slammed the heel of his shoe against the door behind him and shouted, "Meet your new head defense coach!"

He jumped out of the way and thank goodness he moved fast because Max flung open the door and threw his arms in the air.

"Let's get to work, assholes!"

"No fucking way!" Kane shouted. He took off running, and jumped Max, throwing arms around shoulders and almost tossed Max to the floor.

"Easy on the head, idiot!" Max laughed and flung Kane off him as the locker room fell into the madness I'd expected. Behind Max, Kimmy walked in, smiling with tears falling down her cheeks. She was quickly pulled to the side by Emmersyn while the team dog-piled on Max.

"How in the hell?"

"What?"

"We have to deal with you again!?"

All manner of insults and congratulations and shouts of happiness and surprise echoed and bounced off the walls until suit coats were flying as some men whipped them off and swung them in the air. We were jumping on our feet and shouting. Max bear-hugged Ryder with no hesitation. Slapped his shoulder and told him he'd been enjoying watching him play. Ryder told Max he couldn't wait to learn from the best, which only caused an increase in shouts.

It took forever for the room to calm down and there were mothers who had left, the noise too much for their little ones but through it all, Ryann was at my side.

I pulled her into a bear hug, lifted her off her feet and slid my hand to the back of her head, cupping her. "I love you," I told her, no hesitation, no fear.

I'd fallen in love with this woman back in September, in a night, and I was tired of hiding it.

I kissed Ryann before she could say anything, not that I needed to hear the words. Her faith in me, her support, and the way she handled herself this morning with her dad, told me all I needed to know.

She loved me, whether she was ready to say it yet, or not.

***

"WHAT AN EXHAUSTING NIGHT." Ryann turned toward me, her head on the headrest. We were flying through the streets of Las Vegas, and her tired, but happy smile squeezed my chest.

I couldn't wait to get back to her house, strip her out of the Vipers sweatshirt and run my hands all over her.

"It was fun, though. Yes?"

"Most of it. It's exciting that Max is back. I bet the team will love that."

"Max was our captain, the guy we all relied on. Losing him this year was tough, especially why. So yes, it is a good thing. A great thing."

My phone rang, and since it was connected to Bluetooth, the shrill sound made Ryann jump. *No Caller ID.*

I'd taken to answering all of them, on the off chance any spam call could be Arya, needing help. In the last month, I'd tried calling my father every week and he quit answering me.

I had Max back. Ryann's family were working on their relationship with Vik and hadn't killed him tonight, and he was now trying to accept my relationship with her.

All we needed were our sisters to return our calls and things would be perfect.

"Hello?"

A feminine sniff, then a sob burst through the car and I turned down the volume as Ryann gasped, eyes flaring in my direction.

"Arya?"

"Ç'est moi." She sniffed again.

"Englais, s'il vous plait. Ryann est avec moi. Est-ce que ça va ? Are you okay?"

It was so much more natural for her to speak French, but translating would be a pain in the ass.

"Oui. Yes. Sorry, Alix. I am okay. I am here."

"Where? Back home?"

"No." She laughed, and I swore the ring of music that could only be one thing came from her side of the call.

"Arya? Where are you?"

"L'aéroport. Las Vegas. Can you come get me?"

"You're *here* here?"

"It is a story, many chapters." Another soft laugh and sniff. "Can you come get me?"

"Of course I will. Bien sûr." I reiterated in French for her benefit.

"Alix, your car," Ryann whispered, and I glanced around.

Shit. "Hold on, Arya. I need to get another car. It will be forty-five minutes until I can be there."

"Just drop me off, Alix."

Right. Of course. Duh. We were only a few minutes from Ryann's place anyway.

What in the hell was going on?

"Does Dad know where you are?" I asked Arya.

"No. Well, I am sure he will understand. But no... long story."

"Okay. I'm coming. Let me drop Ryann off. It'll be about thirty minutes or so, maybe sooner. I'll be there though, yes?"

"Soon, brother. I will be waiting."

I clicked off the phone, and the music blared back to life. I turned it down and glanced at Ryann. "My sister is *here*. What in the hell is going on?"

"Maybe she needed to get somewhere safe."

"She didn't have her passport or any way to get it, last time we talked. How?"

Her hand came out and settled on my thigh. Squeezing, the firm touch from her helped me refocus. On the road. The moment.

"I'm sure she will give you all the answers you need very soon."

"Right." I dropped my hand from the wheel and pressed it over hers. She flipped her hand and I clasped our fingers together. Bringing our connected hands to my lips, I pressed a kiss to the back of Ryann's hand. Held it to me just so I could inhale the soft, sweet scent of her.

Ryann was calming, and I assumed I would need the calm to get me through the storm Arya most likely brought with her.

MY SISTER LOOKED the same as she had the last time I saw her. Tall and thin, she could have been a model by American standards with her height and shimmering blonde hair that fell normally to her waist. Currently, it was pulled back into two braids that looked like she'd done them days ago, slept on them, and hadn't showered. Her face was bare of her usual makeup, and there were purple moons beneath her eyes when I pulled up to the departure pick-up area and spied her sitting on her baby-pink-colored suitcase. Two more were at her feet, and she had her arms crossed in front of her, hugging a thick sweater to her body.

I honked the horn and pulled to the curb to grab her attention but I was already out the door, before she had stood.

"Alix—"

She called my name, and I yanked her to her feet, wrapped her in a hug I was certain risked crushing her rib cage but she did not protest. She tugged her arms out from between us and hugged me back, a sob letting loose from deep in her throat. "Vous êtes ici."

"I'm here. I am glad *you* are here." I pulled back, and wiped tears off my little sister's cheeks. "You are okay?" I scanned her face, all her body I could see which wasn't much, searching for something.

Clues? Bruising. My jaw tightened at the thought and I yanked her back into a hug.

"Je vais bien. Je promets."

"Good. That is good." There were a million questions I had. How she was here and why topping the list. They could wait. "Come. Come. Let us get you to my home and we will speak more. On the way, you can discuss this long story."

"Yes, brother. Thank you."

I loaded her bags into my tiny trunk at the front, cursing as I had to shove them down while closing it to get two of them to fit. Definitely should have taken Ryann's car. Thankfully, I had some space behind the seats and back window where Arya's small bag fit.

We slowly pulled back onto the streets, and Arya was fighting sleep. I had no idea how long she'd been traveling, why she wouldn't call me until she landed, or when and where she left from so I reached over and gave her a playful shove. "Stay awake until we get home, Arya, and then you can sleep as long as you need."

"Merci." She forced her eyes open. "Je t'aime."

"I love you, too. Tell me one thing... did he hurt you? Either Father or Enrich?

"No. Not like that anyway. I needed to leave though. I could not stay. Stifling. It was stifling, and I would have been miserable and I could not demand again you return and be the same. So I left. That is the shortest version of it."

She spoke it quietly, in French, with sleep making her words slow.

It was enough for me to know for the night.

Tomorrow, I would get more answers.

THIRTY-FOUR
RYANN

"I thought Alix was joining us?"

My mom was busy in my small kitchen, food and brunch snacks covered every flat surface along with bottles of champagne and orange juice to mix for mimosas as soon as Blake and Braylen arrived.

Alix had texted me last night once he got Arya to his place and said she was okay, but sleeping and he'd call me this morning. It was now nearing ten o'clock, and the plan had been to be here for brunch. I was getting worried I hadn't heard from him at all, yet. Not that I didn't understand. Arya probably needed him, but a phone call or text would be nice so I stopped worrying so much.

"His sister showed up last night, from Switzerland. A total surprise, so I imagine he's busy."

"A surprise visit from Switzerland? Is everything okay?"

Leave it to my mom to hear the worry in my tone even as I tried to keep it hidden. "I hope so."

"His sister... what was her name?"

"Arya. He hasn't heard from her for a month and then she just showed up. It's bizarre, to say the least, and the fact he hasn't let me know what's going on..."

I flipped my phone in my hands and tossed it back and forth before resettling it on the counter.

"You love him." She tossed a strawberry into her mouth as she turned my world upside down.

"He told me last night he loved me."

"I'm not surprised. Why did you suddenly go pale?"

"Geez, Mom. Do you have to see *everything*?"

She laughed, a light and tinkling laugh that sounded like bells at Christmas. "I'm a mom, it's my job. Why does it scare you?"

"I've never loved a man except for Dad." Blah. Stupid. I was so stupid for thinking that. They weren't the same in any way.

Understanding wiped away her smile and her happiness. "Oh honey." She wrapped me in her arms and swayed back and forth. "Alix is not your father. And from what I can see of Vik, he's learning from his mistakes and his choices. That's all we can ask of anyone, even if it takes decades. But Alix is different, I can see that. The way he looks at you is precious."

"How does he look at me?"

"Like he knows where you are, every moment you're together. He has his pulse on you, checking on you, making sure you're okay, having fun, whatever. I've been around the man for only a little while and I know that he would have torn Vik's throat open had he hurt you, or any of us last night. So don't worry, whatever it is that's going on with his sister, you two will figure it out."

If only it was that simple.

There was always the chance she could leave and force him back to Switzerland with her. Not that he wanted to go. But I doubted I was enough to keep him here, or hockey, over family and protecting his sister.

"Now. Help me finish this charcuterie board and get the melons balled before Paul gets back with more drinks. I have a feeling today is going to be a day drinking kind of day for all of you and this champagne isn't going to come close to being enough."

"Twist my arm. Cook me food, ply me with alcohol... where's

the mom who used to insist we couldn't have sweets except for Friday cookies?"

"Her daughters grew up and became adults and her best friends."

She kissed my cheek and slid the melon baller she'd also picked up at the grocery store before they came over this morning in my direction.

"Get to balling, missy. You'll need sustenance in you to handle anything that might come your way today."

MY MOM WAS A MAGICIAN. A sorceress. Perhaps a fortune teller. We finished the charcuterie board, assembled the rest of the food on my counter. Paul returned with fresh lattes for us from Starbucks, along with three cloth grocery bags of alcohol, plus a case tucked under his arm.

I'd asked if they were moving in, with that amount of beer and wine and he'd laughed.

But for real. I might have to donate the leftovers to Joey's bar or something because there was so much alcohol in my house. Like I was hosting a party for thirty instead of seven—and that was if Alix came.

Around no one, I finally got a text from him, apologizing.

Late night with Arya. So sorry. We're just waking up.

She can join us if you'd like. Vik just arrived.

I'll see what she's thinking. She's been quiet.

Okay.

My thumb hovered over the "I" key, wanting to type out I love you, but that'd be strange.

He should hear it from my mouth first and not over text.

As soon as I tucked my phone into the pocket at the sides of my leggings, Vik poured himself a fresh mimosa and tossed a chunk of cheese into his mouth.

"You doing okay?" I asked because while Paul and Blake were trying to talk to him, my mom was giving him space and Braylen kept staring at him like he was a stranger and she had no idea what to say to him.

"I think a losing season and the possibility of losing my job, and becoming a laughingstock in hockey might be more comfortable."

"It took me time." I squeezed his shoulder. And he still wasn't perfect. "This is a start."

"Right." He slugged back the mimosa, cringing and I laughed.

"Save yourself from the champagne and grab a beer Paul brought. Please."

"Right. Can't have too many more though."

"You have enough time to relax. Maybe some drinks will loosen everyone up."

"Or start a brawl and destroy all your furniture."

"Man, you are a pleasure and so great at trying to see the positives, aren't you?"

Vik shook his head, gaze roamed the living room. Blake had stepped outside and was on his phone, probably work, and Braylen and my mom were laughing at something on Mom's phone. We had basketball on, and Paul was lounging on the couch, feet kicked up on my table like he was at home.

My phone buzzed in my pocket at the same time the buzzer to my apartment went off.

"That's probably Alix," I said and excused myself to let in the visitor downstairs. Afterward, I checked my phone.

Arya wants to meet you. We're leaving now. See you in twenty.

So, if they were just leaving Alix's, who was coming to my door.

"What's wrong?" Vik asked.

"Nothing, it's just—"

"Oh, look at this beautiful family gathering," Hayden's voice rang out as she opened my door, unlocked from when Blake and Braylen showed up.

She looked fresh off an airplane, in comfortable traveling clothes, but her hair was freshly combed and she'd put some makeup on.

"Uh...." What the *hell*? "Hi?"

She dropped her duffel bag on the floor and kicked it to the side. "No hug for your sister?" She grinned over my shoulder at mom. "Or your daughter?"

"Of course, silly." I hugged her, the tension clear in her body and as everyone said hello to Hayden and her complete surprise arrival to everyone in the room, I glanced at Vik.

He now had the beer in his hand, clenching it so tightly the green glass could shatter at any moment. She hadn't so much looked in his direction.

My mother whispered something in Hayden's ear that had her feral smile wiping off her face. "Fine," she grumbled. "I'm sorry."

Assuming it was a warning and correction, I relaxed.

Hayden could lose her cool, but she'd at least attempt to keep control of it in front of Mom.

"Hayden," Vik called and she slowly unpeeled from Mom and turned to him.

"Yes?"

He headed straight toward her—brave man with a death wish— and handed her a mimosa. "It's good to see you again."

Her head tilted to one side, blonde hair spilling down her arm. "Is it?"

My spine tightened. It was the same thing she'd said the last time they saw each other, but this time, Vik didn't falter. "Yes. I think your company is always a lovely surprise for your family, considering you travel so much. And I, for one, can't wait to see more of your surprises in the future."

He tipped his head, took a drink of his beer, and stepped toward the patio.

I knew Vik enough to know he was taking a minute to gather himself, but when I turned back to Hayden, he wasn't the only one shaken.

Score one for Dad.

"Drink up." I poked Hayden in the side. "You're two drinks behind and we all know you hate being sober in the group."

"Well that's because you all act like goofy little idiots when you have a few free drinks in you."

"Then you better beat us." I stuck out my fingers, pressed them to the bottom of her champagne and pushed it until it was at her mouth.

She drained the glass, smacked her lips together. "I probably owe you an apology for my last visit. I didn't expect to feel so shaken, but the moment I saw him, I just... I thought of all the things in my life he'd missed. All the nights when mom had to make an excuse because he chose to work late or whatever."

"Yeah." I snorted. "You made that kind of obvious. How are you now?"

Because all of that rage, not only was she entitled to, I understood.

"Still feeling like strangling him, but I won't"—she winked at Mom—"because I can do better because I was raised better—"

"Thank you." Mom grinned.

"And I wasn't going to come when Braylen told me what everyone was doing, but I figured, if Mom can be in the same room with him without slitting his throat open—"

"Lovely visual," I interrupted.

"You're welcome." She smiled, showing teeth. "My point, if you can all do this... I figured, I'm tougher than I'd been the last time. I could *maybe* try too."

"That's all I ask." I kissed my sister's cheek and grabbed a plate off the counter.

A mimosa and my current glass of wine meant I needed food in my belly or I'd be passed out before Alix and Arya arrived.

Probably *not* the great impression to make.

"Oh," she sang as I had my back to her. "And maybe don't tell me where your sharp carving knives are." I glanced back at her over my shoulder with an eyebrow arched. "You know... just in case I change my mind."

My sister. Life would be boring without her, that was for sure.

LIKE CLOCKWORK, twenty minutes later, Alix let himself into the building with the extra key I gave him the weekend I moved in. He rapped on the door twice before entering and as soon as he entered, the prettiest, tallest woman followed behind him.

The men had all moved to my couch, and Hayden and Mom and Braylen and I had been standing around the kitchen table, eating food. Listening to Hayden tell us about her latest adventure to Costa Rica—which she'd left early and had to return to the next day.

"Hi," I practically sighed as soon as Alix entered. He'd dressed to impress with black, neatly pressed dress pants and a silver dress shirt. Tucked in to show off his lean waist and the sleeves rolled up to his shoulders that showed off the veins on his forearms.

My mouth went dry at the sight of him, and other parts well, didn't.

He came straight to me, his sister's hand clasped in his and kissed my cheek. "You look beautiful."

I tugged on his shirt. "And you're overdressed."

Behind him, Arya let out a quiet giggle. "I told you," she said to her brother and Alix stepped back. Introducing us.

She threw herself at me, hugged me and my mouth opened in surprise. "It is lovely to meet you. I am sorry I worried you both. Alix is not happy with me."

"I'll explain later," he said.

"Are you okay?" I asked her, because our worry was minimal compared to her.

"Well. Yes, I am good. Tired, and it has been a long few weeks, but yes. I am okay and happy to be here. Happy to see Alix happy, too."

"Well, it's nice to finally meet you." I hugged her again, because she was so pretty and sweet she just seemed huggable and I stepped back so Alix could introduce his sister to everyone else.

Hayden gave him that assessing look she had the other day to which he murmured, "Don't start," in a playful tone and Hayden pouted.

Soon, the men were all watching television, and Arya joined us in the kitchen. She turned down wine and mimosas claiming she was still tired from the jet lag and was afraid she'd fall asleep on her feet, but the more she talked, the more I believed she was truly okay, and that made my heart happy for Alix.

All too soon, the sun was beginning to set, my father was leaving and Paul and my mom were headed back to the hotel.

"We leave early tomorrow, so I need to sleep off this beer," Paul said, patting his stomach.

"We should head back with them," Blake told Braylen.

Her pout matched Hayden's earlier one. "I know. But I miss my sisters."

"We'll see each other again soon," I reminded her.

If Alix made the playoffs, they were planning on coming back for the home stretch of games, and even though it was still a couple months away, it was better than nothing.

"And I promise to take time off this summer so I can be home for a while," Hayden said.

"It's still not the same," Braylen whined. "I miss you all not being close."

"You have Blake," I reminded her.

"Yeah, but he's a boy."

"They do smell," Hayden added.

I nudged her shoulder with mine. "Grow up."

"You." She poked me in the soft spot above my hip, and I squealed.

"Girls," my mother said. She and Paul were at the door and she wore the look of an exasperated mother after a long day of taking care of toddlers.

"We'll behave," we all sang, smiling and telling her we absolutely wouldn't.

"Right. I didn't believe it when you were kids, and I certainly don't believe it now."

We all laughed, even Arya, and I gave my hugs, saving Hayden for last. "You can stay here tonight."

"Nah. My flight leaves at six. I'll get a room closer to the airport so I can take off."

"Okay. I'm glad you came."

She looked around the room. She and Vik hadn't talked, but when someone asked him a question or when he and Braylen had huddled off in the corner at one point, she'd paid attention. She watched every move he made, and she didn't stab him, so I figured it was a step in the right direction.

At least for me.

My sisters had to come to their own conclusions with Vik and I wouldn't blame them if they ended up washing their hands of him. That would be his consequence, even if he was trying to make amends.

But no bloodshed was a good sign.

I walked them all downstairs, gave out more hugs and maybe wiped away a few tears.

"Good man you have up there," Paul murmured when I hugged him for the third time. "And you're a great woman. Strong and beautiful. I'm glad we could be here for you, and I have to admit, I don't totally *hate* Vik anymore."

High praise from the man who'd picked up our trauma and dusted us off.

"Love you, Paul."

"Love you more, munchkin. Be good."

I stayed on the sidewalk until my family left and Hayden's Uber pulled away and made my way back inside to find Arya fighting a yawn, slumped in the corner of the couch, and Alix finishing the clean up my mom and I started earlier.

"You two probably need to get going too, don't you?"

Alix slid the remaining charcuterie board into the fridge. "I was hoping you'd join us?"

The last twenty-four hours had been exhausting and well, a lot, emotionally. I suspected Alix felt the same.

Besides, I was learning there was nowhere I'd rather be than with him, anyway, so the choice was easy.

"Let me pack a quick bag."

"I will go to sleep," Arya murmured, her steps slow and tired but still graceful. "Let you two have time."

I gave her a kiss on the cheek. "Sleep well."

She grinned at both of us. "I would say the same to you but I believe you will not get much sleep at all."

Ryann covered her laugh with her hand.

Sisters. Glad she was here, but if she could also not be, I wouldn't complain. I rolled my eyes. "Good night, Arya."

"Au revoir!" She sang her goodbye and waved her fingers in the air before heading up the stairs.

I waited until she was gone and took Ryann's hand in mine. "Need anything to drink?"

"Only a gallon of water."

She probably wasn't joking. She and her sisters and Jennifer put away more than a bottle of wine each throughout the afternoon. Fortunately, they'd also been smart and kept food in their stomachs as well as small water breaks.

I grabbed two bottles of water from the fridge, and guided Ryann toward the couch. My townhome was simple, with dark gray furniture and black rugs. I didn't have a lot of artwork because

I didn't see the need. I never minded before, but since Ryann had been in her place for such a short time and already it felt like a home, I figured this was one of the reasons I spent time at Kane's next door.

My place still looked like I was moving in.

"You seemed to enjoy today." Ryann nodded, draped her knees onto my lap as she cuddled up next to me.

"It was nice. Weird, and not entirely fun, but I don't know, I'm glad my family came down and even Hayden's surprise visit was good."

"She did seem better."

"I think she's quietly working through some things, but her showing said a lot. And speaking of her sisters showing up out of the blue..."

She tipped her head toward the upstairs, where based on the sounds, Arya was still getting ready for bed in her bathroom. The floor was tile and I could hear her heavy steps and the sounds of water turning on and off.

"How is she?"

"She's been fine this whole time, just hiding."

"Hiding? Why?"

"Because she doesn't want to marry Enrich and my father was forcing her to. He'd apparently put her up to that phone call she made with me, and when she realized I wouldn't return, even for her, she couldn't go through with it. But he'd hidden her passport and birth certificate like we figured, so she couldn't leave either."

"Your dad said they were on vacation."

"Lies, because he didn't want to tell me he had no idea where she was." I sighed. My sister had told me everything this morning when she woke up, and I knew I still didn't know everything. "She was staying with an old boarding school friend, someone my dad wouldn't know, or would never think of, I guess. And she waited until she could get her new birth certificate delivered. Then her new passport expedited. She waited until he left for work a couple days, packed a bag, bought her ticket... and here she is."

"How long can she stay?"

"Ninety-day tourist visas are pretty common." After that, I had no idea what we'd do with her. "We'll figure it out."

Ryann sighed and snuggled into me further. I settled my hand at her hips and squeezed.

"Why didn't she call you at least?"

"Because she was mad at me for not dropping my life to come to her rescue, and then she says she thought it would be fun to surprise me."

"That sounds—"

"Selfish? Spoiled and immature? Yes, that can be Arya. I love her, but she needs to grow up. And quickly apparently."

"At least she wasn't hurt or anything."

"She swears Enrich did not do anything bad to her, but she is angry that he was so controlling and had so many expectations of her. What she was allowed to wear. Who she could speak with when they had business dinners. She says she felt as if he wanted a doll, not a woman."

"Yeah, and that kind of controlling can eventually become worse. It's good she got out."

"It would be better if she had let me know what was happening instead of making me worry."

"True." Ryann's hand skimmed the back of my neck and her fingers dug into my shoulders. "Oh, that felt good."

"I bet I know what will make you feel better."

I had a lot of ideas about how I could feel better and they all involved Ryann, on top of me, beneath me, bent over on her hands and knees in front of me.

"What are *you* thinking?"

She pushed onto her knees, straddling me. "Can you be quiet?"

"That is usually a *you* problem."

"Correct." She kissed away my smile and pressed her hands to my neck, across my shoulders and down my chest until she was pulling my shirt from my waistband. She slid down as she moved until she had my knees spread apart and then she was on her knees on the floor, staring up at me with desire in her eyes that instantly sparked my arousal.

"Ryann..." I glanced upstairs. It was quiet now, and Arya was still dealing with jet lag, but still.

"I told you you'll have to be quiet."

My hands met hers at the buckle. Fuck this. Screw waiting for my bedroom and my bed upstairs where I could do all the wicked things to her in my mind.

This was much more filthy and I enjoyed Ryann this way.

I lifted my ass and we shoved down my pants, letting them fall to my ankles. At the first touch of her hands around my length, I gritted my teeth together.

When she leaned forward and peered up at me, mouth opening to take me and eyes watching my reaction, I bit my lip until I tasted the sting of blood.

And when she finally wrapped her full, slick and pink lips around my cock and sucked me deep, I thought of hockey stats and Max's hairy ass I caught sight of in the shower one time so I didn't lose it too soon.

"Shit," I rasped and pushed her hair off her face.

Ryann was a goddess, both in bed and out of it but when she took control like this, she blew my mind. She drove me crazy as she played with my balls, cupped them in her hand and squeezed with just enough pressure to have my hips bucking off the couch.

The move jammed my cock harder into her throat and she gagged, and moaned around my shaft like she enjoyed the surprise.

I couldn't apologize. I couldn't curse and I definitely couldn't express exactly how much I liked what she was doing without giving my sister nightmares.

So instead, I savored the pleasure of her mouth, the way she worked me just how I loved it without any direction, and when I came, I was barely able to whisper it was coming before she sucked me deep, swallowed, and I released everything down her throat.

"Shit," I said once she finished me off. My legs were trembling and my heart was racing. "That was incredible. Thank you."

Ryann pushed my pants and boxers up to my thighs and stood in front of me, letting me wiggle on the couch to redress.

"Good. Now you have two choices."

"Well aren't you quite the planner tonight?"

She laughed and didn't answer. She flicked a finger in the air. "One, we can go upstairs and you can return that favor I just did to you. Or two"—another finger joined the first—"you can climb into the shower with me, bend me over and take me from behind so we don't have to worry so much about your sister hearing my screams when you make me come."

"Two," I lied...

Because I was absolutely, one hundred percent, going to do both.

***

I HAD LIED TO MYSELF.

I did number one while Ryann was propped on the bathroom counter, me on my knees in front of her while the shower steamed up. Number two happened exactly how she offered in the shower except I'd slammed my palm to her mouth so Arya didn't hear. Option three happened once we were dried off in bed, and I took her again, her knees bent out wide at her side with two pillows beneath her. I took her hard, deep, and slow until she soaked the pillowcases with wetness, surprising even herself when she came so hard she drenched the towel I'd had the forethought to put down.

We were in bed, Ryann curled to my side, hand on my chest, right over my heartbeat. She was lazily drawing shapes and fingers onto my heated skin, kissing me occasionally while my hands ran through her still-drying hair.

"You said something to me last night I didn't have time to say back," she finally whispered and tilted her head so she could meet my gaze looking down at her.

"That is because I did not need to hear it back."

"Do you want to know?"

"Of course I do, someday. There is no hurry."

We had happened fast. In one night for me with a near stranger. Ryann always seemed to need more time.

She slid her leg across me to my other hip and straddled me, her hands landing outside my shoulders and bending over to kiss me.

The move had her sex brushing along my soft dick, which twitched at the feel of her. I'd used her enough already tonight, and I was spent, but my dick perked up as her breasts pressed to my chest and she kissed me.

I allowed her the lead for a moment, but as soon as I opened my mouth, I took over, keeping the kiss slow, I stroked arousal in both of us with the quick but gentle flash of my tongue and my hands fell to her hips, moving her over me, working her slit down the length of my dick until I was hard and wet from her own desire for me and then I was pushing inside of her.

Connecting us once again.

"I love you," she whispered against my mouth. "I love you so much it scares me."

"There is nothing scary about loving me because I will always be here to worship you and love you and care for you."

I stole her retort that would be tinged with fear and worry with another kiss, and as I made love to her, controlling us from the bottom, I kissed her and played with her breasts, and everywhere I touched her whether it be with my mouth or my hands, I repeated all the reasons why I loved her. I promised her all the ways I would take care of her.

All she had to do was trust me.

"I do," she rasped as she pushed off me and braced her hand at my chest. Her hips bucked and her stomach muscles tightened. "I do trust you, Alix. Always."

"Good."

I reached down and pressed my fingers to her clit. As I pinched it, she came, repeatedly chanting that she loved me and trusted me and I vowed to always be the man she needed.

We had a long road ahead of us. My family problems. Hers. Her relationship with Vik. Complications that could arise if I was traded or she took a job with another team. Or what would happen once Arya had to return to Switzerland.

Those problems could wait. They were all solvable—as long as Ryann and I kept loving and trusting and working together.

Hopefully, for the rest of our lives.

EPILOGUE

Ryann

"THIS IS ABSOLUTELY INCREDIBLE. They're doing it."

My eyes didn't stray from the ice rink below us. A minute left in the game, and the Vipers were winning five to three in game five. About to pull off the Stanley Cup win without having to travel back to New York again.

Arya's excitement next to me pulsed as deeply as her finger-nails dug into my forearm.

Peeling them off me, I squeezed her hand. "Keep your excite-ment to bruising your own body, please."

She laughed, squeezed my hand, and pulled herself closer. "Thirty seconds... come on, Alix. Come on."

Her prayer was as vocal as the crowd around us on their feet, the entire arena trembling from the force of the screams and stomps as the clock ticked down.

Behind me, Braylen grasped my shoulders and shook me back and forth. "They're doing it! Vipers! Vipers!"

She chanted, and my head spun. There I was, watching not

only my boyfriend, the man I loved, win another championship, but my father. And despite Braylen's still hesitant attempts to have a relationship with Vik, she loved Alix only slightly less than she loved Blake and Paul. Who were also there, with my mom and Hayden, all of them behind Arya and me. Hayden was slower moving with Vik too, but she occasionally took his phone calls, and she even called him on his birthday in May. Sent him a good luck text before the playoffs started, too. It was progress.

The clock ticked down.

Five seconds.

Four.

Three.

Two.

One.

The buzzer must have gone off because lights flashed, and the entire Vipers benched jumped the wall and rushed to the ice, but none of it could be heard over the sirens blaring and the roar of the home crowd.

I stood with everyone, clapping and cheering. Gabby and the rest of the Taylors were nearby cheering on their brother and son. Gabby rested one hand on her slow-growing belly while tears streamed down her cheeks with excitement.

It had to match mine because my view turned blurry, and I grabbed my mom and hugged her. This hadn't been easy for her, but she too, loved Alix.

"Thank you for being here!" I cried into her shoulder.

"I'm so thrilled for all of you!" She squeezed me back, and we jumped up and down.

Soon, the families were ushered out of the stands by security. The only downfall to dating a hockey player over football? You could jump the stands and rush the field but being whisked away through the halls was even better, more terrifying because the thunder in the arena only increased, shaking the floor beneath our feet, but then we were at the tunnels leading to the ice, and carefully, we stepped out. We'd been warmed to wear shoes made for ice, and with my mom and Arya with me, her linking arms with Lucy, Dominick's little sister who she now lived with while staying in the States on a student visa, we carefully made our way to the ice.

Carpets were being rolled out. The Cup would arrive soon, and then the real celebration would begin. And when we returned to Alix's tonight, where I was spending most of my time instead of my own apartment, we'd celebrate for an entirely different reason.

And still, there was a massive dog pile of men in green and gold, slowly peeling themselves out of hugging each other and celebrating as their families made their way to the ice.

A thick arm, followed by the scent of a man I'd know anywhere, reached around me and flung me right off my feet.

"We won!" Alix shouted and encased me in his arms, swinging me in a circle on the ice. "I can't believe we did it in five games!"

"I knew you could!" I was shouting. My cheeks hurt from the stretch, and Alix still had his helmet on so I couldn't even kiss him. But this moment. This was one I would remember forever.

The last three months hadn't been easy. After Arya arrived and insisted she was not returning to Switzerland, Alix called his dad to let him know where Arya was. After that first phone call, Conrad had nothing to do with either of them except for the occasional call he made to Arya threatening to come to the States and take her back home. Telling her she'd fail because she wasn't smart enough to do anything on her own.

After witnessing the emotional abuse Conrad threw at her, Alix blocked his number from their phones, deleted them, and that was when he started helping her get a student visa. Moving in with Lily came more naturally. They were both the same age, both getting back on their feet, and since Lucy lived in Dominick's penthouse condo all alone, she was thrilled to have the company.

Alix ripped off his helmet and tossed it to the ice. Bright, shining blue eyes met mine right before his mouth crashed into me.

"I love you, Ryann. So much."

He kissed me again, spun me in a circle, and then we were separated by teammates and Paul and Blake wanting to share their excitement. I turned and wasn't at all surprised to see Vik behind me, patiently waiting for my attention.

Where my sisters were slowly re-establishing their own relationship with Vik, mine moved faster. Partly because I worked with him, so I had more opportunities, partly because I could see his constant effort. It made things easier for us.

"Dad!" I threw my arms around him, careful not to knock him to the ice. "Congratulations! How does it feel!?"

"Never gets old, but this moment right here might make it my best win yet."

Damn him for making me cry harder. I slapped his back and pulled back. "You did great."

"Got a good team behind me, and that includes you."

He finally let me go and shook hands with Paul and Blake, took quick hugs from Braylen and Hayden, and even gave my mom a quick hug.

"Congratulations, Vik. Aren't you getting tired of winning all these things?" she teased, and Vik laughed but shook his head.

His gaze touched on every one of us, crowded around him, smiling happily, but that regret of his still lingered easily for us to see as well. "No. I think maybe the best is still to come."

***

IT WAS *hours* later when we finally dropped Alix's gear bag in the mudroom off his garage and kicked out of our shoes. I dropped my purse on the stairs and yawned.

"I'm so tired and still feel like I could run a marathon."

Tonight had been insane. There were celebrations on the ice. In the locker room and family lounge. There were press junkets and champagne sprays, and there was waiting while the guys showered, and some moms had to leave to get their young ones to bed.

"No marathons for me," Alix groaned. His hand rested at my lower back, and he guided me toward the kitchen, where he went straight to his fridge and pulled out a bottle of wine. "I'm not doing anything that involves running for weeks."

Who could blame him? The team had been riddled with injuries in the last month. Alix himself sat out for three games for a lower back injury. He needed the rest.

"How does it feel?" I asked and realized how silly that sounded. They'd just won the *Stanley Cup* for the sixth time in nine years or some crazy statistic like that. "Better than the other wins?"

Alix opened the wine bottle and poured us both a glass.

"It feels like you're high on drugs and like every ache, every pain, every crappy moment and every miserable night of travel was absolutely worth it. And it's best this time because you are here with me, every step of the way."

"Always." I reached for him, grabbed his shirt at his side, and pulled him down to me so I could kiss him. He tasted of fruity wine and happiness, and the fresh scent of his body wash from his shower invaded my senses, and instantly had me burrowing into him. "You didn't want to go celebrate with the team?"

"There will be plenty of team celebrations. And the parade. I wanted tonight to be with you."

He slid my glass of wine toward me, but I shook my head. "No thanks. I'm good."

"Sure?"

"Had enough to drink at the game." Not a lie.... I'd drank plenty of water and a 7-Up. Which really meant now was the perfect time to tell him he hadn't just won a game tonight. But so much more. "Hey, listen, Alix..."

"Hold that thought." He reached into his jeans pocket. "Let me go first."

Go first?

"I should be doing this somewhere better. Something more romantic. But I thought of something tonight while I had been planning the rest of this."

"What are you talking about?"

"When you reached the ice today, I realized something I had not yet considered. I love you. And I want the whole world to know it. Asking you to be my wife is more important than the location, and I have had this ring long enough that I am tired of waiting for the perfect moment."

His words blurred after wife, and my jaw dropped. He wasn't... he didn't mean... did he *know*...?

"Alix...."

"Marry me, Ryann. Marry me, and I promise I will be the best husband, a better father someday than either of ours were, which is not saying much, so I will be the best possible father our kids will ever need. I want to spend the rest of my life with you, and I want us to start as soon as we can."

A sob tore through me from surprise and hormones. I hadn't expected this. Not tonight. Not yet.

His hand lifted, and there was no box, just a glimmering, shining rock he was sliding onto my finger. He kissed me then, and I took it happily, eagerly, as he brushed tears off my cheeks and smiled against my mouth.

"You didn't let me say yes." I laughed against his lips.

"You were taking too long and you will not refuse me."

He was absolutely right. I would not.

We kissed until he bent, lifted me, and settled me on the counter. My knees parted until our chests were fused together, my hands at the back of his neck and his at my cheeks.

"There is one condition." Nerves lit up my stomach along with morning sickness.

"What is that?"

He pulled back, adorably confused. "I will give you anything. Name it. You know this."

I absolutely did. He proved it a thousand times over already.

I took his hand off my cheek and pressed it to my lower stomach where his expression did not change until I said, "I will marry you as long as we get married before our baby gets here."

"What?" His hand at my stomach pressed in. Eyes dropped to our hands where my sparkling diamond on my ring finger glistened.

"I said—"

"Holy shit. You are serious!?"

He laughed, threw his head back, and then he slid his hands beneath my backside. "I have won a championship, a wife, and now you are gifting me with a child. I need to take you to bed before I pass out from excitement."

I wrapped my legs around his waist as he hurried us up the stairs and didn't let go when he bent over the bed, lying me down gently.

"You have made me the happiest man. I did not know life, or love, could look or feel like this. I will reassure you every day."

"I know. And I promise to do the same."

"You already do, *ma cherie*." He kissed me slowly, poured his passion for me and the promises he spoke into my body with his touches and caresses, and we celebrated.

We spent the night, long after the next day's sunrise, celebrating every good fortune we had both earned and found in the last year, and I knew we would both treasure every one of those moments for eternity.

THANK **YOU** for reading and enjoying the Las Vegas Vipers! Need more sports romance in your life? Download Dirty Player, and fall in love with Oliver Powell, the dirty talking tight end for the Raleigh Rough Riders: https://amzn.to/3VMNJ20

. . .

CRAVING MORE HOCKEY? Start the Ice Kings Series today with Playing With Fire: http://bit.ly/2Kyl566

WHILE THIS MIGHT BE "THE END" for the Las Vegas Vipers (at least for now) make sure you've subscribed to my newsletter to receive all information about upcoming series, and who knows, there might be some short novellas coming for these guys, too! https://bit.ly/3nC4exd

THANK YOU

HUGE thank you to Nina and all the incredible women at Valentine PR for throwing your full enthusiasm and support behind me and these books. I've loved working with you and can't wait to see what the future brings us.

Ellie and Virginia, as always, thanks for putting up with my mess and spit-shining each manuscript until it sparkles. Thank you especially during this crazy time in our world for your flexibility and your extra hard work.

Shannon, you're the best. Always. Forever. Your talent is astounding and I'm thankful I can call you a friend.

To my Sweeties! I love you ladies and your excitement for my books!

To all the bloggers who devote their time and passion into reading books, book tours, release events, leaving reviews, promoting and pimping – you are all rockstars! Thank you for all the love over the years.

My family— I love you all to the moon and back. I don't know what I would do without you in my corner, cheering me on every step of the way. Your support is everything to me and I love you all with all of my heart.

To my girl crew— Tamara, Lauren, Niccole, Cassy, and Bree. What would I do without you ladies? Thank you for blessing me with your friendships. My life is a hundred times better with y'all in it, and a gazillion times more entertaining! To the SteelP! May we forever reign.

And last but definitely not least – to you the reader. I'm blown away with every release how much you adore my books. You have made my dream a reality and I hope I can cheer you on with yours. Please don't forget to leave reviews on Goodreads or whichever retailer you've purchased this copy from. It helps us so much!

ABOUT THE AUTHOR

Stacey Lynn likes her coffee with a dash of sugar, her heroes with a side of bossy, and her wine a deep shade of red.

The author of over forty romance novels, many of which have been best-selling titles, she loves being able to turn her vivid imagination into a career that brings entertainment and joy to her readers. Focused on sports romance and emotional, small-town romance, she also loves stretching herself in different genres.

Born in Texas and raised in the Midwest, she now makes her home in North Carolina and loves all things Southern. Together with her ultimate tall, dark, and handsome hero, she has four children. Her life is a chaotic mess that fights with her Type-A, list-making, neurotically organized preferences and she wouldn't have it any other way.

Subscribe to her newsletter so you can stay up to date on all her new releases. www.staceylynnbooks.com

OTHER BOOKS BY STACEY LYNN

<u>Las Vegas Vipers ~hockey romance</u>

Final Shot (free on all retailers)

Game Changer

Dream Maker

Rule Breaker

Shot Taker

Goal Chaser

Secret Keeper

<u>Ice Kings Series ~hockey romance</u>

Playing With Fire (free on all retailers)

Playing To Win

Scoring Off The Ice

Hooked One Her

Hard Checked

Fighting Dirty

<u>The Rough Riders Series ~football romance</u>

Dirty Player

Filthy Player

Wicked Player

Cocky Player

<u>Love and Lies Duet ~angsty slow burn, romance</u>

All the Ugly Things

All the Beautiful Things

Love and Honor Duet ~angsty, romantic suspense

Twisted Hearts

Unraveled Love

Love In The Heartland ~small town romance

Captivated By You

This Time Around

Long Road Home

Before We Fell

Crazy Love Series ~small town romance

Fake Wife

Knocked Up

28 Dates

Weekend Fling

The Fireside Series ~small town romance

His to Love

His to Protect

His to Cherish

His to Seduce

Tangled Love Series ~erotic romance

Entice

Embrace

Enflame

The Luminous Series ~BDSM romance

Dominate Me

Crave Me

Long For Me

Just One Series ~rockstar romance

Just One Song

Just One Week

Just One Regret

Just One Moment

The Nordic Lords Series ~MC romance

Point of Return

Point of Redemption

Point of Freedom

Point of Surrender

Standalones

Remembering Us

Don't Lie To Me – billionaire romance

Try Me – A Don't Lie To Me Novella